So Shall I Reap

Kathy-Lynn Cross

ISBN:978-1-63422-078-1
Cover Design by: Marya Heiman
Typography by: Courtney Nuckels
Editing by: Kathy Lapeyre

For more information about our content disclosure,
please utilize the QR code above with your smart phone or visit
us at
www.CleanTeenPublishing.com.

Because our time together was not enough.
Written for my mom, Linda,
and my mother-in-law, Katherine.
Missing you both has taught my fingers how to fly.
Both of you will always be the drive behind Tevin's
determination and the emotional complexity of Alex-
cia's heart.
Lost physically but always with us:
Katherine 09/2010 & Linda 03/2011

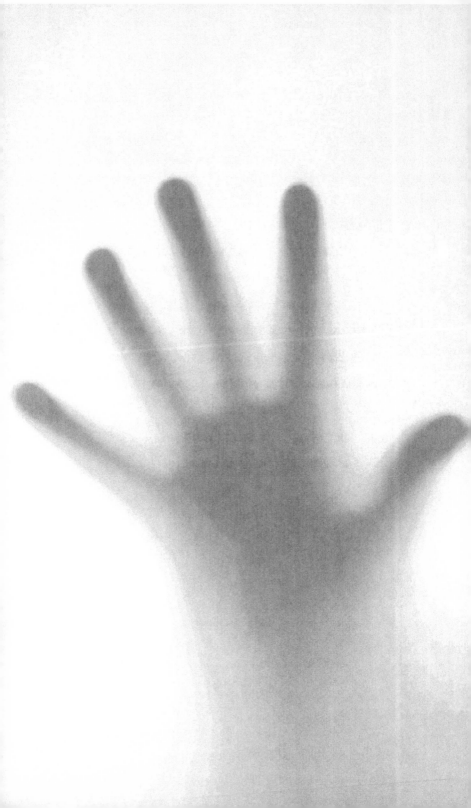

DEATH'S PROLOGUE

The year was 2006 - before all Hell broke loose

HE NIGHT SKY ACROSS THE VALLEY IN LAS VEGAS, NEVADA WAS OVER-laden with stormy, ominous clouds. Now and then, Zeus struck the sky and Lucifer replied with boisterous, rolling laughter. A constant dispute between the Houses of Light, Space, and Time weighed on the clouds, causing cold tears to fall and covering the earth with a bitter blanket of sadness.

We materialized by the emergency room doors as the shroud blended both of us into the shadows. Even though the cloak was never vocal, its energy gave me a sense of silent companionship. Our creator had bonded each Grim Reaper with a minion to provide additional power or assistance when needed. Normally for protection, mine took on the form of a cloak, but it had the inquisitiveness of a child-like Vessel. *Our kind refers to humans as Vessels with disconnect because they are merely temporary containers for a soul's existence.*

Breathing in the promise of cleansing air from the storm, I exhaled heavily while retrieving a cigarette from inside the folds of the cloak. Once lit, I watched the smoke swirl around, becoming lost in thought about this lonely, cursed life. For Ashens, or

Grim Reapers as humans named us, the only purpose for our existence has always been to deal with the last finality of a Vessel's death. At least the importance of this drudgery kept me, my clan, and other Unseen entities from falling apart. Since the options were limited for a being with an immortal existence, we did our job, no matter how grave. *I guess, in a way, it has always given us meaning to an otherwise dull and mundane eternity.*

From a distance, I sensed the targets approaching, but something was off. The soul's flicker of power faltered, and then it dawned on me. *Where was the second soul?* With my focus clouded, I searched in haste for the parchment containing the names of the soon-to-be departed. While exploring its misty folds, I completely forgot to mentally prepare myself for the entity coming to collect and transport the souls, the Bridge Crosser.

In the beginning, the House of Light had created Angels to be guardians, but some became consumed by greed and desire, corrupting their minds. With clear blatancy, many turned against their House and chose to fall. Known as the Fallen, these angel-like entities were treated as unwanted vagrants in the Unseen until they struck a bargain with the House of Space. Because of the pact, they were damned to remain half-breeds, or simply glorified soul escorts, now deemed Bridge Crossers.

Vessels who have escaped death's reach have mistaken Bridge Crossers as true angels for centuries. Filling every branch of literature, they have been described with features of golden, sandy hair, and wings swirled with colors of caramel and ivory. Unfortunately, Vessels who have *seen these creatures* never noticed the slick membrane permanently impairing the Bridge Crosser's eyesight, an indication of something more sinister. *Reapers recognize the dark creatures' glazed look for what it is... a telltale sign of their payment to remain in the world of the Unseen.*

Somehow, through negotiations I never understood, the House of Space forced our kind and the Bridge Crossers to coexist as a team to collect the dearly departed. When a soul's power had reached its expiration date, we were sent to recycle it. Reapers harvested energy from the body and then handed it over to the awaiting Bridge Crosser, no questions asked. After the soul harvesting process has been completed, we are paid with a small portion of the remaining energy to keep us recharged. The Bridge Crosser's job had always been to escort the empty soul back to the waters to be refilled with the power of Creation. *That is how we have always replenished the River Styx, our creator, by helping recycle its purpose to create.*

My cloak slapped me to redirect our focus to the ambulance as it skidded around the corner on slick pavement. The emergency vehicle high beams cut through the shadows, making my minion shudder from the possibility of the living detecting us in our corporeal state. I gave up searching for the parchment with the names of our next targets and took a quick drag from the burnt filter. Lifting a chalk-colored hand, I put out the fire in the middle of my palm, flicking the butt onto the wet sidewalk. *Time for this Ashen to get to work.* The Bridge Crosser would show itself in due time.

Little did I know that choosing life over death would forever turn my existence into chaos... *as if being a Grim Reaper was not hard enough?*

1

TEVIN'S SIDE: THROUGH THE EYES OF A REAPER

*I*N SIN CITY, THE WEATHER FROM JANUARY TO MARCH WAS TYPICALLY dry, so when a rare storm peeked over the western mountain range, I decided to take on a few extra jobs. Flashes of light illuminated the parking lot while I stayed in the shadows and watched. On nights like this, the extra electricity in the air brought a special zing to a daemon's existence. I assumed the emotion called *pleasure* felt like this to the Vessels.

Over the past six hundred years, I watched how useless, emotional fluff-stuff infected my prey. As a spectator, it was difficult to understand these walking human containers and their abilities to make clear, conscious decisions without getting wrapped up in their emotions. I never understood the need for an emotion that could cause weakness. Feeling other sentiments such as *happiness, compassion, and caring* made my stomach pitch. These distasteful, positive emotions could cloud our judgment and cause us to hesitate, damaging the Vessel's reusable power source. As Ashens, the River had forbidden us from experiencing positive emotions. If we botched a job, the Vessel might end up a cast-off or ghost. A misdirected entity added to the Unseen population had always been a strict violation of the first rule set down by our creator, the River Styx. A soul must be severed from the flesh to replenish its maker by returning creation's power so the waters can continue to flow.

Some Vessels welcomed death's presence, ready to embrace their end, which made the task of collection a lot easier. However, most of them fought, clinging to souls that no longer had enough power for them to function. It was always a futile effort on their part in an attempt to change the outcome of their mortality. Watching this process over many centuries had piqued my interest. Occasionally, I wondered what might be waiting beyond the blade of my scythe. Nonetheless, the River only granted such knowledge to specialized entities of the Unseen. All others were not allowed to know.

I fought to discard those random thoughts as I crept in through the shadows of the buildings. Raindrops sparkled in the dim glow of the parking lot, and the sizzle on the previously hot pavement indicated the end of their brief life. Pulling down my hood allowed me to snake in and out of the welcoming lights at the ER's entrance without being seen. Abruptly, I snapped my fingers to keep the dark mist within my cloak still. A slight sigh escaped my lips as the rain slowed to a drizzle. I figured there was time for a smoke before completing the last job for the night and returning home by the time the morning star rose.

Fully corporeal, I leaned up against the windows by the automatic sliding doors, searching for a reason to kill time before working. An evil snicker slipped out at the trade reference as I lifted a finger and whispered before raising the cigarette to my dry lips.

"Spark... burn... fire... thrive."

The words crackled in my mouth with a minuscule amount of power, and the tip of my fingers became hot as I placed the cigarette between two of them and took a drag. Smoke, heat, and then glow. I watched my reflection in the window. The radiance of the ember made my facial features slightly more menacing as it accented the dark indigo marbling in my eyes. Dim parking lot lights mixed with illumination from the exterior ER sign and also highlighted the symbol resting against my chest.

I brought my free hand up to trace a platinum polygon with two even triangular points aimed upward toward the House of Space, where I belonged. All entities in the Unseen wore their House symbol. Essentially, we were collared pets with tags showing others who owned us. The chains were bound to us and could never be removed.

I frowned.

Taking another deep drag, I let the smoke dance inside my mouth for a while. It flowed in and out, nice and slow, with the smell of nicotine lingering like a presence.

An ambulance screamed as it came closer, its sirens blaring in a shrill panic. Medical Vessels beyond the doors scrambled, getting ready for the new arrival. Their timing could not have been more perfect as I waited for the dual soul package to be delivered. This feeling of anticipation reminded me of when I observed the Vessels exhibiting anxiety waiting for a shipment from UPS. *Sometimes, our work requires us on site when everything is about to happen, other times, the jobs find us.* Tonight's pick up and bag should be a basic harvesting… two souls, both requiring a clean sever. According to the schedule, the interval between the two was less than ten minutes. I could recharge, collect, find their escort, and still have time to swing by In-N-Out Burger for a burger and fries before dawn.

While pondering a decision about adding dessert to the menu list, I stiffened. Something was off with the approaching ambulance. A lone survivor from a car accident hung onto life with a small, erratic pulse. I began to mull over the job description because I could have sworn my orders were to collect two souls, not just one. Needing confirmation, I commanded my cloak to hold its shape. Searching feverishly through it for the parchment with the names of the soon-to-be-departed, I checked every inch… to no avail. Tightness built in my chest, but I tried to dismiss the foreign feeling.

The emergency vehicle braked, and two uniformed Vessels exited the cab to pull out a lifeless body. Keeping my eyes on the prize, I followed the pack of annoying savior personnel into the ER as they moved past the doors marked Triage. With the power of my cloak, I willed it to shift my body back to its grim existence. The black, clammy mist from it reached out to touch everything as it slithered around my feet. My minion explored every crack and crevice while I floated forward toward the action.

Once inside, the ER was filled with the commands and demands of the living to save the young, dying Vessel before them. Anticipation was all I could taste as I inched closer to the gurney because time was almost up. In preparation, I swung my arm out in an arc, reaching behind my head to retrieve the reason for my existence. A hollow metal sound resonated as I released the harvesting weapon from its resting place.

A dark-haired Vessel in a white coat barked, "Adrenaline in a 5cc syringe, charge the paddles and hang the IV." Another one in light blue scrubs tilted my subject's head back to begin CPR, and I knew the final moments were at hand. I shifted toward the unconscious form when, suddenly, a voice in the darkness behind me broke my concentration.

"So, Tevin, I didn't know you were working tonight."

Without even a glance, I knew who waited with me for this unfortunate soul. "Thought I smelled roadkill nearby." Moving closer to the hissing whisper, I continued, "I did not think a Bridge Crosser would be here so soon. Running low on your quota of souls, Razor? Why are you here anyway? I thought you only escorted the damned? Probably the worst thing this little one has ever done was refuse to eat vegetables."

"This *little one's* spirit is needed to keep the balance between our worlds. I was specifically given this task by the House of Light. The River Styx requested me to escort her psyche across the bridge, which also gives me the right to make sure the severing is a clean one. I heard you had received the name of this futile creature from the River's Cauldron and figured you wouldn't mind if I observed. Wouldn't want any mishaps. I know the River finds favor with you and your clan's reputation, so I came early to... well... watch you work, so to speak." Razor perched his gargoyle physique on a chair, staying hidden within the corner shadows.

I cocked my head to get a better look at the Bridge Crosser relaxing behind the curtain. In the Unseen, Razor was considered an elite, and he portrayed it well. Even the air surrounding him seemed petrified, making the taste of his presence stale. He was a superior fighter among the Bridge Crossers. If the River assigned him to work with you, it was wise to grim, reap, and then leave.

My skepticism caused an eyebrow to arch. "So to speak? You came here to watch me? That is interesting. Was it not you, about six weeks ago, sitting on top of a red Ford F-150, yelling at me to sharpen my blade with my ass?" Remembering Razor on top of the truck, his face twisted in anger, made the moment of reliving it more gratifying. The daemon within me snarled at the same time I responded. "I do believe you have seen my work, time and time again." Rolling my shoulders back to show defiance, I added, "Now, tell me why you are really here?"

He readjusted the chain with the emblem of his House as if it were pulling on his neck. "You seem to have mistaken me for an entity who cares about your questions. I don't have time to ponder your petty thoughts." Razor pointed, "You need to get your job done and hand me this soul... pristine and intact." At the end of the sentence, his ivory finger aimed at their mark in a mocking gesture. "Please tell me you have had time to sharpen your blade since then, old friend?" He shoved past me, hitting my chin with part of his left wing while he headed for the gurney where the young one desperately fought to keep its heart beating. Razor opened his wings with a sharp cracking sound, similar to a bone breaking.

The Bridge Crosser's reaction caused a strange burn deep within me, allowing the caged daemon inside to stir. Normally, I did not care. I knew not to interrogate a Bridge Crosser, but the room was swimming in uncertainty. *Why was this Vessel so important that he needed a front row seat? This reaping would not normally be worth my time because the Vessel probably did not even have enough power left to snack on. So why would our Creator specifically request Razor on the job? Come to think of it, he never asked about the missing soul?* I was positive the Cauldron had listed two, but without the parchment, I had no proof. If Razor reported back to the River about my lack of knowledge, then the whole clan could suffer. Still, the need to know gnawed under my skin. The only way I could make it stop was by asking the Bridge Crosser about the second soul.

We turned our attention to the humans as they tended to the unconscious Vessel, even though we knew their efforts were moot. I glided over the spotless linoleum floor, floating through two females to position myself for harvesting. Finally situated by the edge of the bed, I prepared for this tiny, grand finale. Sighing with great exasperation, I began the reaper's Death Ritual of the Knell's Toll.

Swinging my tool of trade in one fluid motion from my right side, I held it steadily over the girl's body. My cloak hummed from summoning the innocent essence. White, sheer ribbons stretched from the body, almost far enough to cut in one swipe.

Razor made impatient noises with his wings by the side of the bed and cracked his knuckles over and over. It broke my concentration long enough to glance down at the small one. The child could not have been more than six or seven life cycles old, with golden-blond hair and red highlights. Long, dark lashes blinked above pleading eyes. I watched the mixture of sky blue and green blend together within the irises.

Startled by the tint in her eyes, I began to lose grip on her soul. Through the warped distortion of the spell, it appeared as if she were trying to speak to me. This was unsettling because no human could actually view the creatures of the Unseen, especially not an Ashen. Yet, here she lay, bloody and broken, trying desperately to get my attention. Not sure of what to do, I decided to lean in closer to hear if she were actually addressing me. Certainly, she was mumbling from the pain and drugs. Using the hilt of my scythe to keep her life force suspended above her body, I pressed my ear against her lips.

"Tevin, I have waited for you and have stayed out of the shadows like you told me to." The child's breathless words brushed past my cheek, and I forced myself to face this unfortunate creature. Her gaze stayed fixed on mine while she poured out her heart before it stopped. The girl Vessel broke her stare to look down at her own body. "My soul looks so pretty." Then the color of it marbled and swirled, a mixed sign of betrayal. "Why... are you... trying to take it... now? I thought... you had come to... protect me." Both eyes rolled as her small body fell limp against the sheets.

Multiple doctors and nurses ran around the triage room, yelling commands and grabbing tools that resembled torture devices. The lead Vessel, who I assumed was the surgeon, tore the child's small T-shirt down the middle and swabbed the area over her heart. All at once, the machines in the room sang the same dull tone. The air became potent with smells of frustration and sweat. Dumbfounded, I tried to rationalize what had transpired between us, but logic was stuck somewhere in the back of my throat. My mind could not accept this.

She knows me?

I glanced up and yelled, "Wait."

Thoughts began to race. *She is not gone yet, she knows me. She knows me. What is happening here?* The pull of her heart was getting weaker, and each breath turned into a low rattle. My mind unhinged. *Was I really meant to save this soul?* I could not shake the feeling of dread. I tried to swallow, but my throat felt like hot sand.

A loud crash from a nearby table seized my attention. A petite Vessel in her early thirties pushed toward the center of attention. She wore no makeup and her nails flashed in a rainbow of sparkles. The female waved them in the air, obviously trying to get the girl's attention. What followed next were emotional pleas.

"My daughter, my daughter. Alexcia, Alexcia, Mommy's here. Let me see my daughter." She screamed hysterically. "Oh my goodness. Where is my husband? I don't see my husband."

If her husband was missing, he was probably the second harvest. My cloak froze from her outburst. This new problem made me wonder if I should make a quick appearance at the accident site. Maybe a rogue Ashen had reaped it before, during, or after the crash. Instantly, I cursed under my breath, "Damn the cloak I cast. My clan is going to give me hell if I botch this job over one soul."

I stood mesmerized, studying the frantic being. Her hair stuck to pale cheeks from the combination of rain and tears, and she expelled an overwhelming toxic mixture of hopelessness and desperation. Then her knees gave way to despair, and I watched her drop to the floor. The scent emanating from the mother was like an exquisite funeral bouquet. Simultaneously, it made me parched and spurred my need to feed. Trembling from hunger, my mind crumbled, causing a sensory overload. My caged daemon roared, demanding sustenance.

Pulled by my inner madness from the Bridge Crosser's noise of annoyance, I asked, "What the hell is going on here?"

Razor's glacier gaze fixed on mine as if he were actually

looking at me. Lips curved into a tight, wicked smile as he hissed through clenched teeth. "Are you going to do your job or not? I have a schedule to keep. You do too. It's a problem when the boats aren't running on your time, Tevin. Take her now." Razor's voice was as sharp as his name.

Shock continued running through my body, paralyzing me. Each thought seemed to run on an endless loop. *She had just spoken to me. How did she know my name? What the blazes of hell's fire is going on here?* Not only were my thoughts in disarray... but something dissimilar stirred within me, something I had never felt before. As I drowned in a sea of endless questions, my judgment became clouded, unable to comprehend what it was like to feel needed, wanted. And I certainly could not actually understand the L word these Vessels threw around so often. *Could an Ashen even be allowed to feel an emotion other than the ones attached to death? Was a daemon allowed the ability to...? I shivered... care? Who is this creature and what is she doing to me?*

When the lead surgeon grabbed a scalpel from a nurse, my hands dropped, releasing the soul. Hoisting the scythe into the air, I spun the blade around and popped all the overhead lights. The triage room plunged into darkness, which added to the human chaos, causing them to dive for cover or scramble over one another. Both the mother and a nurse lunged across the small child, shielding her from the raining glass and debris. In the midst of the commotion, I heard the mother pleading for the small child to stay with her. While the masses were distracted, I figured it would be an advantage putting the Vessels to sleep until I could piece together my reality.

I commanded my minion to spin, casting the mist of slumber. *Sometimes a job requires us to get close to our prey or in the middle of a crowd before reaping. This spell keeps the living ones from accidentally detecting us if we lose our ability to remain tethered to the Unseen realm. That is one of the benefits of being able to work between the two realms. Besides, it is best for both parties. The less they know, the easier harvesting is on us.*

Following the inky path of the dark purple cloud as it sped its way through the room, it swirled over and around each face, forcing them to breathe in the spin's magic. Some beings held an expression of confusion and dropped in shock while others fell forward over one another. The two Vessels protecting the child slid to the floor and for a brief moment the mother caught my attention when I spotted a hint of a smile on her face before she curled in on herself. The hesitation I felt toward the mother was odd. Concern, maybe? But I did not have time to check the spin's effect on her. I needed answers. The soul's escort was going to enlighten me.

With the room contained, I commanded my minion to make us solid, and I swung the scythe toward Razor. He pulled his wings back in time, but the tip barely missed his neck, saving him from a sudden change to his existence. In certain circumstances, we might cease to exist. *Angels, daemons, and elementals can be copied and changed when the Creator finds favor with us. Think photocopy or facsimile. Every time one is done, the resolution or quality is reduced. If an entity is so careless to have their existence ended by another, they will not come back as they once were. It's the price one must pay to the River Styx for abusing our immortality. The River always takes it personally if we mishandle our existence, and, therefore, it uses less power when recreating, as a form of punishment.*

With a low snarl, Razor jumped onto a chair, descending into my space. He sent me flying into the medical cabinet doors with a loud crash, scattering bits of shattered glass and medicinal supplies to the floor. Instantly regaining a defensive position, I willed my cloak to blend with the shadows. Razor tucked his wings in as he ran toward the empty gurney on his left, obviously having the same thought.

Confusion had blindsided me. Defiance controlled my

emotions as I flipped my tool of trade around overhead and replaced it in its harness. I needed a new plan for this little soul. The Knell would not be performed tonight even though I did not have a solid reason for protecting the child. Mere curiosity sparked against my reason, igniting a flame of desire. *Could there possibly be a higher meaning to this existence?* Glancing at the bed, I realized my answer might not be with the Bridge Crosser, but with the child. Redirecting strategy, and without knowing why, I mentally prepared to fight for a soul…

Razor's massive wings thrashed, shaking glass and feathers that disintegrated into the air. He stepped over the two medical techs lying on the floor. The humans lay there motionless, still under the mist's control. Razor jumped up on the bed next to the small Vessel. "If you can't do your job, clean or not, her soul is coming with me." Throwing his head back, he unleashed a deep, barbaric roar. At the same time, the thunder from the storm returned for an encore. The Fallen raised his arms and started calling forth her soul.

The small one was too weak to keep fighting. Listening to her words had turned me solemn. I was trying to fulfill the job quota as I had done a hundred thousand times before, but I could not stop staring at her. Past experiences told me she was losing the will to live. The Vessel's breathing went still and a white sheen rose from her body once again. Razor called it out with great speed, but the hatefulness he showed for this child would surely damage the soul.

A plethora of questions clouded my mind, but only one came to the forefront. *Why was she so important to the Unseen?* Ashens were not allowed to ask questions, but with this one, I was determined to get the answer… by force, if necessary. I unsheathed the scythe, this time tilting the hilt to aim the blade low while rushing the winged entity.

My approach toward Razor caused him to break his hold

on her soul. Together, we watched the glistening white cloud of ribbons float back into her body, concentrating on the graceful beating of her heart. In six hundred years, I had never heard a rhythm such as hers. Enthralled by the melody, I forgot about the child's enemy, but a feral roar from behind drew my attention back to the fight. A string of whispered curses filled the air for not ending him when I had had the chance. While I had been enthralled by the child, the Bridge Crosser had changed his form.

Razor's angelic features were replaced by ones with pure rage, and I saw the demand in his eyes. He was not leaving this room without his charge and was ready to challenge anyone who tried to stop him. Naturally, I was at the top of his list. Wings at the ready, he flew forward and slammed into me. Razor had decided to convince me to harvest this soul by force, using his fists. *It takes two to tango, and I am ready to dance.*

A snarl clawed from my throat. No way was I backing down. I wanted him to know it. Razor pushed out both of his hands, latching onto the weapon. Only an Ashen could wield the weapons used for harvesting, and that included my scythe, so any entity from the Unseen who tried to touch a harvester's weapon would burn from Creation's purity. Razor knew that and yet, he wanted this small Vessel so badly, he was willing to burn for it. The stench of his flesh filled the room as we fought for possession of the blade. While we spun out of control throughout the room, face-to-face, our shoulders crashed into the far wall. Jaws clenched, we growled at each other, displaying dominance over the girl. I found footing again by using the corner and sheer leg strength to push back. It was enough leverage to cause the Bridge Crosser to stumble, only for a second. Instinct took over for me, and I looped my right arm under the blade handle to connect with Razor's jaw. His head snapped back with a loud *thwack* as real thunder outside mimicked the same sound.

Razor laughed. "Is that the best you can do?" Sounding gritty and spiteful, his voice could no longer hold any peaceful demeanor. His eyes narrowed as they began to glow a sick, unnatural green. This struggle was being taken to the next level... spiritual. The daemon within me recognized it too and responded with a threatening growl.

Raw power from Razor's unholy aura lit the room, blinding me for a split second, allowing him time to counterattack. He ripped his right hand free by peeling off the seared flesh from the scythe's handle. With all his strength, he plunged a fist into my chest, pinning me against the wall and lifting me three feet off the floor.

Now it was my turn, summoning the minion to wrap around my body. While my form changed to shadow against the wall, I slithered to the floor and slipped past Razor's legs. Whistling to my weapon, the scythe disappeared from the Bridge Crosser's grip, taking with it more burned flesh. I felt the weight of the blade once again resting on my back, filling me with its power. This turn of events caught the winged creature off guard as he screamed out a stream of profanity while holding his other wrist tight. Both hands dripped blood, leaving an acidic, steamy haze around his body.

I used Ashen stealth to reappear behind the Bridge Crosser. With barely a whisper, I recalled my weapon. Now, when the cloak responded, it covered my body and completed the hood over my brow, giving me a thunderbolt of dark power. Fully prepared—I was death, armed with blade and cloak—aiming for the winged daemon.

Razor's senses were still heightened with the faintest imprint of the brawl, and he flattened his wings against his back. The air escaping from around his feathers emitted different octaves of crackling as he turned back with blinding speed to attack me. We stood face-to-face with the blade between our bodies.

Gnashing his teeth in a weak attempt to distract me, he grabbed at the harvesting weapon. Again, surprised at his brash behavior, I momentarily lost my grip when he attempted to snatch the scythe again. Razor flipped the handle end over end. The air in the room screamed as he pushed its velocity faster and faster until the room fell silent. Then I noticed his arm had steadily gauged the silver jagged tip over the hollow point of my chest. Through grinding teeth, he growled, "You will learn your place, demon." Anger crested from within at his disrespectful way of pronouncing *daemon*. Vessels were misinformed and used the wrong enunciation, but Bridge Crossers knew better. It was a strategically placed insult, and we both knew it.

Before my cloak could dissolve from solid form, Razor followed through with his threat. With an outlandish display of overconfidence, he whipped the blade around once, firmly placing the hilt under his arm and plunging it into my chest. A bloodcurdling roar scrambled my brain as the beast inside wanted to make him pay for his actions. The two etched silver roses, meeting in the middle of the hilt, began to pulse a bright crimson. The chain and pendant around my neck became hot. A thick liquid resembling hot tar bubbled up from throat to mouth, causing my body to shudder. Being forced to swallow, I spat what remained at the vile face before me. Hands rising, I used one to swipe across my mouth and the other to clasp around the pulsing silver roses.

A hardened, blood-speckled face was inches from mine. He did not even raise a hand to wipe it. His tight-lipped grin matched the arrogance of triumph through his glazed stare. Razor spoke in a condescending tone, "How ironic, Tevin, that your own weapon is about to displace your existence. Ironic indeed. Poetic justice in a way." His voice trailed as he turned to look at the child, his head making quick, side-to-side movements. "What's possessed you, demon?" Clearly, Razor was baffled by my tenacity. When the Bridge Crosser turned back to face me, the indigo from my eyes illuminated his sneer. "Are you actually protecting her? Maybe you're feeling some kind of emotion?" Razor mimicked me by spitting in my face.

He used the back of his charred hand to wipe the blood from his eyes. Then he cleared his throat to mask the pain from his wounds while twisting the handle farther into my chest. I dared not give this entity a sense of satisfaction with the sound of a single breath as the pain crippled my solid form. All I could think as I looked down was if the River had created Ashens with a heart, I would surely be nonexistent by now.

Heart?

An idea came to me, sharper than the tip of my scythe. When an evil smile threatened to show itself and give away my idea, I kept it at bay. All I could do was wait for the right opportunity to present itself. Death may not be kind, at times, but pride mixed with the art of patience was where I excelled.

With me impaled to the wall, Razor became over confident that I was no longer a threat to his mission. Reverting his attention back to acquiring the girl's soul, he heaved his massive left wing over the hilt and turned, barely missing my face. He limped over to the gurney with hands still dripping blood, leaving a trail of hissing dots across the linoleum. The little Vessel lay there, broken and helpless, taking short, raspy breaths. Razor stood over the orange gurney, apparently unmoved by the small one's condition.

Using the stealth of a shadow, I drew in what was left of my cloak's power. I had never been recopied and was not about to let that happen today. Eternity was all I had, and this fight was worth winning. The shroud worked as instructed, healing my wounds. Although my chest burned, I focused on reclaiming my target.

With true reaper form returned, my corporeal being faded,

leaving the ebony mist from my minion flowing over me. The haze of the cloak fanned out as it searched my surroundings for obstacles. Its wispy tentacles from under the hem scaled up the wall two feet behind me and stabilized us while I stepped left of the hilt. In one swift slide, I pulled the weapon free with my right hand. Razor still had his back to me, beginning the speech in his own tongue, reciting the Knell's spell.

Claws raked against the inside of my chest from the beast losing its patience, reminding me of the daemon I hosted called a Smolder. All Ashens were possessed with one because the River believed an equal amount of power should always be divided. It was the River's method to control us. As a whole, Ashens were worthy enough to handle reaping death and wielding creation's weapon of choice. Our cloaks served us like a well-trained pet and aided us with reaper duties. The Smolder was designed as our dormant daemonic fighting form, unleashed only in dire situations. After a quick scan of the area, I decided the room would not withstand the Smolder's power. That side of me must remain locked as I did not have time to unleash the transformation. This fight was mine alone to endure. Trying to control the daemon within caused a sick feeling of confusion, which made me hesitate. I had never experienced anything like it, forcing my reason to spin out of control.

In all his superior knowledge, the Fallen had forgotten one crucial detail—their kind had a common bond with humans. Both were molded from Light's image, which meant he had a heart. I flexed the muscles in my right arm to jerk the handle free from the wall.

Now.

The weapon turned into a silver blur as I spun it high above my head, allowing me to flip it up and around my left arm. Then rushing in behind Razor, I dipped low to jump over him in a forward flip. The air swooshed, distracting the Bridge Crosser to face the sound while I landed in front of him. In one swift move, I whipped around and shouted, "Razor. Have a heart?" Then I pierced the curve of my scythe into his chest, thrusting it upwards to reach his pumping organ. His blood hissed and fizzled down the blade. I could not disguise the evil behind my smile anymore because it grew broader by the second. "Wish *I* did. What is it like?" I leaned into his trembling body, struggling to hold the scythe in place until the last gulp of air passed his lips.

Quivering and on the edge of dying, his own words seeped from his mouth. "You think you've saved her? You think you've won this? Demon of the Reapers, it has only just begun." More blood sizzled and pooled around his mouth, dripping down the sides. His voice became a breathless rasp as he spoke. "You will... find more harm than truth. With no answers to satisfy... your need for veracity about her will devour you both. And you will run... but all will find her... daemons... angels... elementals. Even the humans will hunt her down if she lives long enough. You will never... be allowed back to your former existence. A demon fugitive on the run... forever wanting."

I was done listening to him. My eyes burned from the untapped Smolder power within me, trying to release. The point of the blade had caught the Bridge Crosser's chain as I ripped it from his chest. Razor's body began to smoke before bursting into a mass of white and crystal blue flames. The fire licked and danced up his skin. Instantly, the Light within him imploded, causing me to release my weapon to shield myself with both hands.

After the spirit of Creation's fire reclaimed Razor's body, the heaviness dissipated and the room felt lighter. A small cough echoed in the room while I bent over to pick up my scythe. The Smolder's curiosity stacked against my own, and I found myself inching to the child. I needed to find out for sure if she really could see me. Leaning over the bed rail, my cloak worked at making my shape more corporeal. Then, very timidly, I brushed the blood-caked hair from her face. She stirred and her eyes fluttered from the touch. I swallowed hard, keeping a chuckle at bay. What if my battered appearance shocks her to death? The Smolder's daemonic chuckle within me bounced along my ribs at the attempted joke. Soon, everything I had fought for was worth the effort while I waited for her to focus on my eyes.

Her breathing became stronger, and she rocked her head slowly from side to side. A small moan escaped her lips, sending a shudder of sensations throughout my body. I licked my lips, tasting a familiar scent but could not place my bony finger on it. The combination drove me crazy while a nauseating mixture of anticipation and confusion swelled. What happened next might be perceived as either a miracle or a curse, and I was hard-pressed to determine which. In her unconscious state, the small one began to speak about me.

The need to help her was like a disease infecting my senses. Was this because of the small one's soul? I knew deep down that something was not right with all this, but I had dropped all preconceived ideas concerning the Vessel. This needed to end, here and now.

"I'm hiding, come and find me. Tevin, you're so cold. Why can't I play in the shadows? Tevin...Tev...Te..."

I staggered back a few steps. Clearly, she was hallucinating or dreaming. But she spoke of being cold and playing in the shadows. Only in my world did one stay out of the unknown. Not all shadows were harmless. I was proof of that. *When had she ever been to the Unseen?* No human could cross into our realm alive. My gaze drifted to the tentacles tugging at the bottom of my cloak, shifting my attention. I needed to regain my thoughts. *She knows my name, but how? I do not remember her. How is this even possible?*

———— ◆ ————

THE CHILD'S PROTECTOR LEANED AGAINST THE DOOR JAMB. THE ADULT FEMALE sighed ever so slightly and clicked her tongue, then cleared her throat. It caused a gut-wrenching knot within my stomach, and I felt her presence tighten around me. *Was it possible she could answer my questions?*

All the inquiries unearthed an unfamiliar female's voice in my head that whispered, "Do you really want to find out?"

My head snapped in her direction.

Wait. She can see me too?

Disbelief filled my hollow chest and the reminder caused me to mindlessly scratch an itch… the area where Razor had impaled me. I spoke cautiously to the female who had addressed me. "You can see me? How do you know my name? And how come my minion will not go near you? Or much less, kill you?" The black tentacles were tinted purple from the cloak drifting to the darkest side of the room. Its demonstration of abnormal behavior made me severely skeptical about this particular Vessel.

She walked with an unearthly style of grace as she answered, "Because you and Alexcia are the same, and yet, you are not. She belongs to this world, for now, like you once did. You were given a choice and chose your path as a Grim Reaper, an Ashen."

My eyes latched onto hers as she approached. The color of them was hidden by a mask of dark circles caused by the stress of crying. An underlying protectiveness for this child was palpable. The little one's mother must have sensed the danger was gone and returned for her daughter. Then I looked down where she had fallen asleep and felt my lips press together. Since I had succumbed to my situation, I never noticed if she had left the room. The mother faced me as I stood over the little Vessel.

When she spoke, I was awestruck, frozen in place. I had never heard of such a thing, let alone witnessed it. "Well, there are many powers I once possessed. Ultimate clarity was one, which enabled me to see the overlapping planes between our world and this one. I was able to wield the purest form of Light. What I miss most is the ability to dance with the clouds." She glanced down at the child and smoothed her hair. Staring past me, both of her eyes filled with memories she had purposely misplaced. Continuing with a sigh, she said, "Sadly, I have been recopied several times while trying to save her life. Each time I return with less power. For this reason alone, we need you... she needs you. Your role in her life holds special meaning since you were once like her. A time will come when she will make a similar choice."

My mouth hung open. "Sorry, I am having a hard time with all of this. First off, no Vessel has ever spoken to me in over six hundred years. I have only dealt with the entities of the Unseen. Secondly, what are you, angel or daemon?" I backed away, uncertain who I was dealing with. "You are not an elemental." I knew that because she did not have nature's scent. She was not entirely human either, nor was it implied. But her aura was distorted somehow. "Yet, you claim... you have died... more than once?"

"Yes."

"How many times have you been recopied?" I motioned with the scythe to the little one on the gurney. "And how did you become one of them?"

"I have died four times, and as you know, only a small portion of an entity dies each time. Unfortunately, you never realize what you've lost until the River brings you back." The sadness in her voice reached out to the corners of the room. My shoulders hunched along with hers as she continued, "The last time the River recopied me, it stripped the ability to summon my wings." Cocking her head to examine my reaction, she chose to go on. "Alexcia's soul is special. The Bridge Crosser spoke the truth, but I'm unsure why they want her power. The Houses are not giving my daughter the chance to choose, and it's such a life-altering decision. Spindled magic in our world smells tainted, Daemon. I believe the Houses have gone mad. Something is very wrong." She inched closer, carefully sliding off the covers of the bed while bending down to gently brush the child's cheek before placing a kiss on her forehead. No question, she cared for her child.

Why was I getting pulled into this mess? I did not even know this child, or why the female was implying a connection between me and the small one. The Cauldron only gave me two names. I was still frustrated and without realizing it, I began pacing. To top it off, there was not enough power to recharge from the Vessel. My aggravation was almost at its boiling point. It was time to go, even if it meant leaving without the souls. I wanted to forget ever meeting these creatures. Maybe I could recruit one of my own to find this human to harvest her another time. Better late than never, right?

I slowly pulled my scythe out and crossed it in front, moving closer to the side windows in case the chance arose to make a quick getaway. Then, it occurred to me. No other humans had entered the room. What was going on? Annoyance was a mask I wore well, "Can you finish with me soon? I am on a schedule and must get back to my clan," I said, patience wearing thin.

"Of course, but you need to listen with a simple mind about what I'm about to explain. Otherwise, it will only confuse you further and I'm too tired to put up with that." She propped herself up on the edge of the bed next to her child and waved a hand in the general direction of a chair across the room. *I guess I'm expected to stay a while.*

Since she had used the proper pronunciation of *daemon,*

out of respect, I agreed to give her five minutes. Coolly, I walked over to the bedside chair. Before I sat, she swiped a hand to her chest, and the chair turned to face her. I blinked and switched my gaze from the chair back to her. The sigh that slipped out was mixed with a confounded, "Really? Enough with the parlor tricks. I have had a really long night." My eyes narrowed as something distracted me as I lifted my fingers to rub both temples. "After being around for hundreds of years, it astonishes me that a daemon can get a headache." I finally dropped down on the chair in one motion. It issued a protesting creak. I fished around in the cloak for a cigarette. If any time was appropriate for a smoke, this was one of those times.

Alexcia stirred in her bed, showing signs of improving. Time, however briefly, was on her side. Her mother leaned back to check on the child, unaware I was about to become the fly stuck in their web. Right about then, I regretted taking this job, but according to the woman, this child was directly connected to me somehow. A thought confirmed the instant frown. *Great, another curse.*

"My name is Rae-Lynn. You are correct that... I *was* part of the House of Light. My husband, who seems to be missing, is a full daemon."

"You do not look like one of the Fallen," I mentioned while patting down my cloak to keep it calm.

"I was once an angel who was removed from the House of Light, not by choice. Although I didn't fall from grace for using free will... it was much worse." The accompanying sigh added pause as she pulled her shirt down mere inches from her throat. A faded scar in the shape of Light's symbol rested permanently just below her shirt collar. At least she did not have to deal with the chain's weight, but it still was an everlasting reminder of the House she served. She continued, "I fell in love with a powerful daemon. We are the classic story of angel and daemon falling into eternal love, pledging our devotion only to each other. You can imagine how well that went over in Heaven, putting the River in second place. I was cast out to live life as a human, with benefits."

As she spoke, I tried to sit still and save questions for later.

"Precisely seven years ago, a miracle happened, I became pregnant. We were so excited because we had never heard of a birth from a union like ours. Everything we'd been told was wrong. That's when we found out that special children with certain abilities are only born from unwanted unions every three hundred and thirty-three years. They are rare, but it does happen. Alexcia was born in the sixth month of the millennium year, on the sixth day, at six o'clock in the morning. Because of her birth rite, and the time when she was born, her powers are tenfold to that of a normal Unseen. Alexcia isn't from only one race but of all three: angel, daemon, and human. It's what makes her soul unique. In the Unseen, she is known as a Child-of-Balance. It is written in the scrolls. If an entity can convince her to make a Bond-Rite to their House in exchange for her power, that contract will tip Creation's control, and make their House stronger. Then they can guard the River Styx and oversee the rest of the Unseen. Do you understand so far?" She glanced at the child again, a worried expression on her face. "If she doesn't pick a House to serve, she is as good as dead, permanently."

Staring at the ceiling, I counted the holes in the tiles and listened to her ramble. All the while, I was trying to convince myself it was only a story. Other entities within the House of Space had conveyed tales about selected child-like Vessels. Whether you believed they were blessed or cursed with specific powers, as the twisted tale explained, they were the only beings that could wield them. *Surely, it was just daemon lore... it had to be.* I blew a few smoke rings and decided to put the cigarette out of its misery.

With thoughts drifting I was brought back momentarily and made eye contact with Rae-Lynn. "This is all fascinating, but the sun is coming up, and a different clan of Ashens works this shift during the day. If they start to wonder why I am roaming around on their time, they might think I am rogue and try to dispatch me."

When I made a move to get up, Rae-Lynn placed her hand on my shoulder. Blinking, I tried to comprehend how fast she had moved from the other side of the bed, to end up next to me. I had not even heard her approach. My insides gurgled in protest. Overwhelmed with exhaustion and a bit vexed from feeling empty, I glared at her, realizing I had lost the chance for a burger and fries.

Rae-Lynn frowned as she used her body to stretch up the length of my torso. Her fingers intertwined through some locks of hair, pulling our faces closer together. Cupping the right side of my cheek, she used the other hand to lower my head and ear even closer to her lips. "Don't you want to know why there's a connection between you and Alexcia? Why it is she knows you? Can you feel the connection when you see her, touch her? Aren't you the least bit curious?" She let go of the short locks of hair as her slim frame slid away from me. Shaking in disbelief, I wondered how an angel could get away with that kind of behavior.

"Okay, I will bite. Why?" The phrase only reminded me of how hungry I really was. The grumbling in my head now mirrored the complaints coming from hunger.

The half-angel turned with soft grace, but her eyes appeared as cold as steel. Mentally, I heard... "You will pay attention." She used her arms to embrace me. As an act of comfort, the feeling was unnaturally warm, which made her touch unbearable. I was becoming nauseous.

Rae-Lynn's voice became soft and alluring. "Alexcia sees you in her dreams. She knew you would be coming for her someday but only as someone she could trust. In her mind, she remembers you as a daemon of shadow, but she is still too young to know what that entails." The woman's nose scrunched slightly. "I suggest we keep what you really are to ourselves, at least until she is old enough to comprehend your real job. Alexcia is ours to raise. My husband and I have that responsibility, but your role in her life is much more complex. Children born of Balance share a bond far more complicated than with another entity or Vessel. And only your unique ability to love can mold her into what she will become... if you agree."

"I do not understand what you mean by *love*." I spit the word out quickly so I could continue with the rest and get out of there. "But more importantly, why me? I do not have time to reap souls and read bedtime stories to an angel-child... daemon... Vessel. Whatever she is. You still have not been clear about how and why she knows me."

Rae-Lynn stepped back and put her hands on her hips. Her smile became peaceful. "Tevin, you were once a Child-of-Balance yourself."

My eyes flared. "You are mistaken. I am an Ashen, a reaper of death, a daemon, always have been and always will be. I have no past memory of living like that." Using my arm and scythe to make a point, I motioned to the Vessel on the bed.

Rae-Lynn walked toward her daughter and took her hand. "All children born with Balance are required to make a choice when they reach the age of maturity. An entity representative from one of the Houses will explain how their powers could benefit in keeping the unions of their House balanced. The child then makes a choice to serve one of the three: the House of Light, Space or Time." Cheeks flushed with impatience. She huffed. "Obviously, I'm not getting through your thick, Ashen skull."

"What does that have to do with me?"

"Dear Reaper, I am trying to explain it to you. Once upon a time an entity closed in on you, offering immortality to use your talent for the good of their House. But you made the choice to trade your life for an eternal existence wrapped in death."

Hanging my head from the weight of our conversation, it was too much to absorb on an empty stomach. The back of my cloak flowed over my body. I felt the hood weave together, covering my brow in shadow. Eyes burning with indigo cast a glow within the cloak's hood. I urged her on. "So you are saying…"

Rae-Lynn's hair framed her face in a cascade of fire red and sunshine gold strands. She whipped her head around to grab my attention as she latched onto my challenging glare. "I'm saying you were once like her."

None of it made any sense. The headache was blurring my vision, along with the added confusion of the conversation. Having more questions than answers, getting pissed was predictable.

I slammed the scythe down in front of her and raised my voice. "So, what are you *really* saying, angel?"

Blinking several times to regain her composure, then for reassurance, Rae-Lynn quickly glanced at her daughter. Steeling herself, she focused on my cloaked form. "How many times do I have to explain? You really were once a Child-of-Balance. Your Vessel form died. Now as a daemon, you tend to the dead."

Shock and denial ran through my veins. "I was never human." The unpleasant taste of the word *human* caused a gagging sensation in my throat.

Rae-Lynn swished a thin finger back and forth in front of my face. She spoke with a hint of pity, her lips full of pout. "Once human… now daemon… forever a cursed child hiding behind death-laced lies."

2

When I took his hand
It felt so familiar...
When I stole a glance
His eyes felt like strength...
When I held a breath
Seconds felt like minutes...
When I welcomed its embrace
I felt death dancing... with me.
—Alexcia

SEVEN TWENTY-THREE IN THE EVENING AND I GLARED AT THE LED lights on the clock as my brain hummed the familiar Jeopardy tune. Struggling for time, I tripped over discarded boots, other shoes, and handbags. With eight minutes to impress, *late Lex-Cee* strikes again. Friday and Saturday nights were normally like this if work permitted. It was an extra bonus when my parents were away due to their work schedules. To fill the void of their absence, I toted a pretty crammed schedule. I excelled at making every mundane minute in my life count, the need to spread myself among two lists was a challenge. A *have to* list was scribbled in pencil and split between serving my junior year prison sentence, and my job at the local coffee house, called the Sip 'N Chug. The other list, my priority *want to* list, penned in ink, of course, for friend time or the next group social. I may not act it at times, but I managed to skip a whole grade. For me, planning was the only way to feel a sense of stability.

I stood in front of the mirror, inspecting the new silver skirt as it shimmered with the glow of the black lights. Pleased with the loosely curled strands of blond that intertwined with the cinder red ones from underneath, I checked the cascade of curls. *Good.* No sign of frizz, so I clipped each side with a comb that matched the skirt I wore. This style added emphasis to my falling mane, hopefully causing the male eye to scan and process.

A black silk blouse with a low scoop neckline tapered down to hug my thin waist. Unpainted lips curved in disgust, noticing the transparent charcoal stripes that lacked at enhancing my chest. Very few outfits helped my features, but most screamed, "She's almost sixteen." At least I was a solid B cup because the absence of sensual curves was depressing. That's when the solution came to me, and a smile replaced the pout as my reflection glanced down at the tissue box.

Around my neck hung the amulet my mother told me to never take off. When my parents gave it to me on my fifteenth birthday, Mom cried while my father hooked it behind my neck. She had cupped my face, told me to keep it close because she explained it was a way to watch over me and show others how special I was. *Eesh*, whatever that meant. The memory still confused me. If my parents had purchased it, ten to one, it was probably expensive. I figured they made a big deal because they didn't want me to lose it.

Unfortunately, the color didn't go with my outfit, so it had to go. What could it hurt? Manicured fingers worked at the clasp as the red garnet rose took on a deep purple sheen. The rose sat perfectly within the gold-roped polygon setting. When the lock released, a quick stir of wind hit me in the face and brought with it a thick heaviness settling across my chest. Straightaway, a sad ache formed behind my eyelids, and it stung, but it wasn't enough to ruin the evening. After clasping the chain together, the lid to my jewelry box opened, making me jump. A knot at the back of my throat made it hard to dismiss the nervous laugh. Placing the necklace into the front slot, it took on a presence making me feel as if I were closing a coffin lid. I sighed and said out loud, "This is ridiculous." The atmosphere changed, and so did my focus when I caught sight of myself in the mirror.

The blouse complemented my long, empty neckline. With my favorite smoke-black choker, it filled the space nicely. Then, I added the matching bracelets and earrings to complete the set. It was needed to make the opposite sex look up, take notice, instead of down where they lost interest with me.

My mom had always told me, "When a wandering eye catches a fancy wrapper, they only want to taste the candy. Make them see you for who you are, not for what you could be right now."

"Freak'n, as if. Who was she kidding?" I said to no one, and my reflection laughed with me. Really, who *was* she kidding? Her closet contained almost every name brand of clothing and accessories known to woman. *Mom, thy name is vanity.* She said it was because of the dress code at her job, but I knew people were judged by first impressions.

I held a breath while I paused. "Just wait," I whispered to myself after making a small promise to the feature staring back. Sixteen was a transformation number. Clasping both hands together, I whispered a pre-birthday wish. The guys would drool for this killer body. Until then, I would enhance and accessorize my slight shortcomings to make up the difference.

My room was awesome if I did say so myself. Painted in midnight blue, I added to the ambiance by plastering about a hundred or so glow-in-the-dark stars I had cut out on a whim after one of my nightmares. If memory served, it had been time-consuming, but the added depth gave the room a three-dimensional feel. A black and silver ceiling fan hung in the middle of the room, and I placed three black bulbs in each smoke glass casing so the stars took on an eerie, light green glow.

A flat black makeup table with silver knobs to accent the half-length mirror stood against the wall. The top of the table, crammed with the latest powders, nail polishes, lotions and face paints, was all my meager paycheck allowed. A black four-drawer dresser with the same silver knobs served as my backup table and sat positioned next to the walk-in closet. Across from the bed, the necessities of life… a twenty-seven inch flat-screen TV and a new PS5-R station so I could keep up with the latest games the guys liked. Myspace was the ultimate place to kill time, or at least help ease anxiety from a nightmare, in case the capacity to rhyme wasn't there. Anger worked well with the seventh installment of Call of Duty—Zombie vs. Vampires II.

On the floor next to the TV, my favorite dark purple bean bag chair sat, where I would read, write poetry, or jot down a short story. It had started as a cure but became a passion. So many of my journals had been crammed with doodles, stories, and poems. My dark side, which remained under lock and key during the day, fueled my creativity at night. The darkness seemed to know how to expose my mind all the time and was a quick fix to suppressing my altered nightlife. It was cheaper than therapy too. No one needed to know where my love for writing had originated.

Draped over the bed, at least ten outfits discarded to the *I don't think so in a million years* pile were sliding off the dark purple crush bedspread. The rest of the clothes pooled on a fuzzy black throw rug where my dad's Rottweiler, Gigi, claimed proprietorship rights. She was dumb but cute. Every now and then she would open an eye to inspect the next item of discarded clothing. Sniff, huff, and then lay her head back down to do what she did best. Snore.

The timer set for 7:25 p.m. on my cell buzzed, chasing away the monster named Mr. Procrastination. With five minutes left, the reflection stared back, and then twirled in front of the glass.

Satisfaction brought a wicked little smile of pleasure from this latest creation. I glanced to the right as if the reflection was trying to tell me to prepare myself. Eyes widening, I took in the condition of the room and looked back at the clock with a sense of astonishment. "Wow. I did all this in twenty minutes? That's a new record," I said, positioning a hand on each hip to survey the damage done by tornado Lex-Cee. Mom was going to declare this area a disaster zone, but for the sake of self-discovery, I needed a new image. Time was of the essence. Besides, I'd rather have the room a mess, than me. I waved a hand in dismissal; my ride would be here soon. The plan was to clean up before anyone walked through the door anyway. In my defense, it would be faster to piece together outfits for school without even thinking. Just roll out of bed already dressed. Simple.

Tod was due any minute. He was my latest and current conquest. So far, we had survived two months, three weeks and four days, but who was counting? Tolerance was a vague character flaw, and I didn't want to jeopardize the evening by not being on time. Being the main star of the school jocks, others waited for him, not the other way around, including me. We both had patience issues and worked on them. Besides that, he was fun to hang out with. Tod was also tall and pretty easy on the eyes. *Trust me, I don't mind the fact my toes have to help me up to kiss him because his kisses are worth the climb.*

High school would be okay if it were me, a cup a coffee, and a good book. The fact I had to interact with the masses was another story. Not that Alexcia Crystalline Stasis will ever be a card member of the popular crowd any time soon, but my fingers have the skills to stay connected. All the Preps, Socialites, Loners, Stoners, Nerds… pretty much anyone with a pulse… have me on speed dial. *Want to know where the liquid flows nonstop, and where an iPod docking system is that blares the latest tunes, then pass me a ten for a keg and follow me.*

If you looked up the definition of a social butterfly, you'd see my pin-up—a red plastic cup in one hand, filled with whatever makes you feel good at the time—a smoke in the other, tongue out. *And yes, I still have my tonsils.* No one could tie me down to a specific clique, but I've always believed there is someone for everyone to hang out with. From the tweens who search for the right image to the ones who don't give a crap. And I almost forgot about the *Inbetweeners*, who jumped from one extreme fad to the next.

Trust me, it's hard to build a rapport when the lambs can't decide which shepherd to follow.

The friends I have are neither sheep nor do we consider ourselves leaders. From the time we uttered the ABCs... to our first PG movie without our parents, we've been there for each other. I cherish them for accepting my true nature, fluttering from clique to clique. Strategically, I made my presence known, sipping the sweet nectar of information, before school, at lunch, and after school functions. *It's how I stay in touch with the five W's. Four of them are questions anyone needs to ask: Who, What, When... the Why is self-explanatory... because we Want to.*

One of my best buds is Jake Harlin Steal, but he goes by the name Ghost because he likes being heard but not seen. His family held him back a grade when he was little. Jake would have been a senior this year, but because of his lack of maturity, he fits in well with the junior crowd. Ghost is almost a year and a half older than me and uses the age difference for leverage when I'm not listening, or he wants me to do his English homework. Jake is the lifeline when playing the game How to Make a Million Mistakes. Sometimes I wish he could be my big brother. *Now that I think about it, I guess he is... in a way.*

Then there's Demetria Kara Stuart, but we all call her Dee. She is perky, bright, and extremely high-strung. The latter is the main cause of her drastic mood swings. Dee looks tiny for her age, but heaven forbid if you piss her off. Trust me when I say, you definitely want her in your corner before a fight. Her one flaw... she's the human version of the Peanuts cartoon character, Lucy. She analyzes everything, gives five cents worth of advice, then wants a tip. Dee has no problem handing out advice to anyone she feels is a charity case, and she just applies it to their credit. She's our very own conscience cricket, for the most part, keeping our little clan from getting into serious trouble. When she's not playing therapist, she rambles. *We presume she loves the sing-song lilt of her own voice.*

The last introduction is for Blakely Violet Sanderson. Miss Blakely takes the cake, frosting, and all. She is gorgeous but hides behind her tomboy name. Dresses in grunge and wears dark colors to conceal her outer beauty, among other things. We are polar opposites. I'm a girl walking on the edge of life, tempted to jump, but she will do a graceful swan dive from the highest cliff without even thinking. Blakely is probably the only person close enough to me for the title *best friend*, but we don't name brand each other. It's only a label anyway.

BECAUSE OF ME, BLAKE AND GHOST PUT UP WITH TOD'S DEMEANOR; WHEREAS, Dee flat out despised the guy. She believed he suffered from a rare condition called *contagious jock itch*. It was a quirk of his. If you asked him a question he didn't know, he would scratch the back of his head. Dee implied he might be infectious because he was always scratching the wrong head. She prayed that I was immune to stupid because he couldn't relate to others if it wasn't about sports and struggled to understand their point of view on things. *My friends understand how I operate which means the world to me. Supporters are very hard to come by. You hang onto them with loving claws, digging in and never letting go.*

Night before last we were getting back late from a gathering by the lakes. My parents expected me to stay home on school nights. If I weren't working at the Sip 'N Chug, the temptation angel would sit on one shoulder and convince me every time. "What the hell, you're not even going to be out that long. Your parents are out of town, go on, have a good time." Our night ended with the smell of burnt rubber after my mom shocked us with a text. She was almost home, my father about twenty minutes behind her. Together, my friends and I raced back to my house at two in the morning only to see both my parents' cars in the driveway with the interior lights off. With the impression of a sporting chance, the evil angel whispered, "Maybe they went straight to bed?" So, I snuck through my second floor bedroom window.

Backup Plan D was a ladder buried in the bushes on the side of the house hidden from the street. If anyone wanted to steal anything, they would only make off with a few TVs, two computers that were about six years old, and a game system I was willing to sacrifice. My mom and dad took their laptops everywhere, so anything worthwhile would be on their person.

After I had climbed through the open window, my hip bumped the side of the vanity table, causing me to lose balance and face-plant into the carpet. A couple of eyeliners and a base makeup case landed on the hardwood floor by the rug. Luckily, those items and my thigh, which sported a three-inch gash, were the only causalities. The black Guess jeans I was wearing came through unscathed. Much to my surprise, even with all the commotion, my parents never asked about anything the next morning.

Gigi sneezed making my body jolt. Perched in the corner

by the dresser was a gift from dad. A hand-blown hourglass filled with fine onyx sand was emptying its used seconds. Another reminder that time was of the essence. Scooping up the blue-black eyeliner from the floor, I added the finishing touches to the glass portrait. I pressed up close to the full-length mirror to get a better view of my ever changing eyes and traced a thick black line around the upper and lower lids.

Only a mother such as mine could say she loved my eyes because they acted like a mood ring, always changing colors to match my disposition. Ordinarily, my eyes were a bright sky blue that faded to a ring of dark green around the pupils. *But geez, talk about being cursed with open windows to the mind.* I brushed the thought away with the glitter powder I put on both eyelids. This particular design made them appear more catlike. Then, I used my right ring finger to swipe lightly under the lower lashes to remove any smudges.

Content with the bold look, I snatched the wayward mascara again, immediately opening my mouth to begin the last process. Carefully, I applied it to each feathered row of thick, long lashes. "Thanks, Mom," I thought while concentrating on the right lower rim when I heard the muffled tone to "Shout at the Devil."

A short gasp came from between pale rose-colored lips. My poor cell had been buried alive and was now somewhere in the pile of discarded clothes singing for help. While waving all ten silver tipped nails in the air, I walked over to the bed in a huff of frustration.

"Great. Now he calls," I mumbled as I tossed myself onto my bed to dig out the beckoning cell phone. Slipping fingers under the purple and black zebra print pillow, I wrapped them around the slender, metallic green cell. It fell silent as it started to vibrate. Tod had left me a text message instead.

Tod: In driveway Rdy 2 go?
Me: B in a jif
Tod: Stopping 4 beer - get your a$$ moving
Me: B thr in 5. Need smokes 2

His reply came with the monster truck's deep revving engine, demanding my presence. *Damn, he needs to cool off with a beer soon or our night's gonna be hell.* We didn't need to start the date with a fight.

I gave my mirror the once-over to make sure the look was presentable before running down the stairs to my parents' room. Rae-Lynn considered it off limits to me. Busting through the door, I slammed the door knob into the wall making a hole the size of a small fist. Rushing was never advised because I lacked coordination, possibly from a disconnected wire somewhere between my eyes and both feet. Breathing slower, I checked the closet door. Thankfully, it was unlocked. Offering myself a pat on the back for courage, I opened it. Digging toward the back where she kept the *no longer in style* items, I found Mom's black Coach Amina high heels. Her black Coach Signature Clip Demi Flap bag complemented my outer wrapper. Thank the stars we wore the same sizes because it doubled my wardrobe... as long as she didn't find out about my system of borrowing.

Sprinting back upstairs to gather my list of needs: real ID, fake ID, wallet, extra makeup, I kept only necessities. Mentally, I checked off each item and gathered everything together to dump into the purse. Opening the bottom drawer to the dresser, I grabbed the tampon box from under my *time-of-the-month* panties to dig out the hidden cash stash. To my way of thinking, most robbers would not take the time to look through feminine hygiene products to score. I pulled a wad of bills out, crammed it into the zipper pocket, and flipped the flap to lock it. With a finger looped through the heel straps, I carried them downstairs, punched in the code on the wall lockbox and waited for the beep. The door popped open.

A silver key ring with a calligraphy style "A" sparkled in greeting. The coolness of the metal ignited a wish for a vehicle of my own, but then again... I wouldn't be able to indulge the drink. It was not up to me to judge others if they made the wrong intoxicated choice to risk losing their rides. Freedom was a responsibility just slightly out of reach as I pictured a silver Jeep with chrome rims and light gray microfiber interior. In Vegas, leather would give me second-degree burns. My cell phone belted out Tod's ringtone from a distance, interrupting my daydream.

Jutting out my lower lip, I puffed a stray curl out of my eyes. The cell was still in my room. Pissed at forgetting it, I dropped everything to bolt back up the stairs, bare feet hitting every other step. Tripping over the mountain of clothes, I heard Gigi's low growl of protest from the disturbance. Snatching the phone from the bed at the same time a twinkle from the hourglass caught my eye. Still in the moment, I watched the last portion of sparkly black sand continue to pour over the small hill. Less than a minute of sand left before the last grain fell. Time pressed, and I yelled at the dog to get out while using a free hand to push against her butt. Wonderful. Drool all over my gym socks. Gross. Then I slammed the door so the miniature horse would get the hint to stay out.

Once again, my feet flew down the steps. By the time they hit the last stair, I was out of breath. After bending down to gather up everything, I stood and snagged the key ring from the hook, closed the key box and opened the front door. Right then, Tod laid on the horn, making my body jerk as if it tried to cough up my heart.

"I'm coming. Damn. Be right there. Still have to lock up." He was either talking under his breath or singing with the Metallica song blaring out of the vehicle windows. His eyes were dark with impatience as his fingers drummed to the song.

I locked up and ran on my tiptoes down the paved drive to the passenger side of the truck. Before I got there, he reached across to push the door open. Dangling the purse and shoes, I rose up into the truck and tossed everything onto the seat. Tod leaned forward to help, and then met my lips with a quick peck. Yeah, he was pretty pissed off, but damn, my chest was aching from the two hundred yard dash, with stairs no less. I pulled the seatbelt across my chest and snapped it in place. "Let's go."

Within three seconds of the word *go*, Tod gunned the engine again, fixed the rearview mirror, and flashed me a half smile.

TEVIN'S SIDE: THROUGH THE EYES OF A REAPER

WHILE ALL OF THIS WAS TRANSPIRING, SHE REMAINED UNAWARE OF MY PRESENCE. With the chill of death so close to her, I figured by now the Child-of-Balance would have noticed our essence. The hood inched lower over my brow to frame both eyes as I observed the child and her playmate from her bedroom window. The cloak mimicked my movement as I turned to the hourglass. With narrowed focus on the hairline stream of black sand fading from sight, I followed the last grain to its final resting place. Licking dried lips, I smiled. "Time's up."

3

Writing in my books is therapeutic but guiding you into one of my nightmares... priceless.
~Alexcia

I HADN'T ALWAYS BEEN A PARTY GIRL. THE SHORTAGE OF REST SOMEtimes got me to the point of desperation even if that meant numbing my brain every night. Maybe the sandman on this route dreaded what lay behind closed lids to deliver his dose of slumber without liquid help from Bud or Miller... or Jack, if the night was really bad. I was under the impression that if I didn't knock myself out every night, my fate would either be in a straitjacket conversing with walls or found dead somewhere. When unconsciousness took over naturally, the dreams dragged the unwilling conscious into a realm of confusion and pain. On most nights, that side of me woke up in a completely different part of the house, bloody and bruised. At least on the terror-filled nights, I'd find myself frozen beneath the sheets. When I spoke of *frozen* related to my sheets, I did not mean metaphorically... literally the sheets are encased in frozen sweat droplets formed over skin and my breath was visible in the moonlight.

To give you hindsight about the cursed beings within the nightmares, picture death's winged creatures, who at first glance, resembled stone gargoyles or mythical dragons. With closer observation, their forms changed into cloaked humans with webbed wings. Mrs. Curiosity then pushed me toward the creatures instead of away from them. When each foot inched closer, I always ran away after noticing their cloaks move and slither, shift and shimmer as if they were alive.

One of the creatures in particular broke my resolve, no matter how hard I tried to scream or break from his bond. The situation had become problematic as his presence devolved my will within the dreams. And this might sound crazy but he was *hot*. When he appeared behind closed eyelids, he could suck the air right out of me, similar to backdraft of a large fire. The way I reacted to this creature made me speculate if I really needed to breathe air in dreams.

It had all started on the night of my fifteenth birthday when the torturous, realistic dreams touched upon an untapped world. The terror visions could not enter my subconscious when I was chemically passed out... a prisoner locked within a caged mind to relive the same frightful dream pattern. With a nervous laugh and a bit of rationalizing, I convinced my brain that it hadn't detached from the nightmare, yet. *To this day, I wake up feeling the little neck hairs stand at attention from his icy breath lingering at the base of my skull, and both legs spontaneously jump me out of bed to open up the black drapes. Street lamps can chase away the shadows posing as demons.* On a few nights, if I was having a dream-terror within a nightmare, the shadowed creatures would hiss from the dull streams of light that passed through the drapes.

Every night before slipping into a REM state of sleep, a falling-forward sensation hit me before the dreams started. This was baffling because most people have the feeling of falling backward and jolting themselves awake before they hit the bottom. But, oh no, not me. The tingling spread throughout my body similar to being sucked into a vacuum, depositing me in an unfamiliar setting; the uncertainty was maddening. This dream state switched my mind on autopilot, guiding me to the same place every time.

The atmosphere was filled with an electrical buzz all around. A touch of warmth lingered in the hands of innocence as it drifted along with the sunlight, kissing the top of the trees goodnight. Tears filled my eyes as I watched the sudden change of scenery become more sinister. The rose colored clouds lost their inviting glow, mutating as they fell to the ground, heavy with moisture. Barefoot, I could feel the way the pebbles in the dirt pressed against the underside of my feet as I walked aimlessly. With the sense of my safety sinking with the sun, I always knew how the dreams would end, with two kinds of sorrow.

The mountain air dropped in temperature as the sun made its last appearance for the day. I hugged my shoulders in a cool embrace, and I remembered an image of a man standing on the edge of the ridge above me. Huge rocks stacked above him outlined an opening to a cave. He held up his hands, giving me the impression he wanted to pull the shiny orb back down so the shadows could consume it.

The sun's demise gave this demon a small thrill as though he enjoyed a game of *What If*. His eyes were ablaze with the possible expiration of mankind so there would be no need for his kind to exist anymore. Somehow, I could sense his thoughts as he pondered. *Would he, as a demon, be able to rest in peace? Could they find bliss in their death?*

Terror wove its way into my mind from being able to hear his thoughts. I found it baffling, though the effect his voice had on my body left me to assume it was responding to his power. A quiet, passive laugh from the back of his throat snaked past those perfect lips, and I became fascinated by how his tongue danced behind white teeth. An odd reddish purple shade licked slowly over lips and hungrily enticed unfounded physical desires. I assumed he dreamed of sharing them with me.

The demon stretched his arms straight up and over his head. Then in an arc, he flexed his shoulder muscles down to the etched six-pack. I held back the urge to trace it with my fingers. A sheer black mist from the ground quivered and swirled around his body. My eyes widened, observing the blades of grass under this creature's feet wither and die. Air lightly deposited the disintegrated ash into his space. Studying the dust-like snowflakes dancing around him, I tried to force myself to ignore the slight wave of his ebony hair as the moonlight enhanced each rusted tip. Closing in mid blink, I reached out to him wanting to weave my fingers through it.

No matter what I did, the demon always seemed aware of everything but would never look down at me. I pictured him scanning the horizon as though expecting to see something or maybe someone. Taking a shaky breath, I cracked both lids. He turned to me, gesturing to come closer. I was surprised to find fear had grown into fascination. The sight of him caused an ache that radiated to the back of both eye sockets from trying to absorb so much of him at once. Even with his perfect features, I noticed a few abnormalities. His lips were a frost-kissed gray, and his nose was slightly crooked to the right. But the gravity of his indigo eyes was so intense, I couldn't stop staring.

The dark creature slowly broke his connection with me by closing his own eyes, keeping secrets for him alone to endure. When they reopened, a haunting sensation appeared, as though he had lost a part of what he was. The vibrant color had been replaced by detachment. His eyes shed tarry tears, turning the irises and pupils a dead black-on-black. Inside the darkness, a sea of white smoke was held at bay with complete self-control. Standing about seven feet tall, the width of his shoulders perfectly matched his build, completing the outer armor. The last hint of sun made his grey skin glow as the night's dew glistened against his tightly flexed body.

The place where he stood fell silent in the forest around him. All creatures waited for his next move. Darkness from the shadows through the trees grew from the lack of sunlight. Twigs snapped and dead leaves crunched under lead feet. More of his kind were coming and the demon prepared for his confrontation.

The same oozing black mist found its way from under fallen trees, boulders, and brush. It covered the ground, chilling me to the bone. Hearing the beat of my hammering heart was excruciating as I pressed palms into the groves above each cheek, wishing for the throbbing to stop. Blood in my veins drummed with a beat that called out to the dead. I was in agony, clutching both hands to my chest, willing for it to quit before the creatures could hear how near I was. Each vein ran thick with panic, and my heart choked to stop its screams.

Instinctively, I wiped the warm trickles of tears. A thought flashed from memory. No, it was blood... bright, red liquid stained my fingers and pooled under some of the nails when I brushed them against my cheeks. Summoning the strength to gaze at him, I found comfort from the demon's stare. Anxiety filled me while tearing apart from our shared moment and frantically surveying the woods.

Swirls of opaque smoke burned my throat and lungs, finding refuge within the strained organs. Pain accompanied with blurred vision made it difficult to focus. Not being able to breathe properly kept my crying down to a small whimper. I forced the pumping organ to slow as my head swam in thoughts. I fell to the dirt, knees first, upper body slumping forward. Desperate for the constant pounding of my head to cease, I prayed for someone or something to make it stop. My arms felt as if water were holding them down. I shook them. Everything happened in slow motion.

A hollow scream echoed from the dense forest in front of

me. Other demons existed too? Even if he weren't here to save me, why didn't he at least get rid of the pain for me? Frustration superseded the panic now. Not knowing where I was, or what was to become of me, I felt completely vulnerable. I'd never thought of myself as helpless in any form, sober or drunk. But here I was, paralyzed with a murky feeling of dread for what was about to happen next. Somewhere, deep inside, a voice cursed for not drinking enough man-made elixir before resting my head tonight.

Wondering how to get out of the grave nightmare, his unknown whereabouts filled me with apprehension and dread. My prime concern stemmed from a sense the creatures wanted to hurt him. The dread came because I didn't want him to lose control and kill me instead. As more seconds ticked away, the fear solidified the possibility of being trapped in that location with all of them. *One thing I was sure of... I didn't want to stick around.*

Those creatures scared me to death. Yet, my heart was trying to speak to me in between the sobs. I had become lost without this demon's help as if there could be no future, not only mine, but everyone's. For me, my life had little meaning, leaving me to question why I had to relive this torment every night. Time drifted in reverse, and I was afraid I might lose my will to exist. I faced my own reality that I was in a place buried beyond blood and bone. A voice very faintly gnawed at me about survival, to keep something in check.

I mentally questioned the voice. *What was my purpose? Why was I being continually haunted by these dreams and drawn to this place and these creatures?* Silence was my answer. More questions bounced around in my brain. Hopelessness ate at the core of my being. My hands found their way into my hair and I began to pull at it while I tried to understand the meaning of this encrypted dream. In my mind, a war raged between knowledge and confusion. I was losing my sanity from the lack of answers, so I gritted my teeth to bite back the screams building from inside my body. If I was really going insane, that was the least of my problems. If I hadn't already, it would be a chance for me to break free.

A faraway sound brought me back to my own Wonderland of Hell. Totally obsessed with searching for my rabbit of death, I didn't even realize it was leading me, not to a locked door, but to my grave. I expected the creatures above me weren't coming for tea.

To the left, deep throaty screeches came from the top of the pines and gained intensity in volume. I used sheer terror to fuel my drive to live. Digging hands and nails into the ground, I forced myself to move, drawing both legs into a crouch, knees under my chest. I shot up like a spring and ran in the opposite direction of the screeching. Fear drove the cool thickness of air past both cracked lips as the burn seeped into my muscles. It created a movement that resembled the way I had always pictured the sound of thunder, not the aftermath of a lighting strike but as a huge, unseen dragon with force and strength behind it.

The curls in my hair had been replaced with tangles from tears and sweat. My hands and nails appeared as though I had driven them into an animal, from wiping away my gooey tears. Blood around the rims of each eye had produced hardened, itchy streaks down my face. I pictured myself as an undead in the latest horror flick, searching the night for a soul.

Although the haze had blinded me before it began to dissipate, I ran faster now that I visualized a path and the sense of direction. It was just the adrenaline boost I needed. Picking up the pace, I soon realized my body was driving me straight for the black mist I'd seen at the beginning of the dream. I had run in a complete circle and yet I felt misplaced. As the mist grew thicker, denser, I continued to move deeper into the forest. The fog took on an odd incandescence as it pulsed in anticipation.

Was it expecting me?

Small, curling wisps of black stretched up from the ooze that resembled melted eggplant. The whole scene gave the appearance of specters inviting participants to join them in a game of Hide and Seek through the trees and bushes. A crackling, similar to a match striking, came from the surrounding umbra. Sparks emanated from the oozing, colored mist. Within seconds, the bark around the base of the pines became engulfed in an unholy fire.

Terror worked its way down and found my inner brakes. Whipping both arms out like sails, they demanded my body stop before reaching the other side of the forest. When I spotted the demon on the other side of the blaze, my eyes filled with liquid determination. His hands reached out motioning for me to hurry. Anxiety, dread, and horror found a room next to fearfulness. It was an emotional, dark gift only he could give if I continued running toward him.

Crashing limbs from the trees behind me was the final push I needed to maintain forward progress. The creatures he was expecting had finally arrived. A sweeping wind from their wings as they landed caused me to stumble. I glanced up to survey the surroundings as I started to fall. I couldn't help myself from locking eyes with him. My hearing cut out. Now a star in a silent film, I mouthed his name in a small plea for help. He stopped gravity's pull by catching me inches from the flames. Heat licked over my skin; the smell of it made my stomach turn.

He had swooped in so fast, it made both ears pop. Seemingly stable, no longer deaf, I stood in front of him ready to face whatever was coming out of the trees. Being so close felt unnatural. Yet, his intentions were obviously focused on me. He didn't want to hurt me at all. I knew that now. His purpose was protection against the demons coming for me. Another sharp cracking came from behind and a soft flutter of air brushed past as his lean, muscular arms embraced me. Excitement in the form of chills started at the crown of my head and rippled down making each rib vibrate. The sensation continued down each extremity, and when leaning into him, I found strength and safety in his shadowy influence.

The sound of feet heading our way on bare ground made me think of shod horses. He stomped his right foot, and one of his arms wrapped possessively around my waist. His other arm rested on the hilt of something thin, old. The object had been made of dark marble with silver thorned vines curving down the handle. In its resting state, a low thrum of power hummed.

My eyes widened as five creatures, similar to my seven-foot-tall protector, were in front of us. The one farthest to our left shuffled his feet and outstretched his wings. Directly in front, this demon curled his torn dragon-like wings and bowed from his waist as a display of allegiance. I was positive his submissive nature was not on my account. The other two, to my right, followed the same gesture, wings curled, heads lowered. Next, the remaining creature stepped forward and extended his wings and arms, dropping his frame down hard on the ground. When his face twisted in pain, the one I leaned against growled, making me want to run and hide. He slammed the stick, burying the bottom into the ground next to me. The cracking along the earth echoed through our surrounding area and the five creatures bent lower.

"I expect more respect from my kind, especially one from my clan." His words were soft but menacing and it almost made me pee myself. My body shook uncontrollably from the inside out. He shifted me to his other arm and spun the scythe blade around me with lightning speed as if he had conjured it out of thin air. *My goodness, he was fast.*

The middle character broke his stare from the ground and said, "You are the only one we answer to. We continue to harvest the souls and fulfill our River's needs without question." Then he sucked in a quick breath. "We are supposed to obey what the Cauldron requests of us, no more." The air moved faster after he spoke again. The others were clearly in pain. The demon protecting me seemed to have control of them. I should have taken comfort in his defense, but found myself scared out of my mind.

One of the demons spoke, "Brother, we will continue to suffer and fight others until she chooses." He pointed to me. "You must open her eyes and release us from going against our nature. We take souls. It's not our place to protect them. Death cannot watch over and protect life. The clan grows weary of this task."

Another one spoke in a bleary tone, "I wish to be relieved from soul sitting and stick to what I do best. Death seeks out and collects the dead. From the moment Vessels take their first breath, the metronome of their life ticks down." He appeared determined to get his point across and lowered his face to hide the anger. "Time is their debt. Death becomes their payment."

Throat muscles tightened, choking me in guilt. The creature's head snapped up and eyes pierced me as if he had yelled, *Stop.* His features revealed a feeling of betrayal, wanting to challenge *my* demon's decisions. The reason for the tension between them was murky, other than the fact that they seemed to be talking about me.

I suspected that shifting feet and arcing wings indicated restlessness among the ones in the half circle. Murmurs of their disagreements were deafening. The protector held me tighter as his laugh lightly prickled down my neck. A new feeling of warmth filled my heart. Caring less about what took place in front of him, his focus remained on me.

"I didn't ask for this." He raised a hand to intertwine his fingers into the strands of hair, lifting them up to his face. Inhaling my scent provided information only he could interpret. I was his and only his. Those mesmerizing eyes raked over every inch of me, making me hurt all over, stirring a sleeping woman inside my teenage body. His salt and pepper wings sounded heavy as they flapped behind his back. The grass underneath me began to decompose and the ground became stone as though life was drained from his presence. My bare feet became colder than they had been, and I noticed frost had formed under them. "It did not start out this way. I was given a job other than reaping. We should be thankful for her existence because it changed our mundane way of seeing death." *What did my existence have to do with them?* I filed the question in a mental drawer for later while he continued to explain to the others, "We do not comprehend most emotions. We do not have a soul. We are doomed to negativity and tied by demise. I cannot explain the force or pull she has on me."

His words sounded hollow and desperate with need, creating heartache. I wanted to help but couldn't shake the jaws of doubt gnawing from within. We seemed to forget about the clan of demons encircling us. Their voices drifted away, smearing together both sight and sound. The disappearing forest continued to be consumed by the crackling fires eating away the edges of my imagination. I craned to meet his face, and he met my gaze, then raised both of his hands. With a feather touch, his fingers traced over my bloodstained face. Clearly embarrassed, I didn't understand why anyone would want to touch my face looking as I did. He slowly bent down, lips grazing my left earlobe.

When he came back into view, I didn't think his eyes could become darker than the black mirrors I'd seen earlier, but the coolness of his stare captivated me as he spoke. "Alexcia, you are my treasure. I will never allow anything to happen to you."

Flames and darkness served as a reminder of the future we faced. Resting both forearms around my middle and feeling defeated, I shuddered. Filling in my view with his unreadable stare, he then glanced away briefly and whispered, "I wonder if a soulless creature is worthy to be bound by a heart, tied to a soul? Yet, as you stand there looking at me, I continue seeing the eyes of the child I once knew. Do you still want to offer me your soul?"

Without hesitation, sorrow for him exploded inside my chest. Thin lines of ink trailed down his cheeks, and I reached up to caress his face while pulling him closer for a chance to kiss his lips. Even for a moment, to give him a taste of my soul.

How did I know him?

I hadn't grasped the words he spoke, let alone the feelings I had for him. Without conscious control over my voice, it answered him for me, "I can only choose what is right and pure. This is my only function. My heart is all the power I can give you right now." I was unsure what I meant, but he smiled at me. The other creatures formed a tighter circle around us and their wings appeared to be dripping hot silver acid that melted into what looked like cloaks made of the same black mist rising from the ground. Without notice, I found myself wrapped within two massive wings.

His wings sizzled as he pulled me into his icy embrace, leaning in to whisper against the inner part of my ear, "They say love knows no bounds. Death only has one boundary, and you cross over it when your heart stops. But written in the Unseen scrolls, it states this one emotion will last even after the breath ceases."

With his trail of words still lingering against the inside curvature of my ear, my composure disappeared. The blankets were wrapped tight around me like a cocoon. If I didn't know better, I would have sworn it had snowed in the room overnight. Shadows were thick and barricaded the bedroom and closet doors. No escape from the nightly terrors. Rubbing the grit from each lash, I unwrapped from the cocoon of covers, followed by flopping one leg at a time to the floor. My mind was clouded in the thick fog making it difficult to push off the bed. I wasn't sure if I'd ever been so weak and chilled from sweating. An overwhelming need washed over me to open the drapes and cleanse the bedroom from the unknown with the glow from the streetlights. His presence remained in the room with me. Turning slowly from the window, it felt as if I were wearing lead shoes. Pushing their weight toward the mirror, I was horrified at the face gaping back at me. I leaned closer to try and comprehend what the glass was telling me. Two small, dried streams of red gleamed on my cheeks. I was frozen in a nonexistent moment of time. My breath caught as I gasped… and woke up.

4

Forcing My Character To Be...

Nonconformist: one who does not conform
Oddball: an eccentric
Rare: marked by unusual quality, merit, or appeal
Maniacal: affected with or suggestive of madness
Anomalous: deviating from what is usual
Lunatic: wildly foolish
~Alexcia

WELL, IT WAS OFFICIAL, THE NIGHT WAS RUINED. I POPPED MY head up while strapping on Mom's high heels as the sense of direction alarm went off between both ears. We were heading in the wrong direction to the party. My head whipped around to stare at Tod, who was singing an off-key version of "Enter Sandman." He loved the metal songs from the eighties, said the drumming made his truck sound more monster-like. The second chorus started playing when he finally noticed I wasn't getting ready, and he looked disappointed when he realized I was staring a hole through his brain.

"What?" he yelled over the guitars and drums.

"You want to clue me in why we aren't heading over to Scotty's place?" I had to raise my voice an octave to be heard over the gritty, deep singing.

We were traveling up Charleston and had passed one of the local hotel/casinos. Luckily we stopped at a red light before getting on the 215. Flipping his bottle-blond bangs while chewing on his tongue, he gauged a reply. "Nope, it'll just start a fight. You'll see soon enough where we're going. I don't want you to start acting all pissy." He motioned with his head at my shoes, pointing out the other one wasn't on yet.

I unfastened the shoe and tossed it onto the black floor mat in front of my seat and stared out the window. No way was I getting ready while not knowing where we were going. Instead, I would remain in the truck, call one of my friends to come pick me up and hang out with them.

The unbuckled seatbelt made the final point with a defiant click, and I swished it away in a nonchalant move. Gracefully, I reached for the borrowed purse and started digging for the metallic green get-out-of-jail free card. When I found it, I grabbed my lip gloss too. After tossing the bag back in between bare feet, I set the phone down in the middle cup holder and leaned forward to grab onto the rearview mirror. Tilting it toward me, I applied a thin coat of gloss, nice and methodically. Tod got a small preview of what he would be missing tonight if he kept up this caveman act. He was going to learn... I was a person, not a prize. Both were P words but hardly interchangeable. Plus, I was making a point. He hated it when anyone touched or moved anything in his truck. I was now in violation of one of the top five major Tod rules and was hoping he hit a bump and the damn thing broke off.

Giving back some Ka-cha, I smiled wider at the thought and almost brushed the stick of gloss across my front two teeth. *Ka-cha is a secret word I made up in place of karma.* I let go of the mirror without repositioning it and wiggled back into the seat. Using my left hand, I reached over methodically pulling the seat belt across the front of my blouse, making sure the click was loud... an exclamation point. After a quick side glance, I noticed he was ready to listen. Tod had begun to simmer in the driver's seat while turning two shades of red.

"Damn it, Lex-Cee. You know I need to see in back of the truck. You should've been ready before I even pulled up into your driveway. Why do you always insist on making a presentation?" The oncoming headlights highlighted his jaw muscle as it twitched. Maybe his brain was on overdrive from so many sentences linked together. "You know how I feel about that. Plus, we planned to go out together tonight. So does it really matter where we're going as long as we're together?" He carefully moved the rearview mirror back into position, his face still holding a look of annoyance.

Anger was one emotion that worked against me because it brought these itchy, red-blotchy welts on my face and neck with it. Smooth pale skin became one color that blended in with the fire red hair strands. Then my best feature would go dry and that made it hard for me to spit the gritty words out. Tonight, I was proud to say, was not one of those nights. I started to feel prickly heat from the welts forming, but he was in my sights as I unhinged for rapid fire.

Narrowing both eyes to black slits, like one of those angry Emoticons you use in text, I exploded. "What the hell, Tod? All I asked was where we were going. You had to be all 1950s and pull the *little woman doesn't need to know* routine. Who and what makes you so superior to me anyway? I like you, Tod, I really do, but I think it's time to call this what it is. You're a Neener-Wad." I completely failed at making up polite curse words because of trying to curb the cussing scale. Unfortunately, the words sounded like playground language at a preschool. "I would call you something else, but you're not worth me lowering several I.Q. points to speak jock." *Oh, my goshness. Did I just do that? Wait? Did I threaten to no longer see him? Okay, maybe now I know why I can't peel my tongue off the roof of my mouth in an argument. It's the body's way of making me shut up before something stupid comes out.*

Not thinking before you speak always comes back to haunt you, like the Internet, once it's out there, you can never completely delete it.

It wasn't as if my heart had a one-way door, revolving was more like it. But I was nowhere near ready for a leash and collar. At school, the boys called me the Eight-Second Girl. If I didn't throw you off while you tried to break me, I might stick around for a while. I knew Tod's hands were getting chafed from the ride. The kisses were good but in all honesty, I was getting tired of trying to buck him off.

We stopped at another red light. In the glow, he appeared to be concentrating on something as I watched him slowly nod to himself. *This is it; I opened the door of opportunity.* With Tod zoned out, the truck seemed to accelerate through the intersection on its own. Driving the speed limit, I seriously thought he was going to drop me off at the next corner. To my shock, he did something entirely out of character.

Tod used the steering wheel to help shuck out of his letterman's jacket, and he tossed it at me while clearing his throat. Both hands gripped the wheel until his knuckles were white. He stared out the windshield, sighing with a heaviness so palpable it vibrated throughout the cab. Tod really appeared vulnerable, setting off every worry sensor, mimicking that high-pitched, balloon ear squeal.

"You really feel that way? Because I don't. I was hoping you would start wearing my jacket tonight and make us official. But I didn't want to ruin the mood by telling you where we were going right off. I already had a feeling you weren't going to be excited about it. Unfortunately, now I know you're really not going to like it." He took his left hand off the steering wheel and massaged the back of his neck. Tod must have been feeling the onset of an Alexcia headache coming on.

I found myself staring at him, similar to a deer's disbelieving look just before a vehicle takes its legs out. Thank goodness,

I was still sitting in the truck. Unspoken words floated in the air around me… intertwining with his. Did the insinuation of, *we should stop seeing each other* get lost in translation somehow?

"Yeeesss…" was my only response as I stared at his jacket. It smelled of AXE body wash and spray. The frown deepened, shifting my gaze from his jacket to his eyes. Then, I remembered where I had stuffed patience. It was getting moldy sitting in the untouched morals box. I stopped the first of many responses before saying something I would regret.

"Got a text from Scott tonight. He's laid up with the flu. Party's off." He cleared his throat again. "We were invited to another party, but I had turned her down because I knew we already had plans to hang with Scott." He eyed me in his peripheral vision so he could still drive and watch my reactions.

Tod hadn't said whose party yet, but he continued, "A lot of people are going tonight, and I hear she has a local band performing." *No name yet.* "No parents, just her older brother from college hanging around watching us, so to speak. He's visiting while on spring break. Picked up a couple of kegs for his sister's party too, showing he's cool with it. So, what do you say?"

A keg or two is good, but I still don't know who she is yet.

"Do you still want to go? No pressure. We can hang out for a while and see how it goes. When the night is over, if you still feel the same way, you can hand me back the jacket. I'll understand."

Okay, I was so getting punk'd. The hidden camera had to be in one of the radio knobs or maybe the handle of the glove box. I didn't want to give the impression I was on TV, or blow my fifteen seconds of fame on a YouTube video titled *Girl Freaks out over Commitment*. He had sounded too understanding during the last part of his little speech. Tod Ronald Isaac Peston was, after all, captain of the lacrosse team, one of the top twenty heartthrobs at the school, and a first-class jerk jock. Well, the last part I ad-libbed because I was still ticked, sort of. Listening to others was not his strong suit. Our conversation had turned uncomfortable. He knew I was a *just wanna have fun girl*, not *you're mine and only mine* commitment one. I felt the need to start putting my shoes back on. Plus, I was still skeptical about why he hadn't told me where we were heading.

"Tod, whose party are we supposedly going to? The beginning of this fight all started because you avoided that one question. I will make this simple for you, and I will say it slow." The words came out bitchy, but the seriousness of the night had turned *carefree party girl* into *broom up her ass witch*. That led me to stir the conversation with sarcasm, "Whose... party... are... we... going... to?" It's good to know a second language. Actually, I was pretty versed in jockisms. Dated a few football players, two from the basketball team and one wrestler. He hadn't lasted long, always tried to pin me before he'd kiss me. *What can I say? I like variety. When you buy a dozen donuts, you don't stick with only one flavor? Yeah, I thought so. See? Variety.*

I did have a little secret though, one that none of the boys in school knew, not even Tod. I was still one hundred percent pure, meaning if I were to walk down the aisle, white would adorn this body even though I preferred the look of different colored wedding gowns. Even black would technically work. Virginity still hung on my key ring. No one would unlock that without my say-so. *My legs weren't unhinged in that sense.*

Tod was turning the black beast with slime green roll bars off the freeway. We still needed to stop at a convenience store before reaching our destination, which I was still clueless about. Miffed and squirming, the seat belt kept locking up. Even the truck made sure I didn't bolt. Agitated, I craved a smoke.

When he pulled into a Circle K Mini-Mart, Tod revved the truck's engine at everyone to move or be eaten. His jaw clenched and unclenched as he parked, mulling over a decision to end his standoff with me and surrender. Cutting the monster's power, the cab light came on, and we fell into silence. Tod unbuckled his seat belt and opened the driver side door. Sliding out, when his feet hit the pavement, he turned to face me but shamefully looked away. He sighed in defeat. "Stellerback invited us."

He slammed the door. Hearing her name had sucked all the sarcastic words from my arsenal. The welts immediately began forming at the base of my neck as I tried to rationalize the situation I was being driven into unwillingly. Did I have enough time to place a call and say I'd been kidnapped? Tod was absolutely right about me not wanting to go. His ex-girlfriend had invited us to one of her bashes? Krista Gene Stellerback was not known for backing down when she wanted something, or, in this case, someone. She wanted Tod back. Everyone in the school knew it but Tod. He had broken it off three months ago, and it burned her pom-poms to ash because she hadn't done it first.

He didn't do it for me. We had the same math class but sat on opposite sides of the room, never even once said *hi*. Actually, he never even looked in my direction. When he first spoke to me, we were attending a small get-together. At that party, we were pretty hammered and stepped outside for air at the same time, so we sat on the front porch steps talking. It was then he told me about feeling smothered by Krista's presence. Tod's leash to freedom had been replaced with her hands around his slip chain choker. He was tired of being her lap dog. Other than going to practice, his job, and games, she had acted like she was his master instead of his girlfriend. In his drunken stupor, he shared with me why he'd stayed with her for almost eleven months. *Let's just say, he got her key. It was a duplicate, but it still fit in her lock.* Knowing that about Tod made me sick. When I got to know him better, I chalked it up to poor judgment. Yeah, Stellerback was only stellar to the boys when she was flat on her back. I laughed at my character stripping attempt of a joke.

When I caught sight of the convenience store door swinging out, Tod appeared from behind a couple who was laughing. I found myself shaking my head slowly at him as he rounded the truck on the driver's side. He looked put out. The clerk must have questioned his fake I.D. because he was only holding up a pack of smokes and a couple of twelve packs of Coke.

He may have thought by tossing his jacket into the ring, he'd won the first round, but I was not going to the party with my happy face screwed on. The plan was to do what he suggested—hang with him, drink some beer—and if I nonchalantly set his jacket on fire while lighting a cigarette, I wondered if he would take it as a sign. When Tod was situated back in the truck, he pulled me into a side embrace and kissed the top of my head. The sigh I released took some of the hope I'd held onto with it.

5

A shadow knocked on my window one day.
I count and hide, but it continues to play.
It leaves questions in the corners of my mind.
Silently whispering answers I cannot find.
Desperation pushes me to numb my fears.
I drink the spirits to stop my tears.
It works to keep the shadow quiet
By the window, it waits patiently in the moonlight
~Alexcia

KEPT QUIET AS WE DROVE UP TO KRISTA'S TWO-STORY HOUSE. *Oh, wait. That's the garage.* Great. I knew they had money, but the garage alone made my house look like one of the three little pigs had constructed it out of sticks and some borrowed bricks.

Although I wasn't ready for this confrontation, I needed to get out of the space in this truck. I required a cup of something cold to drink and a burn of smoke to calm quivering lungs. Besides, I hadn't really dressed for her kind of party but didn't plan on sticking around very long either. *So, did it matter? Nope.*

Tod turned the key off and stuck the ring in the front pocket of his jeans. He leaned into me, looking for some physical makeup time before heading to the presentation of Cirque de Fakes.

Ten to fifteen minutes later, Tod knocked on Krista's front door. It swung open with a backdraft of *teen spirit* hitting us in the face. I wrapped his jacket around me for protection from any liquid mishaps of anyone's inebriated greeting. The smell from a combination of liquors seeping from teenage pores as they mingled and danced to the live music made my nose scrunch up. That caused me to wonder if I smelled that way after a similar night like this. It would explain why, after a call and rescue, Ghost or Blakely would hose me down in perfume. Someone always forced breath mints and gum between clenched teeth before dumping my butt on the front lawn.

The guy who opened the door was tall and lean. I would guess him to be about twenty-two but still attempting to hold onto his high school years. He wore tight jeans and no shirt, which caused people to focus on the rainbow suspenders. It worked for him though and his humorous personality statement ascended up to broad shoulders, working as eye candy, depending on which way you followed the rainbows. My eyes roamed up to his chocolate-brown hair, adorned with plastered spikes, no acne, and a nice set of full lips... not that I was really looking. He smiled at me, causing my temperature to creep up a degree. Why? I had no idea. Both eyes averted to the floor, a nervous laugh escaped. He was wearing flip-flops and dressed like a new-age Mork from the eighties sitcom Mork and Mindy. *I watch a lot of late night TV Land.* In the midst of judging his attire, he made some type of welcoming hand gesture to Tod as he ushered us into the main hall.

The house was huge. A mini casino came to mind. Lights were out in a few of the side rooms, and the bedrooms were probably set up to be used as the hook-up rooms. But other opened rooms seemed to have lighting set on dim, giving me the feeling we were in the bat cave. I liked it in a twisted horror flick kind of way. The party was only missing the climatic ear-piercing note right before the impending doom. That thought reminded me to look for Krista.

Speaking of music, everyone was convulsing to a deep pulse bouncing off the walls. The room had probably been built to resemble an old-style ballroom but was converted to a mini concert hall. Tod put his hand on my tailbone to move me toward the dancing natives. Any minute, someone was going to toss me into the makeshift mosh pit and ask if I would be the next sacrifice.

The guy who had opened the front door did a disappearing/reappearing act. He held two clear plastic cups already producing condensation around the base. I took mine with an appreciative nod. No sense trying to converse over the percussion's pounding beat. I smelled the cup. It was what I needed, so I happily gulped and realized I'd downed almost half the liquid. I'd be happier yet if I could only find a place to light up. While lifting the pack of cigarettes and smiling sheepishly, I tried to look cute.

Our host understood the implication and pointed me in the direction where I was allowed to smoke. My eyes readjusted to the darkness by focusing on an opening across the dance floor. I placed the pack back in Mom's purse, met Tod's eyes and mouthed that I would find him later. Pushing up the sleeves to his jacket, I made little side bumpers to protect myself against the mob of thrashing bodies before making the plunge.

Without a word, Mork grabbed my free hand and dragged me into the crowd. Jutting the plastic cup above me like a shark fin, we bumped, grinded, and laughed our way through the crowd. Hands firmly clasped were now starting to slip from sweaty palms, but he never let go of mine. For that, I was grateful.

We finally made it to our destination, and I took a deep breath of satisfaction. Upon lowering the drink, I hiked Mom's purse securely onto my shoulder. After giving protector Mork a genuine smile of thanks, he nodded in reply. I turned away and pushed past two huge men standing by the open door like bouncers.

When I entered the kitchen, well, I thought it was the kitchen or maybe more like a diner, a ton of finger foods were neatly set out on different colored trays with glasses to match. Two sinks, dual ovens, a huge center island gas stove, with another small sink. The cabinets were stained a luscious cocoa bean color with retro silver and smoked light fixtures complementing the room. A gigantic polished silver and black Sub-Zero refrigerator sat like a waiting monster in the far left corner of the kitchen. On the other side, a long rectangular table made of the wood and stained the same as the kitchen cabinets filled the area.

Gently placing my plastic cup of salvation on the counter, I took a brief glimpse around the room and caught sight of the enemy as I lit the cigarette. A rather large crowd had encircled the table hootin' and a hollerin'. The guys started drumming really fast on the table, and one of the girls slammed a shot of something blue. That was when the volume of the room soared as she pounded the glass, rim side down, on the table. Licking the back of her hand, portraying a cat removing milk from her fur, it roused a seductive inward purr of self-satisfaction from the group. Krista apparently noticed me and stood, maneuvering around the males, her sights set on me.

I cringed inwardly. *Great.*

Just what I needed, a cat fight for everyone to see. How fitting. My dipstick was still a quart of beer too low for this confrontation to take place, so I clung to the Coach purse as a shield and took a slow drag off my cigarette. Mentally preparing myself for small talk, maybe if I exhaled the smoke, she'd get the hint I wasn't interested in playing.

Strutting toward me, she wore nothing but a gold shimmering flap of material to cover her C cups. I thought it might be an attempt at a dress by how the two black rings linked together the top of the skirt. She was rocking slightly in her four-inch, Nine West Craftwork boots. Yeah, she was on her way to being primed for some unlucky guy tonight. Her eyes skimmed over my attire with disgust after she noticed Tod's letterman jacket.

"Lay-Ceeee." Her drunken slur made its way up my spine. "So glad you could come. Where's Tod, you did come with him, right?" She looked past me to scan the room.

"Yeah, he's here." Glancing over my right shoulder, I hinted for her to go and find him herself. "Somewhere, if you can find him."

"Oh, well, here's a little info, Alex-Less. He'll come looking for me, right after he kicks his trash to the curb or when he's done playing with his stank rag doll. Word around is, you can't keep your men. Is that true, little pet? You're all talk and tease? How sad." Narrowed red, rimmed eyes with the same cocoa bean color as the kitchen, zeroed in on mine. Did she match everything on purpose?

I took another drag, blew the smoke toward her face and jammed a pizza bagel into my mouth, to stop me from explaining to Krista how I planned to kill her after she passed out tonight. It would be real easy to hang out until the body succumbed to her alcohol intake and then toss her off the second story. *Drunken accidents happen all the time at parties like this, right?* I even had a statement all planned out. "She was trying to fly, officer. I tried to stop her, but she dove off before I could get to her." Sniff, sniff. Well, the sniffing would make it sound like I meant to save her.

She waved a hand in front of her face, moving it a little too close to mine. Invading my space was a serious faux pas. So, I stepped back to give her some room.

Sneering at me, she said, "You scared, kitten?" Then she took one step forward. The guys at the table were getting impatient and motioned for me to bring her back. I shook my head and gave the guy wearing black shades a classic eye roll. Krista thought I was responding to her. Sticking one of her manicured claws in my face, her voice cracked. "Quarters, right now. You win, I leave you and Tod alone. I win, well let's just say, I will let you watch me treat him as a man should be."

"Are you crazy? Could you really be that drunk? From what I was told, he broke it off with you long before I was in his life. Why don't you let him decide? Oh... wait... he already did." I grabbed her hand and turned it palm side up. Spitting on it, I placed my smoke right in the middle. It made a little *pssst* sound. "Thanks for taking care of that for me. I wouldn't want to burn the pretty wood floor, now would I?"

She screamed and flicked her hand away, shaking the butt of the cigarette onto the floor. *Awe, too bad, but at least it's not going to leave a burn mark.* I gulped the rest of the beer and started to push myself back through the thumping beat so I could find Tod. *I need to get the H-E double toothpicks out of here.*

Not watching where I was going, I ran right into a blue cotton T-shirt. My gaze skimmed up to a familiar face and yet not. His eyes were blue and black, more black than blue. I took a step back to study his expression. Had I seen him before? His features were different from what I remembered, but I really tried to recall from where. He was tall, really tall, maybe six feet or even six two. His hair was dirty blond and the style seemed to fit his face. It was long on top but short around the sides. I could tell he used his long bangs as a shield, concealing him behind locks of hair so he could check everyone else out without getting too close. The shadows playing across his face was what probably gave his eyes such a dark appearance. But there was something about them working as a lure, trying to latch onto something from my past. It was buried so deep, even I couldn't bring it to the surface. In defeat, I sighed as a small shock wave of déjà vu rippled through me. His hair and lips didn't click with the foggy picture my mind was trying to reconstruct. My face twisted in frustration.

"Am I that bad? Damn, I really liked this shirt too." He stared down at me while speaking in a playful manner. A wave of concern crashed over me as I assessed the huge, wet stain down the front of his shirt. Oh, crap. Did he say he liked the shirt he was wearing? In haste to find my so-called boyfriend, I had spilled his drink.

"I am so sorry. Please, what were you drinking? I'll go and get you another one." I grabbed some cocktail napkins from a girl's drink tray and started to blot his wet, wounded shirt.

He stopped me. "How about a dance instead or maybe a drink and then a dance? Do you have a light? I can't seem to find a lighter." Was this guy for real? Wanting to dance, drink, and smoke? I sized him up. He wasn't bad looking but something behind his eyes triggered my pulse to accelerate—not in an excited kind of way—more like if I said the wrong thing he'd kill me and leave me for dead kind of way.

Mr. Blue Shirt took a free hand, and immediately my heart ached from an overwhelming sense of loneliness. I hastily scanned the room for Tod. Once I locked on him, he would be my excuse to bow out of the dance. Blue Shirt escorted me to the middle of the dance floor as the beat became more of a hard rhythm chant. Guys were wrapping around their partners, drawing them close. I eyed this guy, waiting to see if he was going to do the same thing. Instead, he looked at me with hardened features and made my throat feel as though I had swallowed boiling coffee. The chill around me involuntarily caused the little hairs to stand straight up. Pretending to be nonchalant about the situation, I rubbed the top of both shoulders through Tod's jacket to get back the warmth this guy's atmosphere had stolen. As he eyed me from under his bangs with a Cheshire cat grin, I was picking up on his attitude. *What the hell was he thinking?*

All of a sudden, I didn't feel like dancing and used a hand

gesture for a drink. He gave me a quick thumbs-up motion toward the kitchen. My shoulders slumped forward in a small sign of protest. I so did not want to go back there with him. One of the girls from the B squad held a tray of drinks, dancing and weaving in between sweaty bodies. I lunged for her arm, startled when she whipped the liquid goodies, almost spilling them. As they slid across the tray, I helped her out by saving the one closest to me before it fell. A fruity bite hit my nose, figured it was a Jell-O shot, so down it went. That's when I noticed a disappointing noise coming from behind me. *Oh, my goshness. Judge much.* He pushed past me, then turned to grab the front zipper of Tod's jacket. Astonished by his brash behavior, an inside voice asked, "Who is this guy?"

The harsh light of the kitchen hurt my eyes. I blinked a few times to regain normal sight because the Quarters game crowd had dissipated from the table which gave the room a softer feel. A few cliques hung around the island of cocktail food, but it was quiet enough to hear their soft conversation. I hit blue T-shirt with a hard question.

"So, I spilled your drink, insulted you, almost danced with you, but I still don't know your name."

"What's in a name?" He shrugged. "What's yours?"

What is this—a guessing game? With hands on my hips, I gave him an arched eyebrow look. Did he think he was being cute? Yeah, name or I was out of here in five seconds.

He bent down to bring his eyes level with mine and replied through a secretive hiss. "Michael. That is all you need to know." He seemed pleased by captivating my attention because my eyes were frozen wide with astonishment. I couldn't even turn away from him. Then he mimicked me, placing his hands on his hips and arching the opposite eyebrow.

I was still caught under some kind of hypnosis, staring into the never ending pools of blackness when a swirling flash of blue rose behind his irises. Power, intimidating yet tantalizing. My mouth became parched, and I wanted what was dragging me deeper into his abyss and advanced willingly. As I tried to reach for it, he cleared his throat. What he said next was confusing, "He's going to tear up my Bonding Rite. Alexcia, let go of my essence. If you don't, it will take your breath away, and literally my existence."

Michael placed his hands on my arms and lightly shook me to break contact with his eyes. The corner of his eyebrows were straining, trying to close his eyes but couldn't from the deadlock glare he'd started. Now he was gritting his teeth. "Let go of me, Witch. Didn't your parents teach you it's impolite to stare?"

Parents? I knew that word. I had parents. My lids slid down to state the store was closed. The back of both eye sockets pulsed with a pounding energy that left a lingering echo bouncing around my skull, followed by a high-pitched ringing in my inner ear. Both hands worked up to my face as I sucked in a breath, which made me feel awful. Could lungs actually collapse instead of expand with every intake? Quivering from the ice bath my soul took, I struggled to regain my perspective.

"What happened, Michael? Did you feel that too?" I couldn't help but believe what happened between us was easily explainable. Small quakes continued to push out of my epicenter making it tough to maintain my equilibrium. I staggered into his arms keeping my face away from his. My stomach and brain argued whether I should puke or not. Lovely.

A strong, cold breeze swept past, resting squarely between us. Michael held me upright with both feet hanging four or five inches off the ground, and he walked me backward through the massive kitchen to one of the chairs behind us. I heard something scraping against the wood floor with force. He murmured, "Thank you" to someone I hadn't seen or heard. Suddenly, the chill from his fingers around my ribs vanished. My body reacted with the force of gravity as I fell, like a rag doll, onto the chair. Now my butt *and* pride stung. *Damn Isaac Newton for being right.*

Michael reached back and pulled out a chair to sit directly in front of me. Then the ringing started to subside because I could make out the steady rhythm of music. In the other room, the band was attempting a version of "Evil Angel," by Breaking Benjamin. What a coincidence... or not. In the lyrics, the singer asked an evil angel why he couldn't breathe, then the metal rhythm strummed. It made me consider the last thing Michael had said. Something about, if I didn't stop, I was going to find myself unable to breathe? I couldn't make sense of him, me, or the situation. In need of liquid escape, I caught the attention of one of the girls in the kitchen pouring shots. As I motioned for service, a girl with ink-blue hair that was styled in a pixie cut picked up her tray. Her white leather miniskirt was so tight, I was sure she thought it was an option for birth control. She overly rocked her body to the music as she approached us, held up the tray of rainbow colored shots and smiled.

I sighed. "You're my savior, thanks." Returning a smile back at her, I placed my fingers around the pink cream liquor in the little glass that read, *Slam it and Forget it.* I was now praying for this drink to do just that... make me forget.

Michael took three drinks from the tray. The waitress frowned at him and huffed, spinning away from us on four-inch heels. Her round was going to be pretty quick since we took half the tray. I nodded at Michael, mentally telling him to tip the poor, overworked cheerleader. He sighed and dug into his front pocket, tossing a crumpled wad of money onto her tray. I watched as she sauntered past the bouncers outside the kitchen door, nodding and smiling again. That was when it dawned on me that all the girls serving here tonight were actually from the B-cheerleading squad. Talk about underage sweat shops. Krista was working the girls during her party. I wondered if she promised them a spot at the royal round cheer table.

I was brought back to reality when the guy in front of me coughed after downing the clear shot with the gold flakes. The guy licked his lips in a savor the flavor way. "That one gets me every time, must be the gold. Light can't live in the dark, right?" He laughed. I didn't get it and only shrugged at his one-sided joke. Stand-up was not his calling. My tongue felt heavy as I swirled fingers around the rim of the shot glass before wrapping a hand slowly around it. Michael's face blurred slightly as I forced to refocus.

Michael picked up another shot and held it up, looking at mine. "You gonna make a toast with me or what? I feel awkward holding this up with yours still in your hand."

I set the drink down, then pulled Tod's jacket off and placed it over the back of the chair. Throwing my purse on the floor, I cleared my throat while turning back to him and picking the glass up again. "I'll make you a deal. I will toast with you if you tell me what the hell just happened between us."

Michael curled his lips. "Deal. To the dimensions I guard. May they once again be in balance."

"What?" I blurted out. He laughed, guiding our raised glasses together. Both rims clinked when they connected. I nodded slowly and sipped the cool liquid. It rushed into my belly, catching everything inside on fire before sliding across home plate. I was swimming in befuddlement, and now alcohol, as we slammed our glasses down. My voice scratched from the after-burn. "So, what happened?"

"I think you were falling for me." He held his fingers over the top of the third shot… making rings with his index finger, dipping the tip of it into the glass to put it in his mouth, slowly sucking on it. It turned my gut more than I wanted to let on, so I swiped the drink from under his fingers and made it disappear. I coughed and wheezed trying to make my throat open up. With hands banging on the table, I leaned forward to find my breath. He smacked between my shoulder blades a few times. Then, had he chortled chortle? Or something close to it.

I looked at him through tear-filled eyes and found him holding back laughter. "What made you choke? Upon looking back, the answer I gave you might not have been very truthful or fair of me. My fingers were wandering... well, you understand what I was implying. Oh, I know." His black eyes flickered in amusement as he continued, "Or could it be from your poor judgment in reaction to the first two?" He kept laughing as he spoke, and then snorted, which normally I find as a cute quality in a guy. This time his voice sounded like mocking. "So you know." He gestured down at the empty shot glass. "That one, I'm pretty sure was straight Jim Beam." Michael's dwindling laughter came to a sudden stop, and he took on a more serious look. "Can I give you some fatherly advice?"

I shrugged and winked, displaying indifference. I was starting to feel flirty, an effect from the sudden rush of sleep elixir. Looking away from him, I noticed Mom's Coach purse was nowhere on the floor.

My eyelids fluttered. I was feeling a good buzz, but wouldn't say drunk, yet. I kicked out and glanced around for the purse. Not finding it, I slumped back in the seat. Michael bent down and magically pulled it out from under his chair. I held his actions in question. Leisurely looking at him through mascara lashes, I sighed trying to keep certain thoughts in order. The resulting words were spoken with a slight slur. "Mike, can I call you Mike? Mike, may I ask a personal question? It's a big one. Do you think you can handle it? I mean, you're so straightforward with me, figured you wouldn't mind a few more answers... uh, questions?" Yup, I was feeling it, but before I completely lost my sanity, I needed at least one answer.

He smirked, realizing I had bought a one-way ticket for the

smashed express. Michael's expression spoke volumes. He had nothing to fear from me and my mundane questions.

I took that chance to use some reverse psychology. Scooting the chair closer to him, I maneuvered one knee in between his legs, to create more of an intimate space. Feeling possessed, I found myself creeping up his hard frame, then cupping a hand to his ear. I whispered, "What are you, exactly? You know." I traced a finger up his leg to get his attention. "Michael, what's the price to dance with death?"

His body went rigid and his breath caught. "What did you say to me?"

I started laughing in his ear. "I so got you. You thought I was going to fall for one of your lines." I snorted and rocked back in the chair, placing both hands on my lap and tossing strands of hair back in triumph. Instantly his actions caught me off guard and caused me to sober up a bit.

Clamping down hard on my right wrist, he jerked me toward him. He spoke with his teeth welded shut. Freezing air slithered down my back. "I tire of child sitting. You have no idea who or what I am. Here's some advice, little Vessel, stay sober and stay pure so I can get back to my real job." When he let go, I thought I saw flakes of frost where his fingers had touched.

I jumped from the seat as I raised a hand to slap the crap out of him. Instead, I found myself retreating, with one hand still up as a shield. Blackness pulsated through his body, emanating from his head like a shroud or cloak. Blinking several times, the image started to fade. Tomorrow morning it would be a drunken memory.

I made myself break away from his creepy aura. This guy was bad news. Why do the weird ones always find me? I needed to find Tod.

Michael appeared in front of me. Keeping his eyes lowered, he handed the purse back. "Alexcia, I was out of line, I didn't mean to come on so strong. Sit back down, have another shot, forget what I said before. If you still want your questions answered…" Michael's words seemed strained as he let the rest of the thought hang in the air.

"I just need to find my boyfriend and maybe get some air." At that moment, air was a good idea. The clouds rolling through anxious thoughts had turned gray, and I could tell a storm was brewing between us. Twisting from his half committed embrace, I stumbled only to recover methodically putting one foot in front of the other. He yelled over the music, "Don't go with Tod. You'll be riding with death and yours will come just as swift." His reaction was proof this jerk was drunk. I had picked the right time to cut ties with him.

Lost in the sea of bodies, a beacon appeared through the sparked up haze of the room. A familiar face from school, Melanie Crisspike was leaning on a few of Tod's teammates, Brad especially. This was great. People I knew. They were huddled halfway between me and Tod. At least I would be with familiar people and away from Mr. Creeper. Pushing through the waves, I sensed Michael's presence right behind me.

I waved and yelled, "Hey, what's up?"

Mel saw me and returned the gesture. A cool, thick breeze came from out of nowhere, the chill of it felt like a warning. Something grabbed onto me and was slowing down my progress across the dance floor when one of the guys saw I was in trouble and extended his arm—becoming a lifeline. When his beefy fingers entwined in mine, a sigh of relief puffed out, and he pulled me to safety.

The lack of nicotine worked on frayed nerves. I needed to get out of there. Raising my voice as loud as possible over the band, I said, "What's everyone doing? I think I'm ready for some air." An anxiety attack threatened to happen as I tried to get Tod's attention from across the room.

He was surfing the waves of people from the other side of the room. Tod was double pointing to the front of the house in an overly dramatic move. He sang with the band causing me to smile. Then I saw someone hand over his letterman jacket. Oh, Damn. After the Mr. Creeper incident, I didn't even think twice about it. Crap.

"Where have you been? So much for hanging out." Smiling, Tod pulled me in close and brushed my lips with a soft kiss before he continued, "There's a group of us going up to Red Rock for a bonfire. Krista's brother is buying the beer before heading up there, it was his idea. How about it?"

I pouted. He knew what I thought before I had a chance to say anything. Cupping my face to lock our gaze, he bent down to whisper, "No, Lex-Cee, she's not coming." His words were soft. "I heard about what happened in the kitchen and know for a fact Krista's passed out. She's still the same and will never change. I know I don't want that kind of one-sided life anymore."

Glancing at his letterman jacket, I felt a twinge of guilt for leaving it. When I stared deeply into his eyes, I tried to use the guilt to stir up some kind of emotion. He held up the jacket with questioning eyes. With a coy smile, I took it from him and slipped it back on. Then I found myself rambling. "I'm sorry. I'm not used to having it. I took it off after dancing. It was so hot, ya know? I didn't mean to leave it." My incoherent button was jammed, pathetic. Damn, if anything, loose lips meant I was trying too hard. Moving past *I like you* should have come naturally... the way breathing happens. Why couldn't love be the same way for me?

We headed for the door when a familiar feeling of frost stirred the air in front of me. An overwhelming sense of fear sparked my flight reflexes and continued to push my group to walk faster. Melanie tripped and laughed over her encumbered motor skills, obviously drunker than the rest of us. Could the night get any worse?

Once we pushed our way outside, I heard the guys talking about who was going with whom when I felt the coolness again. It could only mean one thing. Michael was somewhere nearby. A sob caught between panicked emotions. Why was I so afraid of him?

Tod and one of his friends, someone I didn't know very well, were climbing into the truck. How did I get stuck with Sally-Drinks-A-Lot? She was draped over half of me while trying to stay upright. I wanted to make it to the truck and get the hell out of Dodge, not caring where we ended up. Even the idea of going home sounded better than staying for another second. We were almost to the monster truck beast when I thought I heard a low growl. I turned to find Michael coming out of the house, making a beeline in our direction. I picked up the pace and hollered at the guys. Tod's friend opened the passenger door and pulled his rag doll into the cab. Tod moved around and got in on the driver's side. I had trouble gaining a footing in the Coach Amina heels. His friend grabbed my arm and pulled me up. "Hey there, have we met? I'm Brad Stu. I play on the varsity soccer team."

I used a smile to say, *hi*, nice to meet you. My grip said, *now get me into the freakin' truck.*

Another roar and it sent every fear emotion I had into overdrive. I used the seat belt across my chest as a security blanket and glanced out the side window to see Michael's features change. He was covered in shadows, even with the moonlight spilling overhead. Sliding forward, I placed both hands on the back of Tod's seat and yelled, "Go now." He revived the truck's heart and we sped out of Krista's driveway.

I needed some reassurance and peered between a few fingers out the back window. For once, being speechless was a blessing because I couldn't explain to anyone what I'd seen that night, other than the fact the alcohol might have impaired my vision. Michael was dressed in a cloak. He had wings arched behind his back and was shouting for me to come back.

Where was Scotty when I needed to scream? *Beam us up, now.*

MICHAEL'S EYES: FROM THE EYES OF A REAPER

I STOPPED RUNNING AFTER HER. SHE WAS ON THE WAY AGAIN TO MEET HER demise. How many times must we save this creature? I didn't want to do what I knew I was ordered to do if things went wrong. Our problems would be solved *if I killed her.* Unfortunately, that thrill would have to wait for another time and place.

Swiping at a lock of sweaty bangs with the back of my hand, I then reached for the cell and dialed the number.

First ring. He picked up but didn't say anything. Figured.

"It's Michael."

I nodded in response to the swift onslaught of questions.

"I know, but she was crispy and flying tonight. I couldn't convince her to stay put."

The voice on the other end of the line was scorching down to the eardrum. I held the cell away until he was done. He gave me a small reprieve before I physically reported to the head of the clan. My ear might completely be removed then anyway. F-ing great, so looking forward to that.

While I blew out a thin trail of black mist, the Smolder I contained snarled as a reply. "I know. I screwed up. She pissed me off tonight trying to come on to me and crap." Heat from the speaker cooked every last nerve. "No, I didn't act on that. She is your problem child, not mine. I only watch her when you make me. Yes, yes, I know what she is. Doesn't mean I have to like it."

I started walking away from the loud drumming and the soul-filled Vessels. Soon enough, I would be sending them to the Ever After. "Yeah, I know where you are. I know. I will take your job. I'll be right there. From what I saw when I held her hand, you have about twenty-one minutes before it happens." I checked my watch to be sure. "That should be about three minutes to midnight. Yeah. Eleven fifty-seven." I nodded again in agreement with his instructions. "Don't worry. I will make it there on time." I hung up the device.

He can go and save that unpleasant, foul-mouthed, broken creature. She was his problem to watch over, not mine.

I am an Ashen, death's personal wielder, the Grim Reaper from everyone's worst nightmares. I reap the souls of the living. I do not babysit them.

Frustration rubbed my scales the wrong way. With a snarl, I allowed the black mist to surround me, to remove the blending spell and reveal my true form. Opening both wings with a thunder crack and adjusting the battle axe I used for reaping, I lifted off into the cool night sky. A stripped-naked thought danced as evil while the night's cover enveloped me. Settling into the role I meant for, a half-cocked grin crept across my face. *This is what I do best. I take souls.*

6

TEVIN'S SIDE: THROUGH THE EYES OF A REAPER

SEETHING, THE VOICE INSIDE MY HEAD HISSED. "SHE GOT AWAY, again."

I snapped the cell phone shut and heard the plastic buckle under pressure. Placing two fingers on the bridge of my nose, I closed my eyes tight and swayed in frustration. The feeling of agitation only began to subside when I used the motion to calm the daemon within. Tainted judgment disgusted me more than the Ashen I had sent to watch over the child. The caged beast from inside forced me to release my anger into the chilled unknown, detaching from the noticeable emotions of torment.

Michael was right. It was my task to personally watch over her. His noncommittal attitude toward guarding the Child for the past ten years was infuriating. Plus, he was the type of daemon who enjoyed playing with his food before he killed it out of boredom. Michael did not see her the way I did. To him, she was only another soul to harvest. Alexcia was like a well-placed pot on a stove and the water inside it represented her spirit. Michael enjoyed turning up the flame waiting for the water to almost boil over. Then, when she was about to blow, he would stir her pot and start all over.

I should have known better than to send him to keep an eye on her, but the rest of the clan were attending to their own assignments. When Michael had called to inform me her name appeared in the Cauldron's waters, I was already on another harvest and needed to feed. Unable to be in two places at one time. I knew better, but my lack of energy trumped *Child sitting*.

Michael was the only Ashen who had extra time and seemed willing after I disclosed she was attending one of her friend's gatherings. His quick acceptance for the task was the red flag I had completely overlooked. Michael's zeal toward anything was a sign things were not going to go as planned.

I whispered a curse to be carried away with the next whip of air. "Damn the cloak I cast." Those harsh words melted the specks of snow in front of my mouth.

The bus and train were scheduled to collide around 12:02 a.m. and Michael had said her ticket was punched for 11:57 p.m. Besides, the crash location was on the outskirts of the city. Whereas, Alexcia's winding path to demise was in the opposite direction. Not even a Time Bend could move me fast enough between both reapings. Some forces of magic were bound by basic rules. Unbreakable ones.

A multiple harvesting was a complicated and delicate task, not one to be rushed by any means, especially if some of the souls were supposed to pass at the same time. I have never liked passing up certain responsibilities, but deep down I knew Michael could handle it with ease. The Ashens in my clan were still fairly new compared to most daemons of our kind. Approximately six hundred years was a mere stone skip across the lake of our time. Actually, that was a guess since I stopped calculating around five hundred years ago. At some point, counting became mundane.

With the position of clan leader, my powers alone could harvest hundreds if the job required it. Michael was considered my right hand or second in command. It was not a question about him being capable or that I was worried about his ability to get the job done. He existed for assignments like the one I had dropped in his lap. In that particular instance, a slight possibility existed that he would get caught up on the high from so much work. A severing ritual was capable of spurring a contact high from the overabundance of life force collected during the Knell. Each time our death weapon of choice connected with a soul, the power mix would feed us like a daemonic jump charge. To be honest, I was really looking forward to recharging tonight. *Michael should be able to take a month or two off from his reaping duties if he remains well-grounded and does not lose control.*

We did not need the River's attention with us by making more Casters. The ghost population was already booming from so many botched jobs. If I saw another TV show about the "Other Side of Death" or "What Happens after You Die?" or the ones that go hunting to prove the paranormal exist. I shook my head in a small fit of laughter from the next thought I had. If only these Vessels really knew what chased them, even during daylight hours, we would have more souls to harvest simply from them being scared to death.

Tonight the River was requesting to refill more power than the norm. I had heard a rumor, by thread and thimble that the River's flow was slowing down again. This was another reason I wanted to perform tonight's task personally. A reaping of that magnitude would require a flawless, orchestrated style since the performance would happen in front of the audiences of living and the Unseen.

The Bridge Crossers had always belonged to a single part of the network of the Unseen realm. Being angels once did not assure they would agree with the Constant of Light's rules. Since they chose to have free will, and in doing so, damned themselves to the world of serving. Now banned from the House of Light, and too pure to survive in the depths of the River Styx's sepulcher, they had no choice but to make a Bond-Rite with the head of the House of Space, Lucifer.

Becoming a Bridge Crosser was their atonement for retaining certain freedoms. They were not the most patient of half-breeds and had kept to strict guidelines about keeping schedules because of the gondoliers. The souls they were required to escort across the bridges to the boats needed to remain on time to ensure the empty power source was replenished to the River for recycling. Therefore, Styx kept flowing and the life cycle continued.

The River Styx was known as the Infinity Constant, and one of the main rules for the Unseen included: To never disrupt the flow of the river. To my knowledge, that rule had been in place before the Constant Light was created. The River Styx never stopped creating since the dawn of time. My job was to make sure Ashens continued to harvest the souls needed so the River's power could be evenly distributed through the act of recreating.

I understood why everything stayed the same because of the River. And I knew the rules and why I existed. This job was not going to jeopardize the clan over some special Vessel. That particular Bond-Rite situation was jarring each nerve. Pushing a free hand through tangled hair with an added sigh, I thought of how and why my job description had changed. It infuriated me beyond confusion.

What I did not know was why our clan had been bestowed with a new description entitled Child Welfare. This assignment had created questions about being the head of our clan, reaping the dead, and still finding time to save Alexcia. The next thought oppressed my daemon brain with a growling voice. *All this power and for what?* The answering voice sounded much like my own, with jaws wired shut. *For nothing.*

When I met Rae-Lynn Stasis, little did I know our chance meeting would cast me in the main role in *A Daemon's Adventures in Babysitting. I can justly say, it has been an interesting ten years, but who's counting?* I was shocked to find out that the child's parents, for the most part, were from the Unseen.

Alexcia's mother was once the Angel of Water. Her ability was to free a being from their fears. When Rae was tossed out of heaven fifty some odd years ago, she was stripped of her wings and turned half human. The child's father was a full-fledged daemon. He used the name Max Stasis, but it concerned me how my cloak shivered whenever we were in his presence. It was as if my powers were cautious of him. That kind of uncertainty always clouded judgment. Then there was a nagging sense I had seen him before, but the time frame and situation eluded me. The fact alone that I have never been recopied was enough reason to stay as far away from him as possible. In the reality of dealing with death's finalities, universes were not far enough. When it came to addressing their daughter's issues, I only conversed with the one who thought she held my leash… Rae.

Max and Rae-Lynn committed a pure sin by falling into an emotional bond that would link them indefinitely with each other. I never believed in the word love. Simply stated, "I believe it is a fictitious human word for their own imaginary emotions." Anyway, the result of their sin was conception. As such, the child's blood had a portion from both the House of Light and the House of Space coursing through her veins. The Unseen call the offspring from these special unions, Children-of-Balance. A decade ago, I found myself in the wrong place at the wrong time, and now I was the overseer of one of them.

A part of me regretted the night I had stepped into that hospital room. At first, it seemed I could only covet a tiny Vessel on a gurney with a soul to fulfill the job requirement. When she spoke to me, it caught me off guard as I made eye contact with her. *Be the devil take it,* her eyes stopped me in mid-sever. Then I found myself fighting to protect her from a true Unseen asshole, Razor, one of the Bridge Crossers. He was extinguished, thanks to some quick thinking. Unfortunately, over the years he was replaced by others in the Unseen who tried to tip the balance of power. Angel, daemon, and elemental alike wanted claim to the child's soul before she could choose. I blame temporary insanity for accepting this role as bodyguard.

Shock skittered across my skin as a sound of laughter echoed from the snow-topped mountains. This stopped the re-cap of the *what if* era. Poor child, if she only knew her Guardian Angel was none other than a Grim Reaper. *Ashens are the harvesters of death, stealing a human's last breath by separating soul from body.* The simple thought lingered because separating soul from body was my only task back then. A sigh of defeat followed.

It had been a complicated situation juggling between death's dealings and saving one life all the time. And this particular Vessel had never made it easy to save her butt. It became more difficult the older she got. The girl had been forever creative in choosing her venues.

Alexcia took after her daemon father in the stubbornness and mouth department, which made her a magnet for trouble. I completely understood how she tended to get on not only Michael's last nerve, but the whole clan's. Controlling the urge to use my scythe when dealing with one of her situations should have netted me more respect from her parents. Truthfully, there were times I wanted nothing more than to harvest her soul myself.

The most unsavory part of guarding had been when one of us was forced to save her ass by putting her into a manageable state. That involved drugging her by using the mist from our cloak as a sedative. Once we had her in an embrace, she was baked within seconds, ready to be served. The mist allowed her to still function while we barked out commands for her to follow. One thing in our favor was that Alexcia could not retain her memory from events taken place in our presence. *Unfortunately, with every pro there is a con.* One side effect of the mist was her mouth tended to runneth over and turn her somewhat violent. On occasion, the child acted on her aggression as though she was untouchable, even from us. After taking care of her little incidents, and shortly before passing out, she would steal a glimpse at me. Her presence would plunge into my core like a serrated blade cutting away at the cage where part of my power, the Smolder, lay dormant. Thank the Houses, she was never coherent long enough to succeed in freeing it. *As an Ashen, the price for eternally dealing death is a portion of our sight. Part of our power we carry is called the Smolder. It is what fuels our abilities, but blurs the edges of our sight, so we see everything draped over in a haze.*

After hundreds of years looking through the fog… when it was removed, the sharpness tended to stab the back of both eyes. Alexcia's power clawed its way through, burning away the cloudy areas of my vision. Which, for a brief moment, caused me to see the crispness of her features before the smoke returned again. Thank the stars, she was not strong enough to keep it going for both of us.

I cursed at the memory, "Damn me to hell's fire and back," because that was where I ended up every time. She would send me straight into the depths of my own hell and burn with an unnatural feeling for her as it engulfed every thought into pure chaos. I never understood these mixed feelings for this child. As an Ashen, I was not supposed to have emotions toward Vessels. The angel side of her power had always been hidden behind her eyes—truly the windows to her soul have frozen me dead in my tracks and accomplished the impossible—control death. *Until her, no human or animal has ever been able to stop me from harvesting their soul. The child does not know what she is, let alone the power that lies dormant behind those eyes.*

From the beginning of time, our orders had never changed: Do not get attached to a Vessel because eventually the soul will be returned to the River. They were not made to last forever. Casting a glance up to the midnight blue sky, I could still picture how her eyes looked up at me from the hospital bed. Wide, scared, confused but laced with a trust in me I never understood. I gritted my teeth as a low rumble from the beast within wanted to be released from its prison. Standing up straight, I figured I should get started. Changing from one form to another takes time. Unfortunately, I was running out of those golden seconds. I looked at the time and noticed it was 11:43 p.m., less than fifteen minutes to get to her.

I loathed the process of switching from reaper to battle form as a Smolder. Even though I enjoyed having my minion close, I knew this would be for the best. Unlocking the possessed side of me and its abilities would be to our advantage if we should run into trouble. Tonight could possibly become ugly. The thought brought an evil tug forcing me to smirk. In Smolder form, I could slip into the darkness undetected by her assassins. This altered appearance would also allow me to see the different time dimensions by tearing the overlapping plains apart. It was how I planned to reach her because the Smolder's power was more like *how the crow flies* but on speed. The only drawback was if there were not a lot of Time Obstacles in the way. Not everything moved through them the same way, especially when the dimensions overlap.

I slipped the crushed cell phone into the back jeans pocket and quickly made a mental note to get a replacement in the morning. Finding my footing as I started scaling down the mountain, I jumped, making the edge of a ledge on the right. I landed like a cat on all fours and cocked my head to judge the distance from there to the ground below. It was not far. I figured about ninety feet give or take, so I focused on the sounds from a nearby waterfall. Then I stepped off in a crouch, forcing the mass to fall faster, slamming onto a patch of dirty snow. Dust-

ing off the snow and mud, I summoned my minion to shift me
from my blended-Vessel appearance. When the cloak was done,
I watched it slither to the edge of the canyon. Now naked, I felt
the wind coughing up the remaining ice and snow into places
where it should not be. I clapped both hands to psych myself
into morphing. No matter how awesome the power, the more
magic summoned caused the pain returned to the user tenfold.
The practice was referred to as compensation, and I was once
told, "Get used to it."

Rounding both shoulders into my body, the action made
a massive crunch as bones started breaking and fusing into a
different skeletal structure. Time for my Smolder to appear. The
tips of my wings' blades tore through flesh and jutted straight
up and out. I loosened the folds by lightly shaking my torso back
and forth so they would start to open. The action was followed
by several hissing sounds as blood dripped down the edge of
each webbed appendage and back. Concentrating on morphing
into something from a medieval nightmare, I finished unfolding
the massive wings and pushed them into the air behind me. They
expanded to about eighteen feet in length at rest from shoulder
to cusp. Extended, they added another six. The wingtips were
as sharp as folded Japanese steel but stronger. Drawing in a jagged breath as the warmth of blood ran down ripped skin and
over new scales, snapped me from the pain stupor. My shoulder
blades and spine expanded in size to support the weight of the
massive wings. Sucking in another quick breath, I bent down
toward the icy ground and into the pool of blood I had made.
It appeared more like cooked tar across the gravel and melting
snow. I dug fingers into the steaming puddle.

That was the worst part of the process as my frame crumbled to the earth like a rock slide with a sudden impact. Birds
from the surrounding trees took flight from fear of the unknown
quake. A sudden howl from the unbearable pain rebounded

from the back of my throat as hair and skin melted away, revealing dark purple scales highlighted with red. My outer layer materialized as burnt skin before it faded into more scales. On my head grew a set of hollowed horns that curled down and out over pointed ears. I had never really looked at myself in this form but guessed the horns were about two feet in length even with the curls. Arms, legs, hands, and feet cracked and popped in unison, creating a single sound for everything. That move had taken about two hundred years to perfect.

Face morphing was last because it was simply a couple of good, hard shakes for the snout to extend. A hiss of laughter slipped off my forked tongue as I stretched out front claws and wet, leathered wings so they could dry out before I took to the sky. I yawned and slid my massive jaw back and forth before snapping teeth together with a loud crunching sound. This part of the transformation made me appear as a mythical, winged serpent. The drawbacks were the odor. When fully morphed, I reeked of sulfur, and the air around me smelled of rotting corpses with a hint of stale sea water. For centuries, I had re-enacted this process, yet, the pain was so unbearable that within the birth of a second, I always wished for my own grave.

This evening's mountain chill resembled a soft kiss on the breeze and left an aftertaste of Winter's Remembrance in my mouth as it melted. The smell of that unique rose swept through the trees and swirled through the black mist coming up from the holes I had made in the ground with all four claws. I extended the canopy of wingspan so my minion had room to flow around me. It was the closest thing to an embrace, but I endured the searing pain and accepted it as a price for the existence. I opened both wings wider to invite the sharp stings of whipped up snow and ice. Nips from nature's teeth sent a chill down each scale and a sneer exposed my canines. It was a welcome torment after the disappointing turn of events.

Time was my nemesis now and I needed to carve it up, to make it there before hers was up. I sniffed the winds to pinpoint the direction of her scent, figuring about sixty– to sixty-five miles away through this dimension. Crap. I needed to haul ass and tail. Dropping the top of each wing would help scoop up the air around me. Using my back hind leg muscles, I pushed the ground out from under me as both side extensions cupped the air. I was airborne.

Flapping silently, I tried to clear my head before the battle by filling my chest cavity with the frosted heaviness of night, ridding myself of the weighted questions I had concerning the child. To imagine for a brief speck of time... the power I felt as death's wielder was not designed as a Vessel's savior. Slowly, I unhinged both rows of teeth while slitting my eyes to keep them from tearing as I collected more of her scent. I used her fragrance to fuel me while pushing every muscle to their maximum velocity. Then I started to pull apart both dimensions, looking for a bend in time to merge back into her world.

Some of the mountains and trees I had moved to the lower and middle plains worked on splitting my vision. The atmosphere started to work against the wingspan as a separation within dimensions changed the velocity of air molecules. This was making the density of the air either feel too heavy and sticky or too light and very thin. I growled with deep frustration as I pumped faster to gain altitude trying to adjust breathing and speed.

Zipping in between the tall pines, limbs of the trees snapped and crashed as they fell to the ground. That particular commotion was the cause and effect of the sharp bone protruding through the wings, slicing through the dense forest. I tried to lift up above the trees. Occasionally, I felt a splat hit an area on my chest from an unknowing bat or a small night bird that took a wrong turn and crossed my flight path. Something in the dark smacked into my snout and made me sneeze a fizzle of fire. *A lot of power is required, so I rarely use the fire ability. Besides, the core smolders for days. No amount of Tums will extinguish that kind of burn.*

Locating the bend to her dimension, I tucked in both wings and slipped through with ease. A new aroma brought me back from daydreaming. The stench hindered both vision and lung function as I detected a foreign chemical. It was still not as potent as Alexcia's scent, but if my nose was working correctly, she was heading straight for it and it was aiming at her. Either way, whatever was coming was inevitable.

I roared at the darkness around me. The fire burning from behind my palate escaped, licking up the sides as gray smoke plumed from my nostrils. I was still about eight miles away and the mixture of smells continued getting stronger. The possibility of not reaching her in time was making me crazed with an unfamiliar sensation of sinking in sorrow.

Buckling each limb, I positioned them closer to my mass for less wind resistance, pumping legs forward as though running. Pushing out with my wings, I used every scale on them for an advantage. I ground both rows of teeth until I could taste blood as a reminder of the Bond-Rite I had made with Rae. Protect her Child-of-Balance at all cost. I had never broken a vow. I would keep her from harm even if it meant losing my own existence in the process.

7

Sleeping eyes seal my fate
Dreams of terror cannot escape
Choices I suspect can manipulate
Our journeys beyond death's gate
~Alexcia

THE SATELLITE RADIO CLOCK ON THE DASH BLAZED 11:51 P.M. IN neon blue as the truck rocked side to side from the gusts of wind trying to push us off the road. Tod murmured an apology every now and then. It was either meant for us or the truck. I wasn't sure which. He jerked the steering wheel in the opposite direction of the wind, to no avail because it tossed us back into the right lane.

My lips froze into a permanent pout as I listened to the guys talk about the difference between lacrosse and soccer. A small, defeated sigh slipped out. I should have gone with my gut and called one of my friends to come and pluck me out of the Wonderland of Hell. It was my own fault for choosing door number two in haste. The white rabbit's bonfire get-together was looking pretty lame because the narrow path scared me more than taking the wrong one.

As childish as it might seem, my favorite book had always been the original works of "Alice's Adventures in Wonderland" by Charles Lutwidge Dodgson. Most people would know his work under Lewis Carroll. I've always had a habit of quoting from it or using some flamboyant phase to make me feel better. The story reminded me of the fairytale family life I once had with my parents. Catching my reflection in the truck's window, I watched the smile fade as a memory of my dad surfaced. He was reading the story to me at bedtime when Mom was away on business and became upset with the book when he couldn't make sense of the plot. I remembered laughing at him as I explained, "Chaos is what makes life fun." I was six and needless to say, he never read it to me again. I watched two raindrops streak down my two-dimensional face like unspent tears. If anything, I learned that the narrow path implies no room for error. I figured if one wrong mistake would send me down the rabbit hole, why fight destiny? Take the plunge.

A boisterous roll of laughter from Tod bounced me from the daydream. Brad had tossed me a rope by telling Tod a joke, and I used the symbolism to pull myself from the memories. When our group had brought up the Red Rock bonfire party, it sounded like a great escape from the hostile scene. I also didn't want to stay with the blue shirt creep either. Something was very *off* about him, and he seemed more like an older brother being put out by watching his younger sister. My gut said, *stalker*.

Chin on the back part of my left hand, I leaned my forehead into the cold glass with a *thunk*. Eleven fifty-three glowed from the dashboard like a casino marquee. It also reminded me we had been on the road for almost twenty-five minutes. I should have peed before we left. While crossing my legs tighter, I tried to think of other things.

The radio could barely be heard with the truck sounds and the wind, but the guys blasted it because some old band named Guns N' Roses was playing. It was going to be a whole hour of their songs and us trying to decipher what they were singing about. Since the static was coming in clearer than the songs, from what I could make out, the lead singer was singing about a disease he'd caught in a jungle? The rhythm was catchy, but it caused my hearing to become impaired from the hissing speakers in the back seat. The reception was so horrible it was making the drive seem even longer.

Leaning toward the middle console, I mumbled a quick *sorry* to Brad and twisted to face Tod. I used my best voice of reason and kissed his cheek while I tried to get him to change the station or plug-in one of our iSlims. Brad agreed with me, pulling out his iPhone VII and plugging it into the black two-in-one USB three-point five millimeters Audio Charger Cable for iPod/iPhone. *Yes, I know my gadgets.*

Brad began talking to Tod about this new band he heard on one of the satellite stations. He liked the song so much, he had downloaded it. *Great.* Then Tod smiled and motioned for him to connect it. I screwed on a *fine by me* smile and pushed back into my seat. An exaggerated sigh slipped out.

Damn.

I was outnumbered since Melanie had passed out next to me, behind Brad's seat. The crease on my forehead deepened as I watched her shift and moan. Her mascara had smeared under her eyes and the sparkly fuchsia pink lipstick was a faded memory. Melanie moved her lips and laughed under her breath reenacting her drunken dream. *Yeah, this was going to be loads of fun.* Sarcasm dripped from every internal word.

A cramp made its way up my left thigh, adding to the fact I needed to pee, and it didn't help my mood either. To occupy empty minutes, I searched for my purse, did a contents check, then tossed it back on the floorboard. My chest was a bit warm, so I decided I no longer needed Tod's jacket for protection. Attempting to shuck out of it, I heard him clear his throat. *Okay... I'll keep the damn thing on.* Jeez. I rearranged myself, pulling on my skirt and shifting the sheer blouse so it was no longer twisted. When I was done stretching like a kitten, I scooted my butt back into my time-out seat, letting out a soft, defeated huff.

The truck hit a puddle and the tire's complaint to the brakes was to let out a quick screech. We lurched forward, and I looked back to see where I dropped my stomach. I pulled up from the corner of the backseat to make more room since Melanie was stretched across hers and most of mine.

My mood flashed into existence like lightning with words sounding as heated. "How much longer until we get there, Tod? I'm feeling cramped and a bit claustrophobic back here." The leather squeaked as I pushed my right knee into the back of his seat. A little reminder of my discomfort. Lex-Cee wanted him to get the point.

"This is sick. Where in the world did this weather come from? You know, Bro, I don't remember hearing anything on the radio about rain..." Brad let the rest of his sentence roll out. "Especially this kind of crap." He placed his hands on the dash while leaning closer to the windshield. Peering up into the plethora of clouds he added, "You may think I'm crazy, but it looks like it's starting to hail."

I was too caught up following Brad's gaze into the unknown to notice Tod's reply to his passenger was distracted and remote. "I'm not sure it's hail." He leaned toward the steering wheel craning his neck while surveying the night's sky. His breath fogged up the glass while he spoke. "The rain is getting harder to see through. I can only make out a few feet of pavement past the headlights. If I don't find the place by midnight, we'll head back."

Tod was trying to sound reassuring to those of us who were coherent about our impending situation. I looked down at Melanie and felt a twinge of regret forming in the back of my brain. To be passed out right now was a blessing in disguise.

In the distance, I could barely make out two pinpoints of light appearing and disappearing in the darkness. I eased the girl over toward her door and shifted my legs to the left. Leaning closer to the guys, I tried getting a better look at what Tod was dealing with. A small prick of fear made its presence known by raising every hair. I pulled Tod's jacket back around me for an insulated hug as streaks of rain and hail made seeing practically impossible. Never mind trying to see the road. It looked like we were four wheeling in the desert, mud as far as the headlights could reach. The night sky was gone, replaced by a horror scene from a motion picture. I put my right hand softly on Tod's shoulder and dug all five nails into his seat with my left hand. At that moment, I realized I was stone cold sober. *Lucky me.*

"Maybe we should call the night off and turn around anyway. I'm not really in the party mood anymore. Plus, I have to pee. What about you Brad?" I turned to him with pleading eyes. *Please change Tod's mind.*

"No, I don't have to whip it out yet," he said without turning around, still focused on the weather. My jaw unhinged. Oh my goodness. That was all he heard, that I had to pee? Brad was looking out his window up at the sky. Yup, it was official, he was as dense as a redwood. This situation called for a direct approach with Tod.

I looked at the clock again, 11:55 p.m. "Tod, I really have to go. Maybe if we make it to the Red Rock Observance Center, I can find a bush and then we can head back. It's not even midnight yet. We can still spend some time together. My parents won't be home for a couple of more hours. Maybe raid the kitchen, go up to my room and play some C.O.D. How does that sound?" At that moment, I would have rather been zoning out by killing zombies instead of drinking problems away.

Tod started to answer when we all took notice of the lights ahead. They were definitely headed our way, getting closer, brighter each moment. I took them as a sign of salvation because I hadn't seen another car pass us for several miles. At least we weren't the only crazy people out here in this crap. Maybe they were looking for the party too and got lost or decided to head back because of the weather. I frowned but tried to think of the situation optimistically.

The unconscious girl beside me started to moan and smack her lips. Melanie brought one hand up to her stomach and the other to her mouth. She was coming out of her alcoholic-induced dream. That meant one of two things; she was either going to be violently ill when she woke up or she had a severe case of cotton mouth. I was hoping it was the latter and certainly not the former. I didn't need to be stuck in the back with Sister Upchuck. The thought gave me an idea for a new approach, especially since we were in Tod's precious, pristine truck.

I softly coughed and tapped Brad on the shoulder. "Ah, Brad dear, I think your date is going to clear out her stomach here in the back seat."

Tod whipped his head around and his hands on the steering wheel followed, doing what it was told. Jerking hard to the right, the truck then skidded to the left. We all slammed to the opposite side of the cab. A limp Melanie flew onto my side and knocked me in to the passenger door. When my head smacked the window, the door handle bit into my ribs. I screamed, Melanie came to and met me with the same reply, blinking wildly. Brad braced himself against the dashboard with one hand, the roof of the truck with the other. Tod let out a string of curse words, forcing the monster to obey its master.

The tires were slipping and catching the asphalt as the weather seemed to match the tragic mood blasting its way into the space we all occupied. Lightning flashed brightly, then an immediate thunderclap caused the cab lights to flicker. Both ears popped, leaving an intense ringing that blocked out everything happening in the cab. The scene played out frame by frame.

When I regained my balance, I pushed Melanie off me. She

appeared shocked and dismayed towards her surroundings. I wasn't sure she even remembered climbing into Tod's truck, let alone most of the night's debauchery. I barely understood the guys raising their voices to each other on what to do next. I was sure they couldn't hear very well either. Another flash of lightning and the entire truck shook from the sound wave. Everyone's screams were drowned out by the roar of thunder that followed almost immediately.

The oncoming headlights were getting closer and the vehicle seemed to be almost on top of us. My eyes widened at what I saw. To stop the pain and tears, I pressed four fingers into each eye socket. The pepper spray sensation made me instantly nauseous, and I opened them against my better judgment and tried to focus. Whatever was coming toward us was huge and was swerving from side to side taking up most of the road. A halo of shimmering light encircled the moving mass, and we were on a collision course straight for it. A hitched breath caught in the back of my throat followed by a very cool, calm, rational voice. I clenched my teeth from the intense reverb pinging between each eardrum.

Look at what your fear caused, doing what you do best, only thinking of yourself. Your boyfriend can't even keep the truck on the road in this weather, and you chose to distract him, to get your way. You've sentenced everyone to their grave. Enjoy the rest of your ride. See you soon, in hell.

Water filled my eyes making the burning subside. I looked around. Everything still moved in slow motion. Melanie was crying and looking around as if she'd been cast in a horror flick. Brad turned to face her while yelling at her to calm down. Terror showed in his eyes, and when he reached for her, I noticed his fingers shaking. I glanced at the rearview mirror and met Tod's eyes. In between the ticks of a second hand, I understood what Tod was trying to say. The truck was fighting him, protesting against staying on the road. His eyes apologized because he didn't think he could get us out of this mess. Most of all, I felt he was saying that he was in love with me. He blinked, and I lost our connection.

The walls I had built between us began to crumble. I sobbed and poured my soul out that night across the highway, pleading with them all to forgive me. I hadn't meant to create such a catastrophe. Nobody was supposed to get hurt or even die on account of my selfish fear. Feeling the harsh sting of reality, I tried harder to be heard. I screamed prayers out into the air. For all of us... for the people we were about to instantly meet. I would have gladly given my life to replace one of their souls.

I noticed the clock in the dashboard flickering and fading as it tried to stay on. I thought how fitting... our time was about to run out. I whipped my head back and pleaded for someone, anyone, to hear my cries.

"Please. Make it be swift. Please. Please, forgive me. Please... I'm so sorry, I'm so sorry... I'm... so... sorry." I struggled to make myself heard over the truck's engine, the weather, screaming children and now the sound of a meteor striking the front of Tod's truck. Without notice, I was answered, but not as I had hoped. Something hit us hard. The front of the truck buckled. Tires protested to move forward while the bed of the truck raised off the road. Glass cracked and shattered, and somewhere behind me, metal bent under pressure, peeling the roof of the cab away. Instantly, hail mixed with pieces of safety glass fell into the cab of the truck. The wind whipped around Tod's new convertible truck and transported us into the night's version of hell. We all looked up and started screaming out of confusion. But what I saw actually made sense, and I pressed both lips tight before he thought I wasn't worthy of his mercy. *Why would an angel come for me?*

No. It was my own personal demon, here to whisk me into

the unknown. Could this be the atonement for the ones who might die? The wind must have carried each sorrow-filled request straight to his ears. I was going to save the others by him taking my soul as payment. This beautiful creature would make everything right. He was huge and had wings so large they bled into the blackness above us. Menacing would be a proper first impression, but as I forced myself to look harder, focusing on his face, two indigo orbs bore into mine. Burning bright with a sense of determination, this demon met my stare with understanding. Death loomed but with a warming sensation. A blanket straight out of the dryer came to mind. I desired its warm embrace, accepting me as an offering in place of my friends.

Mesmerized by his presence, my body tingled as I raised my arms in acknowledgement, willing to accept the price. A glint of anticipation behind his eyes matched the flickering lights of the dashboard clock. I would try to shine as long as I could until the very end. Eleven fifty-six began to disappear.

Kill me fast is all I ask.

Mentally I made my final request as the supernatural being lunged down and scooped me up with its heavy claw. I gripped it with renewed hope. When I turned to face the dark angel, he broke his stare and looked down at my friends. A bone-chilling, black mist filled the space between me and them. The vapor was thick with a purple cast and tasted like hot asphalt. Their screams were cut short and heaviness overtook my body. Darkness wrapped its cold arms around me, weighing me down with its lifeless hold.

What have I done?

Sadness filled in where fear had cracked me. An overwhelming feeling of mourning took me prisoner. As I faced the last moments of my life, specific memories burned like flash paper. A first kiss, my first oral report, scenes from birthdays appeared to run backwards, the last memory was my parents smiling at me. Then recollection turned to driftwood caught up in the rapids plummeting down to the Ever After. Thoughts scattered from consciousness as I crashed into the waves. My inner voice reflected on a fact… I would never see 11:57 p.m. Then, death's undertow claimed me.

Or so I thought.

8

TEVIN'S SIDE: THROUGH THE EYES OF A REAPER

I WAS FLYING SO FAST MY WINGS DID NOT MAKE ANY FLAPPING SOUNDS. When I spotted the truck, she was barely keeping it together. From four miles away, I heard her voice and the three children with her. About five miles ahead of her vehicle, an eighteen-wheeler had started slightly weaving side to side. Faint sounds reverberated toward me from the driver of the truck. He was beginning to fall asleep at the wheel.

The chemical smell gripped my throat, making it even harder to press forward on the way to her precarious situation. Once again I found myself fighting against my nature and the River's rights to claim her soul. The aroma of sweat glands, burning fire, and blood were not enough to cover up the new scent rolling off me. It was fear. I redirected the emotion and turned up the flame of anger as a distraction. How could it come to this? My existence alone made the word *fate* a real fear to other beings. Here I was, the messenger of dread. Instead, I allowed fear to push me, control me. I detested losing or being controlled and did not believe in panic controlling one's fate, yet it was riding along with me.

Prying both eyes open, the pain was welcome as the sting from the vapors pierced to the back of my skull. I wondered for a brief instant if the kids plowing down death's path could smell what awaited them only three miles ahead. I was aware that one of the male Vessels in the pickup had some importance to the Child. She called him Tod. My memory filed his name away as someone of importance because she spoke to him in a sultry voice. Hissing behind tight lips, it was unbelievable I would find humor in that situation. *In German, Tod means death.* How ironic, I had to literally save Alexcia from her date with death?

Real time seemed to have slowed both vehicles down, but I knew it was an illusion. Their movement shifted and my sight became distorted as the air took on the feeling of liquid. Time rippled around both of the trucks, and I could make out patches of its actual reality as the altered configuration shimmered from the disturbance. Now I knew which House was making another attempt on her life. An elemental being was nearby, trying to boost the time frame by escalating the big rig's speed. The elementals must have gotten wind of me coming because I could sense about five of them. I sniffed the air for some new snacks. Two Wind Evokers and two Water Raisers. Unfortunately, an Earth Sculptor was also present. Taste of the last one still lingered in between a few back molars. The memory of clamping down triggered a gag reflex. That one had turned to sand as I closed my jaws. My stomach lurched, pushing bile up at the thought of gritty sand still wedged between my teeth. I had tasted his pasty grime for days.

I knew I was going into this with an advantage since they could not see me in this form. At least for the time being, I had a chance to surprise the elemental assassins. The night dripped with so much sweet irony, it started to make me nauseous. I scanned the road and across the terrain. The scouts were not far from the potential crash site. They could not wander too far from each other or it would break their connection. I smiled with a wide row of teeth, another advantage. If an elemental was out of range from the ingredients they used for magic, an alternate outlet was needed to draw power; hence, two of the same elementals worked side by side. I had to keep in mind their target was on the ground. That was why the Earth Sculptor was working alone. He was in his element. Most of the Unseen, from the House of Time, were at a huge disadvantage when they were out of their elements.

Without water for miles for the Water Raisers to draw from, the Wind Evokers needed to be off the ground to have the full potential of their magic. The House of Time was as powerful as the other two houses. It might be interesting but if Alexcia walked away from the scene alive, it would still count as a win, more or less. The odds of one of them ending up as a thorn in my claw were pretty good. Time really was working against us and not as a stupid metaphor.

I readjusted to focus on the ground because the Earth Sculptor was starting his attack. The floor beneath me buckled and cracked near the base of the red rocks. The sand rose and fell, taking on the motion of water. Waves of sand were heading toward the road where the vehicles were expected to collide. I made a mental picture of the ground on the road because the area was covered in a cascade of debris. Dirt and sand swirled high in the air around the trucks. The Wind Evokers were doing their part now, blinding the drivers so they could not see the road or each other until it was too late.

I flew higher to get a better vantage point because I could not make out where the Water Raisers were or what part of this production they were going to play. It worried me, and I started my descent to the top of the dark red rocks below. The closer I got, the more I picked up on the smells and voices. Mr. Eighteen-Wheeler was on the cusp of slumber, and the children in the pickup were beginning to complain to one another about never making it to their next destination. I could not hold back the smirk as I snorted in agreement with them. They could not be more correct about their situation. I gulped clean air before flying down to the base of the mountains, wanting to be ready for the Wind Evokers once I entered their plain. They would sense me as I breached their magic with this wingspan. I still could not pick up on the water elementals and it was beginning to piss me off. I shook my mane silently, allowing a brief second or two to prepare for battle. Bending down and pulling my wings in, I dove. The air rushing through both horns caused a high whistling in my ears. I tried to ignore the distraction and turned focus on which elemental to eliminate first.

Checking the distance between the trucks... they had roughly three miles until impact. *Damn.* What were the water ones up to? I figured the wind users were going to be the first of my targets. Looking from side to side, I spotted them on top of one of the Sculptor's dunes. They had positioned themselves above a loose layer of rocks for a poetical slide, perhaps? I factored it into the rapidly unfolding events.

Plowing into the brash winds, I barely made out the elementals' faint whispers. It was not possible to understand their languages, but they knew I had arrived. Obviously, females... from their stature and stance. One moved her hands into the winds. The other was half bent over, holding her stomach. That was the one I wanted. She used her arms controlling the wind, but the magic was coming from the one learning forward. Through the haze, I saw she was pale and sick. The nature of my beast was telling me to put down the weaker one first. Far be it for me to be the better daemon by doing it right.

Cupping my wings into the tormenting air and swooping in a half circle to come up from behind, I realized I had underestimated my foes. The bent elemental whipped up to face me, spread out her hands as a quick smirk crossed her lips. Caught off guard, she shot me with a blast of air knocking me off balance.

I roared.

Smoke billowed from my snout as I fanned the folds of skin to use them like air breaks. My roar tipped off the Earth Sculptor. "Shit," I growled mentally. The Sculptor waved his hands in front and the ground grumbled as a hole formed. Then the strangest thing happened, he dove in as the hole closed behind him. I hovered, waiting to hear the burp. When nothing came of it, I figured he had bailed on the others. Thunder rolled from my chest, a form of laughter. I found it humorous there was such a thing as a smart elemental. A gust of wind flipped me to one side. The action served as a reminder this was far from over. The females switched places and the sick one used the other one's power now. Screaming, she spun around and hit the rocks with her air. They exploded in a crumbled heap on the road beneath the dune.

I hissed at the Evokers. Claws out, I used the webbed extensions to pick up speed. One of them would get hit with everything I had. Longing for their screams of death, I charged. The pale elemental lunged behind her counterpart as she watched my descent.

The standing female raised her hands up and down in a fast motion. I felt the gust about to take me and rolled out of the way and ducked to the left. Leaving my wing halfway out, I pulled all four legs under me, pretending they had succeeded, adding to the deception by free falling.

Whichever one remained on the ground whispered something, and the standing girl laughed as she turned to look down at the other. This was my chance. I was low enough to the ground now. Opening both wings to their full width, they slapped against the air. The elementals did not have time on their side anymore. I reached out with my right claw, wrapping it around the closest Evoker and squeezed until I heard her spine break. She went limp.

Feeling numb looking at the nonexistence elemental, I

turned to the screeching sick one as she tried to stand up in the sand. Without a link to her power, she was at my mercy, or so I thought. Her mouth worked with fervor as she conjured the last of her magic, using the rest of her counterpart's power. With the winds of a cyclone, I crashed into the ground, and the sound waves from my impact distorted both plains.

Everything seemed to be moving in a thick, sluggish motion, as I watched the airflow around me change. Sniffing the air as I tried to stand and on three claws. I threw the limp Evoker away from me and watched her disintegrate before hitting the ground.

Then the sky became murky as the clouds rolled over their intended target of interest. Barely making out the drivers, I knew they were equally hindered by the same visibility troubles. Taking flight right now could be risky because I was unsure how high the dust cloud reached. While trying to figure out the dilemma I got myself into, the ground began to quake. A deep bellow from within the dirt was eerily familiar. It was the sound of a huge mass moving toward the surface. Instantly, the air was thick with debris, making it difficult to breathe.

I was disoriented and enraged. This needed to end now. Stretching out to flap away the film around me, I was struck from the side with a huge force. I blacked out for a second. Crazed, I craned my neck to face my attacker. Claws gripped into something gooey as I tried to gain traction to right myself. Whatever had me trapped, bellowed a low rumble and bent down to meet my gaze. *Holy Daemon!* Every scale bristled from the realization that the Earth Sculptor had changed into... *me.*

I was out of time and had fallen for their ploy. Shock filled the core of my being. The Sculptor chortled, noticing its rolling boom was identical to mine. How had he stolen my thunder?

Disgusted with the dirt elemental for even thinking he could be one-third of what I was caused the upper palate in the back of my throat to close. The air sacks were close to bursting. Rage boiled over and, I let this dirt kisser have it. Fire streaked from me hitting it square in the chest. *Feel the burn, asshole.* The fake copy flew back with a thud, and the Sculptor flapped his sand-molded wings to put himself out as he dropped to the ground and rolled. Scrambling to my feet, a roar was ignited deep from within, making my own eyes tear up. I was consumed by anger. With legs tight as springs, they vaulted me into the air.

The water elementals had begun working the clouds, making them rip apart to let the downpour begin. An impending rock slide became a patient predator waiting for its prey to come to it. Now I knew where the Water Raisers were. I could smell them in the air not far behind me, riding on the back of the fuel truck. That was why I could not track their scent. Masked by the chemicals from the silver and black tanker, they must have had a plan B in case the air elementals failed.

The smell of charred ground filled my nostrils and trigged a memory that curdled stomach fluid. I landed hard on top of the cool sand, and it buckled under my weight. I roared again as a sign they could not defeat death, and then stomped to make my point. The grimy brown dragon took to his feet. Made of sand and dirt, I figured his wings were too heavy for him to take flight. So, I took the opportunity and launched myself back into the sky. At least it would clear away the smell and give me some time to think. I hovered above the battle, waiting for an opportunity to present itself. Using the dirt elemental's disadvantage, he could not move his neck fast enough to focus on me in between the stars.

Looping back around where the last wind elemental had been, I was struck on the head with an idea. If he were going to portray me, he must eat the same as me. Pushing above the stinging winds, the sickly wind elemental was trying to hang on to the last of her power. I could feel her bite of power in the wind whippings she hit me with. Uncurling my wings, I coasted silently through the elemental's wind screen while honing in on the Evoker. She was using a blending spell in her breeze form. It was a last ditch effort of her magic. The purpose of that design was disruption of her power to jam the attacker's radar senses.

I clamped my jaw shut so I would not give away my position to the remaining assassins. The beast within me wanted nothing more than to tear them apart for even thinking they could touch Alexcia's soul. It was my turn to flip destiny's coin in our favor.

Fury raked and bristled each scale with small quakes. My sails jutted out from the adrenaline boost. I was getting a recharge as the rains began to fall. It pelted me, making threatening sounds from the drops as they hissed and fizzled. Oozing, black tar seeped from the wounds made by the Earth Sculptor's claws.

This fight was no longer about them killing Alexcia. It had become personal and related more to Ashen pride being bruised than protecting the Child. Her safety had now been placed on the back burner. These elementals were not just attacking her but trying to put me down like a rabid Hellhound. For this intention alone, they were going to meet their Creator by either my claws or jaw, whichever caught them first. I felt the heat from the Smolder's powers begin to glow from behind both eyes. A long time ago, I had been told by another daemon that when an Ashen reached the cap of their power, our eyes illuminated with deep azure. I represented a lighthouse in the sky, warning others to retreat from my presence or meet their death.

The sound of squealing tires across the wet asphalt made me stop breathing and the whip of reason cracked against my skull. A familiar voice found its way back. *What was I thinking? Screw my pride. The Child. I must protect her.*

I locked in the distance between each vehicle and tried to

judge if I could get to the Water Raisers before they caused more road damage. The Earth Sculptor spat out a threatening hiss and reared up his front legs to make him appear bigger than me. He started to charge toward the road.

Right. Not going to happen.

Time for plan B. If only I had one...

Falling back on improvising skills, I had to figure out how to take two of them out at the same time and fast. It was the only way to make up for the lost seconds and still save the Child's soul. Folding in the outer appendages, I held them tightly against each side so I would free fall to the ground below. Stretching out my senses, I located all four elementals. I did not want to become distracted and lose sight of the fuel truck because I knew the two water elementals were on the back tank, somewhere. Less than two miles before impact. Space, be damned. I let gravity do its part by embracing me with unseen hands guiding me to the earth's surface.

I heard a time tremor beginning to implode during my descent. It resembled a circular motion of distorted heat vapors. That form of power was the House of Time's most used weapon. Time would literally tick down. From the center of altered time, reality began to eat away at the barrier of displacement and when time caught up with itself, within the set circle, it sent out a shockwave making your ears pop. My ears were ringing from the echoed sound bouncing off the canyon walls. Everything sped up to real time again and I realized the ground was not going to be a soft landing, but I had less than a wing's flap to recalculate everyone's fate.

My serpent tail whipped and snapped in the air, making its presence known. It was made up of the same scales as the rest of my body, covering every inch from horns to serrated tip. It cracked the air again, telling me it wanted to be heard. An evil thought painted a smile across my snout. My tail was plan B. I opened my mouth for a blood-curdling screech while reshaping my form on the way down. I opened the right wing and kept the other one tucked to the side so I could make a quick change in the flight path.

Squinting as I hit the whipped up sands, I focused on the lone wind user. She moved to a different sand dune closer to the side of the road. I moved down as close to the sand as I dared while flying. Moving on the terrain, I noticed out of the corner of my eye that the ground elemental was approaching from the left. Cocking my neck toward the Sculptor, I blew fire to slow his pace. Swinging to the right of the sand dune, the Evoker was sprinting toward the two-lane highway. I flew up fast, cutting off her route, making sure I was looking at her pale face. Her body went slack, from weakness or finding herself cornered. I was not sure which, nor did I care.

With the Earth Sculptor heading in our direction, I had only one chance. She started to run again. I landed behind her and whipped my tail down beside her. Making sure to slam the tip of it from the right to the left, I wanted to get my point across. She turned to face me. I curved my tail around her legs and took them right out from under her. Raising it high above her, I jammed the barb into her stomach. The air became rancid from her rapidly decaying shell. Tail muscles pushed her harder into the ground until the appendage cracked around her body. I placed my face over hers, unleashing rage with a single earsplitting roar.

The Earth Sculptor never slowed down, but that worked well with my plan. Having the wind user impaled on the tip was going to be useful so I tucked her and my tail under the fold of a wing and rolled to the right of the dirt dragon. He coiled his neck and roared. Wrong move. I jumped onto his back, used one claw to grab his snout and the other to secure his neck. He bucked and roared again fighting against my strength as his feet stumbled. Gravity helped out as the impostor fell forward with a grunt, repositioning to face me. I placed my snout next to his and growled as saliva hit the ground sizzling. He opened his mouth to respond, and I flipped my tail out from under the wing and crammed the decaying Evoker down his throat, then bolted straight up in the air. He started to get up and shake when he realized what I had done. The scream he unleashed filled the night's sky, followed by the inevitable. The explosion was deafening, adding to the mix of falling clumps of dirt and rain.

With no time to revel in my triumph, I landed and ran to the spot where the crash was supposed to take place. Lifting one of my claws to block the headlights of the fuel truck, I saw the Water Raiser's position better. The texture of the rain had changed with the drastic drop in temperature. Hail was restricting my vision and making it impossible to see more than a few feet in front of me. I let the gray, almost black, smoke filter through grinding teeth.

My nose pointed me in Alexcia's direction, and I took off running on the wet pavement. The children in the pickup could see the lights of the oncoming truck by now. I could tell from all the screaming. Hers was the loudest scream, but it was the one I listened for. The truck swerved and banked up on the gravel a few times as they barreled forward to their end.

I took to the air as their headlights washed over me. Alexcia was asking for forgiveness from the other children. Why would she feel their death was her fault? She did not know who she was, did she? Her crying and pleading rubbed up my scales in the wrong direction. I roared as her friend Tod gunned the engine to his monster truck. Wait till they all get a load of Alexcia's monster.

When I slammed into the front part of Tod's truck and threw myself over the top of the cab, I dug claws into the back window and used nails to pull the top of the cab toward me. The move was similar to opening a large can of sardines. Kids screamed at me, as I knew they would. Alexcia started to but suddenly stopped and stared at my inhuman face. Her eyes told me everything she was feeling. For only a few ticks, time had no control over me. The beast in me was acting of its own accord as it growled at her with disdain. That's when I took the opportunity to lunge, snatching her up. She did not even falter as she embraced my talons to steady herself. Alexcia had managed to shock the thrill of death out of me this time, gazing at me as if she knew who I was even in this horrific form.

As I turned away to depart, I remembered her pleas for forgiveness to her friends. Since their expiration date could not be changed, I gave in to her requests for the Vessels she called friends. I took a deep breath and blew my cloak's mist into the cab so the kids would instantly fall asleep before impact. The mist would drift into their bodies and contain their souls. Then I could collect them with their last exhale.

Feeling her weight shift in my claws, I used the hood of the truck as a launching pad to take off into the night sky. Frozen water and air rushed us as I climbed higher into the hail-spitting clouds. She needed to be far away from the impact.

I was not even forty feet in the air when the blasting of the horn from the fuel tanker bounced off the red striped mountains. Air brakes were now making sharp squealing sounds when they locked up from hitting puddles of slippery mud and rocks. Since the driver had overcorrected, it jack-knifed around Tod's truck. As it clamped around the vehicle, I whispered a promise of a quick death for each Vessel. My power glowed dark and fatal while the cloak's mist came forth from the truck in a hiss. Using telepathy to guide it with blinking speed, the mist covered both cabs, consuming the souls of the children and the truck driver. The jolt from the power surge made my mouth water. I summoned it immediately, inhaling the mist containing what was left of their souls. I would keep what remained of them safe until I could find the Bridge Crosser in charge to take them to the gondolas.

The second explosion of the night plumed in an array of red and black shades. Appearing as a mushroom cloud, it lit up the night sky similar to the way a morning star changes the clouds before it wakes from slumber. Next, there was a searing wave of heat followed by sound waves crashing into me. If the water elementals had not evaporated by that time, they were long gone.

Using webbed wings to cocoon us as we fell back down to earth, the child sighed against me. I looked down at her, matching her sigh in a low rumble. With sleep taking over her from the leftover mist, she mumbled and snuggled deeper into my winged embrace.

With the veil of narrow sight ripped away, I absorbed every inch of this human child, completely taken aback by the way her features had altered since I had last seen her. She was not as small as I had remembered. That was what I got for passing my duties off to others. Her hair was much longer and she was curvier in places not previously there. Alexcia resembled her mother in ways I could not put into words. I was instantly hit in the gut with something resembling a forbidden feeling. Could it be for her? It did not seem right and made the inside of my stomach quiver. I have never had any other emotions toward the living other than the ones related to taking their lives. Never. Even though I knew, with every state of my being, I did not have a soul to power a heart to conjure up meaningless emotions. *What could I possibly feel for her?*

I growled in confusion. What was this Child-of-Balance to me and why was she messing up my existence? I was taught that emotions make humans weak with their complexity and are seemingly unpredictable. How could I even fit into her life other than as her Unseen daemon caretaker? Why would I even consider any other option?

Feeling helpless, as if the human girl was falling without me wrapped around her, I could not shake the new emotion of wanting to be near her. As impossible as it seemed, a connection existed somehow. Not just by this Bond-Rite her mother and I had made, but by a link of power simmering between us. I needed to figure it out because the questions had been stacking up for the last decade, and I could not ignore them any longer. The decision was made before she took another breath... I would see to her safety myself. She had become my Child-of-Balance, even though she threw my own world off balance. From that day forward, I would protect her from the Houses of Time, Light, and Space. But most of all, I would protect her from me: the River Styx's death dealer.

As I gazed upon this creature, the reality of the situation loomed heavy. She was saved without even a scratch or the scent of fear before facing demise. My face contorted from smelling something foul. It was the closest look I could manage under the circumstances. I was going to have to stage her part of the accident.

A strange heaviness took hold of me while I tried to flip around to land with her cradled in one claw. My weight smacking into the ground was masked by another explosion made by the gas tank from Tod's truck. I fanned out both wings to shelter her from the heat, then released a low rumble of protest when she turned toward one of my talons and began to snore. Damn, maybe I used too much of the cloak's slumber spell. At least I knew the children in the truck had not suffered.

The smell of fuel was not as strong now, so I knew the fire was going to burn without protest. This meant she was no longer in danger, from neither the vehicles nor the dead elementals... only me. I limped over to one of the closest sand dunes to the left of the small truck. Laying her down, facing up toward the heavens, she looked like a discarded child's toy. Her clothes were torn and even charred in areas, but the jacket she wore covered up the important parts. It was good for me because it meant I would not have to stage the fire part of the accident. Her hair was in tangles but still framed her face in a way that complemented her features. I was starting to feel sick knowing I would have to ruin her perfect skin and maybe break a bone or two. Shaking my mane, I relaxed long enough so the bristled scales would return to normal. I closed my eyes, trying to convince myself the sick feeling was from the Earth Sculptor I had tried to eat the last time.

No Vessel could have walked away from a disaster of this magnitude without some damage to their outer shell. I was now on *stage and clean up* duty. This part was mandatory if the assignment was botched. She had to look like a survivor, ripped from the jaws of her own demise.

With a quick flick of my tail, I shattered some windshield glass. I used my mouth to scoop up the glass, wet sand, and some small pieces of torn metal. Positioning just above her, I opened my jaws. The fake debris did its job covering her with dirt and small cuts on the exposed skin. I winced, looking at a few that actually did the job too well. She was bleeding pretty badly from a ragged piece of metal stuck between her neck and collarbone. Another wedged into her right thigh.

An inner roar jolted me forward which made me react without thinking. Quickly, I licked her throat, then moved my snout down toward her leg to do the same. A soft hiss came from her neck as the saliva cauterized the wound. The smell of scorched blood and skin was heavy around her. As the bleeding stopped, I sniffed the air. She smelled and looked as though she had been thrown from the force of the explosion. Observing the wound on her leg, I lowered my nose, making a cautious effort to only touch the deep gash. I finished staging the scene by pacing around the body trying to make a groove in the sand to appear she had been shoved into the ground and then blown the rest of the way to safety.

To think that about an hour ago, the opportunity to break her would have snuffed the agitation, but now I struggled against normal resolve. The clan might toss me over to the Bridge Crossers if they knew my conflicts about this situation. Claws firmly placed into the scorched sand to steel my nerve, I lifted the right front foot to place it on her arm. The leg froze.

While the fires burned, I found myself putting the child first and everything else second. Tonight I was looking at our situation differently. As long as we shared an entwined future, she would remain unharmed. A silent vow drifted in thought from me to her. My clan would never use our harvesting weapons to claim her soul. At least she was safe for now.

From the canyon's entrance, the sirens pierced my ears. I had always hated that sound. Help for this lone survivor was on its way. Bellowing toward the stars helped me detach from my corrupted emotions as I stepped on Alexcia's left arm and broke it.

9

Pretentious
Mortality takes my hand
I sense the weight of acceptance
Why must I have to bear to stand?
Alone
My hand now empty
Acceptance is discarded and rejected
The whys no longer matter when the future
Repeats
~Alexcia

I DRIFTED, COLD AND EXHAUSTED. IMMERSED IN DARKNESS, I WAS disoriented and chilled to the bone. The sensation made me think of water... somewhere. I sank deeper into the inky whirlpool where the voices coming out of the pool's center were nothing but static. With the current sucking me deeper, I couldn't tell if they were calling out to me or if I should try to swim away from the distorted sounds.

Surely, I was broken as I tried to push away from whatever was calling out to me. Bad idea. Crap, this was beyond agonizing. *New plan, move to the voices and hope for the best.* I was already dead, what did I care?

I was shocked to find out there was an afterlife. Mine wasn't at all like fuzzy kittens with automatic weapons or unicorns barfing up Skittles. Was this my punishment, to swim through this ink for all eternity? Feeling a bit jaded, I had always been told I would burn in hell, not drown in it.

If I thought I had been hurting before, nothing would have prepared me for what was coming. Kicking through the thick liquid pain took its sweet time to finally greet me with vigor. It crept up my neck while I pushed deeper toward the voices. Twisting to see what was gnawing on my collar bone, I realized both arms were stuck to my sides. Straightaway the gnawing turned to scalding as bits of flesh burned down my right leg. Whatever held my left arm in place had jaws made from molten iron and the pressure was about to snap it in two.

Several nerves were firing into my brain that I was in trouble. I bucked forward as pain followed every movement. It swam around, flowing from neck to leg with the same burn and pressure. What the F was attacking me in the dark? How could I fight against something I couldn't see?

Pain and Panic, from the movie *Hercules*, kept me company. Blood pounded in my ears, the heart's response to my brain telling me someone's dread was one of the voices calling out to me. Anger was next to arrive unannounced to this little get-together. All too familiar with its presence I tried to make the jaw muscle work to grind out the emotion.

A thick, metallic taste pooled instead of salvia. I tried to cough, but something pressed down on my tongue. Dry, cool air trickled down my throat, and I made out a soft, rhythmic beat along with the static. It sounded mechanical, and I heard air being pushed into something hollow.

My consciousness was about to be sentenced to do hard time. The pull to give in to the darkness was strong, but somewhere deep in the abyss I was stronger than this creature which I assumed was trying to drag me into death's hold. Seizing these emotions, they formed into a pinpoint of light. I screamed, "Get your ass moving." A solid presence began to obey the demand.

Both eyelids fluttered faster than a hummingbird's wings. Mentally, I placed cognizant in one corner and spirit in another. *Ding.* The conscious part of me came out swinging, grabbed my spirit and punched the crap out of it. The physique responded with eyes snapping open. Imaginary strings yanked my upper body forward while a free hand grabbed something foreign protruding between dried lips. Startled, I wrenched out the breathing apparatus, the scream that followed the plastic tube shredded my throat.

Awestruck, I had survived. Now I really was in hell.

Forcefully making my lungs accept air again, I coughed violently. My left side was weighted down by something heavy and thick. Shrilling alarms filled up the room with whistles and screams, followed by a voice shouting through a speaker. Someone was coding nearby. Blinking through crusted tears, trying to focus on my surroundings, stillness soon filled the air as I struggled to breathe.

I was instantaneously greeted by my mother, two men in white lab coats and three or four people wearing scrubs. Everyone frantically worked on or around me, checking vitals and comparing them to the machines I appeared to be hooked up to, then discussing medical issues with my mother.

Rae-Lynn stood absolutely still in silence as the doctors and nurses spoke about protocol and what to expect with future recovery. One of the nurses explained to me how the morphine drip pump worked. She finished her show and tell demonstration by placing the pen-like device in my open hand and clicking it. Her doe eyes held sympathy as she patted my shoulder with reassurance.

It wasn't difficult reading about twenty different emotions, all passing within seconds, as Rae-Lynn dabbed at the dampness around her lashes with dad's black silk handkerchief. I knew it was his when I spotted the gold monogrammed MS in the corner.

I froze.

It was up to me how I handled this situation... with a grain of salt and lemon if my mother were the only one handling it. If Max were involved, it meant I was in a serious predicament. Either I had died and was brought back or I was on the verge of dying. More than likely, by the time he was done with me, I would wish I had.

Cautiously scanning the hospital room, I narrowed my gaze and made out a towering figure leaning in the corner... my father. The darkness seemed befitting of his aura. With or without the black slice of cover, I knew he was dressed in one of his dark, Italian business suits.

With the silver glint of his company cell phone resting against his face, he fit the part of a villain in a thriller movie. Eyes set in a winter vex stare, fear frosted over thoughts. It whispered against the nape of my neck saying I was going to be his next victim. The instant, warm sensation between my legs indicated he had literally scared the piss out of me. No matter how bad I wanted to crumble, I would never express to him how much he intimidated me. Rae-Lynn, I could handle. Max was a completely different story.

My eyes rolled as I failed to prevent the weight of being alive from knocking me backward in the hospital bed. I was alive but feeling a lot like road kill. As soon as the laugh escaped, reality killed it. I was alive... but how about the others? Where were they? What had happened to them? Whatever the outcome, memories from before the crash would replay as a nightmare for the rest of my life.

The questions rushed out in a gritty whisper, "Where is everyone? When can I see Tod? Did anyone come for Melanie or Brad?" Tears slipped down the sides of my nose and cheeks. I had known the answer before Mom rushed to the side of the bed. Rae-Lynn's eyes were rimmed red and her irises spun pink spider webs attaching themselves to each corner.

She cleared her throat, attempting to stay calm, and forced the sound of reassurance with her reply. "I'm sorry, honey. Everyone was gone by the time the EMTs and fire trucks arrived. It was a miracle you survived. They said you were thrown about hundred and fifty feet away from the crash." Her voice trailed to a small quiver. "Tod didn't make it, Lex-Cee. None of them did. Not even the truck driver who fell asleep at the wheel." She shook her head slowly and reached for the hand with the IV attached to it, motioning Max to bring her a chair. Rae-Lynn patted my hand while emotions exploded within me. The dam holding back the river was now raging rapids. Remaining bound in bed by guilt, I let the tears consume me until I drowned in the pain of realization. I had killed them. The winged creature was nothing but a fleeting wish of a dream for hope my friends had been saved. I had asked for their forgiveness. More than ever, I needed a smoke and a drink.

Max slapped his cell phone case shut while carrying a chair over for my mom, then he walked to the opposite side of the hospital bed. Today, his eyes were deep blue with the onyx threatening to overcome it. They were telling me he understood what I was feeling, but I still had some explaining to do.

"Alexcia, I know it's too soon to ask you about details, but the officers have been checking in every hour or so to see if you were going to pull through. They want to speak with you, child." Like always, his discussions started out sincere but ended putting me in my place. I went from a person to a possession within two sentences. It was comforting to see my near death experience had brought us so much closer. I turned away to face Mom for reinforcement.

I could never hold my own against Max in a fight, but I knew Rae-Lynn could. He was wrapped around Mom's little finger and hated it with a passion but knew better than to fight it. Whenever he tried to beach himself, my mother's feelings for him always pulled him back out to her personal sea. I loved that Max and Rae-Lynn got along, but why did they have to be on opposite sides of my compass? She was the sun; he was the moon, the dark side of it.

"Mom." I caught the first sobs and reined them in, hiccuping through tears. "Can I talk to them tomorrow? Can't you explain to them I just heard about my friends? Please, please, it hurts so badly." I hiccuped again and didn't know if I could deal with it so soon and relive what happened that night. The knowledge of loss swam in pools of emptiness. A quiver of air slipped out. "How long have I been like this?" My eyes started to sting again from the pressure building up behind them. Rae-Lynn's face took on an uncharacteristic expression. Whipping her face away from me to make eye contact with Max, she motioned back at the bed never directly making eye contact with me. Instead, Rae-Lynn chose her words guardedly. Max had an air of concern about him, but his eyes stared at the wall, the floor, the bed. That was all, never at me.

"Lex-Cee, I know you're upset. It has been about three days since…" She let her words trail off into silence for a moment. "Don't worry about anything else right now. I will talk to them and see if we can make an appointment. Baby, do you have a headache? Want me to call a nurse to come in here and give you some pain medication?" Her fingers pulled lightly on the sheet.

"Mom, I was in a life-threatening accident. I *f-ing* hurt all over. I have a cast on my arm and a brace of some sort on this leg. Plus, my neck itches whenever I turn to look at you. I must have stitches somewhere on that side too. My skin is getting itchy and hot. A case of welts is about to be delivered to me. I just found out my friends are dead. Everywhere outside and inside hurts, so a headache is the very least problem. Plus, all I have to do is press this little button." I was holding out the arm with the cast on it, dangling my salvation line. I heard pain medication was better than drinking. I'd test the theory out later if the nightmares came back.

"Still, I have to ask. Can you bear with me? Did you see anything that night that might raise questions? Or maybe something… out of place… in here, possibly?" She sounded far away. Mom was normally so grounded, so sure of herself. The concern in her voice sent shivers up my spine and even hurt. Damn.

Surely, I would have sounded insane blurting out about the demon coming to save me and in turn, dooming everyone else. All I needed was to tell them about the winged creatures that came out every night to visit me in my sleep. They would never believe me anyway. My eyes were really beginning to burn. Crying must have dried them up and now they were disintegrating into volcanic sand. The lights in the room were adding to the pain. When I held up my right hand, it pulled the tape around the IV drip, but that didn't stop me from placing it over my eyes.

I wanted to see Blakely, Dee, and Ghost… to hold them and tell them I cherished their friendship. The lump that refused to dislodge in my throat reminded me how raw it was. That was it. I couldn't take how broken I felt. I knew it would mend, but my heart was slowly dying. The demon had cursed it that night. I assumed it was my payment for beating death at its own game.

In a flash, memories from that night passed behind mental eyes. I was wearing Tod's jacket and wondered if I still had it on when they found me. While turning away to get Rae-Lynn's attention, I asked, "Mom, this may be a weird question, but was I wearing a jacket when they found me?"

She drew in a small breath. "Ah, yes you were. They gave us a bag with all the belongings. Your father took it home. Most of your clothes were ruined, but I do remember seeing a sports jacket, it was in fair condition." She looked confused.

Biting back sobs because his jacket made it and he didn't was insane. He would never wear it again. I wanted to see Tod and fight with him, telling him to quit being a jerk. What I wouldn't give to laugh at his stupid jokes or reach up to kiss his lips, stare into his eyes and tell him I would always care for him. Realizing even in death, I still couldn't say I'd loved him. I didn't think it would be right for me to keep the jacket since I had been thinking of giving it back to him at the end of the night anyway.

I was pathetic.

The lump in my throat turned into a jagged rock stabbing me every time I tried to swallow. My thumb fumbled with the medication button as I pushed it until I felt the coolness rush through the vein. I lay there, wishing I had Dorothy's ruby slippers to transport me back to Oz because this reality held nothing good for me.

10

Thank goodness, I broke my left arm and not the right Because writing is therapy and for me not to have the ability would have damaged my soul.
~Alexcia

THE FOOD LEFT SOMETHING TO BE DESIRED. I WAS HELD CAPTIVE AT Summerset Hospital and was finally moved to a decent room. The drawback? I had to share it. When I was wheeled into the room for the first time, she introduced herself as Willow Glasston. She snored. But, I was told I did too. Blakely had confirmed it the last time she came to visit and woke me up to tell me so. I kind of felt bad for the woman sentenced to share the room with me. Every time someone came into our room, she complained her chest hurt and was having a heart attack. The nurses and doctors would reassure her by explaining she was experiencing a bad case of acid reflux.

Rae-Lynn took a few weeks off work to keep me company and to help at home. When I fell asleep or was tied up in the bathroom, Mom would go over and talk with my roommate. Willow seemed to enjoy the attention Rae-Lynn gave her and nicknamed her Angel. "Angel, can you get my glasses? Angel, can you turn off the light for me." She didn't know Rae-Lynn very well. I love my mom, but she was far from the ranks of celestial beings. I never saw anyone come to visit Willow, and it made me appreciate the people around me a lot more than before the accident.

Father was another story. He left the day after I went from

needing a coffin to remaining in a hospital bed. I'm sure he was pissed the latter was costing him more money in the long run. They gave me some excuse about the Dow dropping and it was imperative to save their asses, I meant their assets. *Don't get me wrong, I love Max. Usually, we have this wall that separates us from becoming dad and daughter.* I came to terms with it a while ago. For some reason, our titles changed to father and child.

We had been close... before the accident I'd had when I was six. I don't remember what happened, only that our relationship had changed shortly after that. I still remember the long walks we shared. He would point out and tell me about the animals, plants, and trees. Max knew a lot about nature and seemed to want to pass the knowledge down to me. He would even come into the playroom for tea parties or to color in one of the Disney princess books I owned. Max sparked my imagination with stories about how, someday, I would be a princess like them. I loved calling him dad. *But, I believe he sees me as a piece from his art collection or one of his business suits. A possession, something to own but that one day will be discarded.*

I stared out the window as small, insignificant tears rolled down both cheeks. It was unfathomable I could still cry. The past six days, it was all I had done. I was cursed to live future days soggy for eternity. I leaned over to the rolling hospital table for another tissue. *Max should tell his shareholders to invest in Kleenex. Their stock would go up and he would have me to thank for supplying the need.*

Mom left to get us some real food. I had begged her for any kind of take-out close by. After she removed the lunch plate lid and saw the over-cooked meat cube that could pass for cardboard, she agreed. I desired something greasy and salty.

Rae-Lynn had been going above and beyond for me. No one would ever find her without her laptop, Blackberry Sonic and collapsible iPad. She was always busy with her job as a full-time journalist. Actually, she worked primarily as a freelance reporter, but her work had been picked up by several magazines and a few out-of-state newspapers. *I'm pretty proud of her. She has looks, talent, and a good marriage. Max and Rae-Lynn look like a matching Ken and Barbie set. They make a very good living too.*

One desire was to have them around more, instead of having something tragic happen to bring us together. But then, I wouldn't have had the freedom to hang out the way I did. So, something had to be sacrificed for our lifestyle. *Family time is a have to, when we have the time to. Most people don't get that.*

Willow rolled over and mumbled something under her breath to remind me she was there. I turned up the volume on the small TV facing me so I could focus on that rather than her. A familiar face came around the corner about the time I was getting ready to change the channel.

Blakely sauntered through the door wearing her standard black zip-up hoodie, and dark blue jeans two sizes too big, held up by a huge, black belt. While inspecting the rest of her clothes, I noticed her white tank top underneath the hoodie. A cream-colored stain the size of a baseball showed on the front of it. Then it hit me… caffeine. She was carrying three cups of coffee, accompanied by a brown paper bag from the Sip 'N Chug tucked under her other arm.

The Sip 'N Chug coffeehouse, owned by Mr. Sipton, was my place of employment. I was certain it burned Blakely's butt that the owner probably made her pay for our goodies… even if he knew she was buying it for us. I hope he was at least giving her the fifteen percent employee discount.

We greeted each other with a smile when I saw her placing the cup holder onto the table. Her expression quickly turned into a frown. "Dammit. This is my favorite tank too. Look what your stupid coffee did to me. Napkins, I need napkins." She reached over to the tissue box, pulled out a wad of sheets, and repeatedly dabbed at the unwanted spot.

"Hi to you too. You're a lifesaver." I reached over to grab a cup and she smacked me, leaving a two finger welt. It hurt enough that I impulsively rubbed the top of that hand against the blankets. "What the hell? We drink the same coffee, heavy vanilla, light mocha with a shot of espresso. Now what gives? Can I reach for the pastry, or are you going to cut off the hand next?" I was eyeing the brown paper recycled bag while still rubbing the skin. It was going to leave a mark.

"Crap, Lex-Cee. Don't they feed you around here? You're always acting like you're starving. I didn't see a sign out front that read, *We Do Not Feed the Patients*." She took the lids off the coffee cups to let them cool. "Where's your mom? I figured she could use a cup too. I got her a regular strength joey." Blakely pulled out the napkins and flavored Stir Stix. My boss, Mr. Sipton, thought it was clever to change the word sticks with an X on the Sip 'N Chug menu. A small frown formed on Blakely's face.

Curling all four fingers to forget about the sting, I asked, "What's wrong?"

"I forgot your Cinna Frog Stix. I could have sworn I asked him for one. You can have my Slap Ya Lemon one, I guess." Her frown deepened.

"Forget it. I'm thankful you're here and brought me fuel," I said, motioning toward the coffees.

"Oh, I'm sorry Lex-Cee. I wanted to give you the right one since I spilled it. And now I forgot your Stir Stix." She grabbed the full coffee instead of the one dripping coffee tears from the lid, "Here."

"Thanks, Blakely. Are you sure?"

"Of course, I'm not the one laid up in this sterile insane asylum. I'm sure it's worse than being at school. Since you're watched all the time here, it's the least I can do." With narrow eyes, she turned slowly around and let out a slow breath. "It's kind of creepy, even with all the flowers. How do you breathe in here?" She handed me the hot cup and opened the bag of sweet goodies. Saliva pooled as she pulled out a powered donut placing it on the napkin across from me. Licking her fingers, her other hand reached back into the bag for her dark chocolate iced one. I wasn't too crazy about chocolate, but it was her favorite and especially dark chocolate. *Yuck.*

Welcoming the warm vapors into my nose, I felt them tease the other senses and took a huge sip, allowing the life-giving liquid to give me a quick charge. I leaned back into the bed and sighed. "This is awesome. Thanks so much for all of it. Rae-Lynn should be back any moment. She went to get us lunch." I lifted the cover on the food plate and watched Blake's nose curl up. She looked at me with a new understanding, and I knew by the look on her face she would be waiting for me to show up with food too.

We laughed and put the cover back down. Willow asked us to use our inside voices. Blake narrowed her eyebrows and reached for the curtain separating our areas, pulling it around the bed as she whispered a generic apology. Normally, Blakely would have told her to shove it up her ass and mind her own damn business. I think the reality of an old person in a hospital bed went against her usual need to be blunt.

She grabbed the chair from behind her and made a temporary bed/work space and sat down. I looked at the time and noticed it was only 12:20 p.m. "Ah, Blake darling, aren't you supposed to be in last period? Don't you think Ms. Kyto will miss you? P.E. won't be the same without you if you get your ass thrown out of her class."

"Don't worry about it. She won't care when I tell her I came to rescue her star pupil. Tennis won't be the same without you either. How long before you can come back to school?" She was knocking on the cast and pulling out a medium black Sharpie.

I took another quick sip and set the cup on the table. "The doctor said I can go home in a couple of days. I won't get the brace off for about another week, but I can use crutches in the meantime. The short arm cast is another issue. Four, maybe five weeks before this arm will be exposed to the light of day. It sucks, but at least it wasn't the right one. I can still move these fingers with this kind of cast, but I have to be careful when using the crutches, one wrong slip and my butt's back in here."

Shifting over to one side of the bed, I moved the arm so she would have better access to the cast. "Hey, are Ghost and Dee coming by today? I haven't had my daily dose of *I told you so* from Dee, with a sprinkling of sarcasm, courtesy of Ghost." I readjusted the thin hospital blanket so I wouldn't be flashing anyone walking in. Moving was a chore with one side not working so well. I reached for the cup again.

Blake flipped the hair out of her eyes and tucked the rest under her hoodie. "They said they would stop by after Ghost finishes his hauntings at work." Dee is going to catch a ride with him, so you'll have to wait a few hours before you get your fix. Now hold still."

Every day she added something new to her expanding artwork. She was sticking her tongue out while moving the pen in small, pointed triangles. Intensely watching her draw the mouth of the shark reminded me of the donut. Without thinking, I leaned forward placing the cup on the table and snatched the powdered sugar one. With a mouth full of smooth sugary sweetness, I heard a disappointing huff.

"Dammit, Alexcia, tell me when you want something or need to move. Now I will have to draw a hook or something out of the shark's mouth. Crap, I will have to remember to bring a red pen tomorrow." Blakely eyed her work, "...and a blue one too." She sat up waiting for me to finish chewing. I grabbed a napkin to wipe the powdered sugar off and made a slight cough while reaching for the coffee cup. I gave her a smirk and cradled the cup close for protection.

"Are you done yet?"

I gave her a look of *really* and nodded. Blake went back to work on her dot-to-dot.

The TV was dismal, showing nothing but how-to shows and news. Balancing the coffee next to my right hip and using a free hand to pull the remote closer, I kept pushing the up button, channel surfing, to kill time while Blakely created her new masterpiece. That was when a picture flickered into focus. A feeling of dread stopped my finger on KSNV Channel 3.

The news anchor was finishing her intro when the next story caught my breath. Cameras highlighted a dark highway and several emergency vehicles with their lights flashing in the background. Not realizing I was shaking, I pushed the volume plus sign on the remote.

A news broadcaster at the scene held his rain attire so the wind wouldn't claim it. The accident he was covering resembled a small nuclear test site and what was left of the mangled vehicles involved reminded me of corpses. Scattered fires were still burning in the tumbleweeds and Joshua trees were being snuffed out by fire hoses. A video camera scanned the carnage of what was left of the wreckage. Then a man's voice sliced through my memory, mixing with familiar images as he covered the story.

"...about a week ago this horrific scene could have been avoided if the driver of a fuel truck had taken the time to pull over and use a rest stop. Three teens and the driver of the big rig were killed. Only one passenger in the oncoming pickup survived this crash. Getting behind the wheel with an insufficient amount of sleep and driving under poor road conditions to make up time seems to be on the rise. Could companies soon be held accountable for pressuring their drivers to meet impossible deadlines? Or will the freight companies leave the truck drivers to be accountable for their own actions? Unfortunately, Hank Timberman and three teenagers paid the price. Tune in for a look at these questions and more on Channel 3 News at Five."

I didn't see Rae-Lynn holding out the tissue box. The room grew colder, and I wasn't hungry anymore. She had gone to In-N-Out Burger. Normally, the smell would have had me barking like Gigi and begging for a fry. Today, nerves trumped food and I grabbed the pink puke tray and let go. Blakely jumped back and started timidly patting me as she made little gagging noises. Rae-Lynn sighed and set down the bags of food in the chair. She walked over to push the call button for the nurse's station and asked for someone to bring in a new blanket, hospital gown, and a couple of washcloths. Then she took Blakely's spot, moved the half empty cup back to the table, and held back a few locks of hair as I deposited used coffee and donut in the bowl.

Thoughts of remorse hit home about the poor dead driver getting the blame. I knew... I had killed them all. How on earth was I going to live knowing I should have died right along with them? After draining myself, both physically and emotionally, I sat back. Wiping the corner of the hospital gown across my mouth, I motioned to Rae-Lynn that I was done.

A candy striper came into the room with a smile and carrying the requested supplies. Rae-Lynn returned the smile and said, "Thanks," while reaching for the stack, indicating she would take it from there. The overly cheerful female waved and disappeared without comment.

"I'm sorry, Mom. I know you went out of your way to get us food. I will try to eat it after my nerves have settled down." The voice coming out of me sounded raw from undealt emotions and gritty from using my throat backwards. Blakely and Mom looked at each other at the same time as if they were sharing a secret. They both nodded as Rae-Lynn held out a warm, wet rag to me.

I wiped the tears away when I noticed they were still staring at me. "Www... hat?" I couldn't help sounding paranoid. Both of them stood there, in silence. Blakely broke her stare first by bending over to pick up her pen from the floor.

"We need to discuss some issues. I wanted to address them closer to the end of the week, but I'm not sure there will be a right time, so..." Her voice trailed and Blakely sat on the bed next to me and placed her hand on my knee. "Tod's mom has informed me about his funeral. It's more like a wake since they can't bury him. Law enforcement assigned to the case are treating it as a vehicular manslaughter and wouldn't release his remains because of evidence problems. I guess things were pretty tied up until yesterday. His family is from different corners of the country and even some live abroad, so they are waiting for everyone to get here. The service will be in a few weeks.

"Funerals for the other passengers, Melanie Crisspike, and Brad Stu, are being held at the end of the week. I told both families you would probably be in the hospital for at least another week, and I gave them our condolences."

More water escaped from under both lids. *Really, how many tears can one person cry?* I missed Tod terribly and wished he were here to tell me one of his stupid jokes or sing one of his silly songs. I felt bad for the others because I knew of them and yet I didn't know them well enough to feel more than regret.

Mom took a breath. Misunderstanding the reaction I was having to her talk, she continued, "I can try to arrange it if you want to go to Melanie's. It's in five days. It will require me shifting around my work schedule, but I can manage it if the doctors are okay with it as well."

I rocked *no* in a silent reply, and turned toward the window and cried internally. Why couldn't I have died right along with them? Why did I get spared and not any of them? Then memory recall brought up a clip from that night as it flashed a picture of the demon. Why did it let me live when I had asked for their lives to be spared? I damned myself for what I did to them. This was retribution, for me to relive the night over and over again. The only thing good about recalling new nightmares was that I hadn't had a normal nightmare since I'd been in the hospital. Credit probably went to the painkillers for driving the creatures away. The pills had worked as good as drinking the horrors away. At least under a doctor's care, I was doing it legally. This incident reopened old issues I wasn't ready to face. I made a loud sniffling sound, and Blakely handed me another tissue.

Jolting us from our somber mood was a hammer knuckle knock on the door frame. We all jumped, including my roommate. Willow had been concentrating on her unflavored gelatin cup while I was sick and crying.

"Is there an Alexcia Stasis staying here?" The guy was trying to look through smashed, blond bangs, caused by his cap being pushed too low across his brow. I couldn't make out his eyes. His voice sounded hurried. I guessed he was in his late teens. Standing about six feet with a slight tan, I surmised he probably actually worked outside with the plants. His medium build filled out the ivy green polo shirt nicely. I was slightly embarrassed about someone asking to see me at a time like this. I could star in a Clear Eyes commercial and, I reeked of regurgitated food.

Rae-Lynn raised her hand in a *put it here* gesture. Maybe an overactive imagination could explain the sudden plunge in temperature, but I couldn't dismiss why I was covered in chicken skin when he entered. The chill caused me to pull up the white cotton blanket. It also hid the mess. Blakely and Mom never indicated the change, so I figured shivers were a side effect of getting sick.

The delivery guy carried a long, iridescent pearl box with a small, plastic window on the top corner of the lid. With his free hand, he tugged at the brim of his ivy and white cap in greeting. Handing the box to Rae-Lynn, he shot me a wink. Underneath the box, he held an order confirmation form and receipt. "Ma'am, I'm from Spring Is Beauty, Floral Decorating and Arrangements Service. I have a delivery for Alexcia Stasis." He glanced back down at me and I felt the crimson rise.

"Do you have a pen? I can sign for her." Rae-Lynn gently took the box from him and placed the pretty rectangle down across both legs. Instantly, all the little hairs stood at attention from its touch. It was like a block of ice, which sparked internal curiosity. As I observed his attire, an even mixture of bewilderment added to the interest when I noticed he wasn't wearing gloves. How on earth was he handling this without protection?

I watched my skin change to different swatches of pink as the box sat there. Someone needed to move it before frostbite made it stick like dry ice. Nonchalantly, I lifted the good leg and watched the box as it partially slid onto the blanket. With lungs quivering, I slowly released a white cloud into the air. *I could see my breath.*

Blakely made a clicking sound with her tongue bringing me back to the floral commercial unfolding in front of me. Gazing up and down, I did my own personal scan and downloaded his image to memory. She reached up and pulled her own hood off to let the locks of straight, light brown and ash blond cascade down to her back. Her hair was gorgeous. In the sunlight, it gave off a brassy gold shine that said, "...and I'm worth it."

Wow, I couldn't believe it, crushing over the flower guy. A lazy grin made her face appear like a twelve-year-old instead of the grumpy sixteen-year-old we all knew and loved. I found myself snickering at Blakely's twitterpatedness over the buck that came out of the forest, or, in this case, the hallway, bearing flowers.

Maybe I should give her one flower from the box in remembrance of this rare occasion. She never took the hood off or liked herself enough to care about her appearance around others. Blakely never showed all of her face or body if she could avoid it, and here she was bursting out of her cocoon. Her beauty could not even be compared to a butterfly's. She was gorgeous. It was a damn shame she didn't see her reflection the same way others did. I knew part of her problem was because of her father, but we didn't discuss her issues often.

Blakely fluttered her lashes. "Where in the world are we going to put that? She has her own flower shop going on here. You know, maybe we can sell tickets to come and see Lex-Cee's *soon to be withering garden*. Tickets going fast and so are the flowers. Better hurry." Hunching forward, she put her hands in the pockets of her hoodie and started surveying where they should go. Tossing her hair in a *notice me kind of way*, I rolled my eyes.

Quite a few floral arrangements and a few stuffed animals adorned the windowsill and nightstand. I had to say, I didn't think I knew enough people who cared. Apparently, I did. The high school faculty even sent a bouquet of lilies. Most of the teachers didn't even like me.

A few days prior to this latest delivery, Mom, Dee, and Blake had taped up the surplus of get well and sympathy cards. The wall behind me looked like a section out of a Hallmark store. The sympathy cards were from people who knew Tod and I were closer than friends. I bit part of my lower lip and corrected myself. *We had been a couple* but didn't advertise the exclusive part of our relationship.

Along with the gifts came the visitors, most of whom were acquaintances from school or the party circuit. Of course, my closest friends and Mom kept me company every day. Except Father, who left the night I'd awakened from the coma.

Max would call Rae-Lynn every night to get an update. She would make excuses for him, work was too busy or there was a threat the market might crash. As long as I was out of danger, he would see me after the hospital stay. *Thanks for caring.* One of the big teddy bears was supposedly from him, but I knew Mom had picked it out and signed his name to the card. *Way to cover.*

Clink, Clink, Clink.

The sound snapped me back to our current situation. Blakely was moving some of the vases around to make room for another floral arrangement. The box looked like a seesaw, leaning partly on the leg brace. I couldn't stop eyeing the box even though I knew what people said about the cat being curious. I was in a hospital, so if it started killing me, I'd be in the best place to be curious, at least.

The chain attached to the pen was hitting against the clipboard as Rae-Lynn signed for the package, and the guy was shifting from foot to foot as he waited for her to be done. He probably wanted a tip too. I would want something for having to carry a parcel with the ability to freeze your fingers off. *Rae-Lynn, quick, give him money so he can buy a decent pair of gloves.*

A puff of air escaped from his lips as his eyes fixed on mine. I felt my lungs lock up from the pressure of his gaze. His face held a flicker of pain while mine was going to melt off my skull. I didn't understand the strange connection going on between us, but I knew from our obvious discomfort it was not good. He broke away from our challenge of wills and cleared his throat while Rae-Lynn handed him the clipboard. She bent down for her black laptop case where she kept her wallet.

"So how are you doing? I heard about you and your friends on the news." He spoke to the floor and not directly to me.

The laugh I made sounded empty. "Ah, yeah, it's hard, but I'm taking it day by day." This uneasy emotion we shared made the feeling of worry deepen. *I might have to persuade Blakely out of pursuing this one. He could end up being a deadbeat and then what? Blakely finds out she bought a chance to visit Hurtsville, that's what.*

Then he turned so I could see the name patch on his shirt. My heart seized up and screamed. The alarm mentally trigged so loud my eyes started to burn. The same eerie coldness from the night we met encircled my rib cage. The name *Michael* was embroidered in the same green as his work shirt. Memories from the party slammed the brakes on, forcing small talk. Chilled sweat was making the hair on my entire body stand on end. I couldn't believe I was face to face with Mr. Creeper again. I wanted to sob from the way fear grabbed me whenever he was around. Why was I so afraid of him? Why?

"I only have a ten. This is your lucky day." Rae-Lynn's hand held out the bill when she noticed how he was staring at me. She cleared her throat while waving the money in front of his face. "Excuse me, Michael, is it? Thank you for your time, but my daughter is not feeling well and I have to change her linens." The fanning of her fingers slowed once she observed how zoned out he was. With her free hand, she moved her chair back, side-stepping around to position her body directly in front of him. "Thanks again. I'm sure she will love them."

Michael snatched the bill from her fingers and shook his head. Staring at the floor, he took steps to leave the room. Blakely's sigh sounded deflated, but she had no idea what he was like. I drank with the guy. I should know. When we had some time alone, I would fill her in. He stopped suddenly at the door, appearing as if he had heard the silent thoughts and spun around.

Blakely squeaked out a quick whisper, "Oh my goodness. He is tempting."

I, on the other hand, wanted to pull the blankets over my head to make the bad man go away.

"I'm sure I'll be seeing you around. You take better care of yourself..." The last part to me was under his breath, but I heard him loud and clear from the doorway, "...it will make my job much easier if you do." He tipped the brim of his hat and turned to Willow. She was sipping from a small milk carton when he spoke to her next, "Willamina Glasston, I'll see your act very soon. You take care for now, hun." He turned back to us and bowed. "You ladies have a great day." Waving the ten, he said, "Thanks for the tip."

I peeked out from under the covers and made myself really look at his face. Eyes burned with horror-filled tears from what I saw. Something black with a purple hue wrapped itself around his body, then slithered up and over his shoulders. I had to be losing my mind. Was that thing alive? Did he know it was there? What the hell was going on? I was a deer caught up in the darkness of it. Adrenaline kicked in the fight or flight feeling, but where would I flee? It was time to show some teeth and bite. Fighting was the answer.

Steeling myself for a confrontation, I spoke right back to him, "Well, thanks, Michael, for the flowers. I'm sure I will see you around, as well." I sat up straight and nodded, indicating I had remembered him from the party. My heart was trying out for a triathlon. I couldn't control the calisthenics it was performing, flipping between each rib. It was making me short of breath and dizzy. The two black holes staring at me were pulling on a layer of consciousness. Those eyes made me start to falter against what little fight I had mustered to stand up to him.

He nodded back, and in a menacing tone, spoke my name upon leaving, "Alexcia." Soon he was around the corner with whatever misty thing was trailing behind him. After his departure, the air in the room turned instantly warmer.

Willow sat there with the straw stuck to her bottom lip as it quivered. She had a far off look on her face, and I couldn't tell if she had blinked at all since he left. I turned away from her and looked back at Rae-Lynn and Blakely.

Mom bent back down to her laptop case and pulled out her cell phone. Blakely was still silently wishing for her creepy knight in khakis to come back and rescue her. Rae-Lynn pressed only one button which meant she was calling Max. *Why now?*

The box reminded me it was still there as the coolness drifted through the covers. I reached for it when suddenly Rae-Lynn turned around and snapped, "Don't touch that."

Then she tiptoed to the bathroom for some privacy. Her eyes took on a darker shade, reminding me of anguish. Mom must have forgotten to tell Max something I shouldn't hear. Shrugging, I lightly touched the corner of the box to test if it was going to bite. Blakely's grin turned inquisitive peeking through the lids window.

"Well, come on. What's in there? We need to find out who sent this. The box alone looks incredibly expensive. I would even keep the box after the flowers died if it were up to me." She used one of her black chipped nails to pry open the side of the lid.

While I worked on the left side, I remembered the manicure I had treated myself to before the party. Most nails were broken and the polish had been worn off some of them. My pinky nail had snapped in half and hurt when it rubbed against the sheets. I was holding it out at an angle so I wouldn't get it caught on anything. Not being able to use my left hand was such a bother. Good thing I had Blakely's inquisitiveness to help me out.

We both lifted the lid at the same time. A light breeze drifted out of the box like whatever it was had greeted us by taking a breath to say *Hello.* I looked at Blake, "Did you feel that?" She let go of the lid, and I tossed it down to the end of the bed. Something was wrapped in pearl frosted tissue paper similar to the outside of the box. Light pastel colors caught the fluorescent lights and shimmered. The paper had a smooth, cool crispness to it. For some weird reason, I had the urge to taste it. Both of us were smiling. At least that was a nice feeling for a change.

A white envelope with crystal flakes was embedded in the paper toward the bottom of the box. Blakely slipped it between two fingers and tossed it over to me. Our smiles were widened with anticipation. What did this mystery person send me? It was making us reel. I carefully pulled the corner to flip it up and slid the card from its holder. It was made out of the same material as the envelope. Someone with script handwriting left a message... not a *get well...* or a *so sorry.* Just three words and a letter. *See you soon, T.*

"Ah, Lex-Cee, who's T?" Blake came around to read from over my shoulder. "I don't know anyone by the name of T, do you?"

We looked at each other trying to see if one of us could remember this someone of a person. He obviously knew me. My name was unique and most people misspelled it without the "c." Blakely tugged on my arm. "Hey, maybe he left a number on the back side?"

I flipped it over. Nothing. "I wonder what's under the paper. Here." I handed her back the card and began to peel the tissue away. The same scripted handwriting graced a four by six piece of calligraphy paper. I lifted it out and held it close so I could read it first. My heart felt giddy when I realized it was a poem. I read it over and over until the words were burned into memory. Feeling the card between my fingers was surreal, in a way. I didn't know anyone who would be able to afford these flowers, well, except Max. I knew from Rae-Lynn's demeanor that wasn't the case. I read the poem in a whisper...

To Kiss Remembrance

Where winter's breath is felt on skin,
It grows alone, feeling the bite of wind
Where snowflakes fall so not to bruise.
It dreams of someone's touch of dew
Where the air is crisp and dries one's tears.
It longs to protect what it wants to hold dear
Where life cannot go but death can follow
It wants to remember why it fights for tomorrow
Where its roots drink from creations flame
It needs just one kiss to remember thy name.
From: T.

I finished the poem with a breathless whisper, "…from T."
The *from* part of the poem was signed with only one letter glaring at me. Both forefingers and thumbs holding the card felt as if I had plunged them into ice water. Blood drained from the top half of my core, making each leg throb from the rush. Where tears would have made tracks by now, both cheeks felt more like wind burn from skiing. All I could do was sit there reading the words over and over in silent disbelief. Dumbfounded, swimming in disbelief, I tried to make sense of the poem. The words seemed to reach out to me. Someone was sending me a message, by way of frozen flowers and a stranger named T. What was scarier… he was trying to communicate with me by poetry. Another indication this person knew me.

Blakely was getting impatient with me. Reaching over my shoulder, she whisked the sheet of paper away and read it to herself. I recited it word for word along with her moving lips. As I watched her mouth, a male's voice was overlapping hers with every syllable. He sounded far away, like beyond a dream. And yet as they recited it together, I knew in my heart, he was nearby.

When she finished, tears formed in her eyes. It had also spoken to her and an emotion of lightheartedness came over me. As quickly as it came, the feeling was replaced by a sense of emptiness. Something had been lost or missing. Facing me with small self-made rain drops on her face, Blakely smiled and handed me back my note.

Bringing both of her hands up to her face, she wiped under each of her lower lashes with her third finger while clearing her throat. "Damn, we know one thing. He's right up your alley, Lex-Cee. The guy can write." Blake used her hands to push the chair against the hospital bed and turned it so she could face me when she sat down. "I don't know what you felt, but it made me glad to feel sad or something close to sadness. So, are you going to see what's in the box, or should I grab the lid and close it?" She was pretending to lean over both legs to replace the lid when I bolted up, and without thinking snatched the box from its resting place.

Pitched into an Arctic sea, my body reacted as though I had a light case of hypothermia from the dip. With teeth beginning to chatter, I replaced it between Blakely's arm and the right leg brace. I couldn't understand why I was the only person affected by this thing. She touched the sides of it trying to raise one end up so we both could look at the same time. Blake showed no signs of being cold, not one shiver. Why could she touch it with no ill effects? But, when I did, it turned me into a frozen Push Pop. I wrapped each arm around myself for some warmth. "You go ahead. I'm feeling a bit overwhelmed and am tired of this arm hurting. The medication must be wearing off."

"Are you sure? I mean it's your gift. You should be the one to see it first."

"Go ahead and unwrap the damn thing. I'm getting bitchy, and I smell. And why is she taking so damn long on the phone? Rae-Lynn." By using her name, I was hoping for a quicker response because it irritated her. I was cold, tired, hungry, upset, and done trying to figure out who this mystery person was. *I mean who sends frozen bouquets and encrypted messages?* The need to get out of these puke smelling blankets and gown was greater than mere curiosity. Sealing myself off in mid blink, I inwardly wished one of them would get the hint to warm up the coffee and food. I didn't care what was in the box anymore. Whatever it was, it didn't like me touching it. Hence, the freezer burn sensation whenever I tried to hold it.

My friend, with her mouth unhinged, gawked at me like she didn't know who I was. The bathroom doorknob made a popping sound indicating Rae-Lynn had locked the door when it slowly opened. Willow made little sniffing sounds from her side of the room. With my tongue glued, I couldn't muster up the word *sorry*, to either of them. I was done with all of this.

Blakely's face reminded me of a scolded puppy and it was enough oil to unlock my jaw. "So sorry. I'm getting restless and this adds to it, ya know?"

Mom had a frown on her face when she saw the opened box on the bed. Rae-Lynn looked as though she aged ten years behind the closed door. This meant the conversation with Max must not have gone well. She slowly closed the cell phone and brought her face up to meet mine. I grew worrisome when I noticed she had been crying. Why? Oh, no. Was I going to die anyway? That explained why I keep getting cold. It probably was insufficient blood flow. My lower lip was beginning to quiver as I waited for her words to hit me with the horrible news. Blake turned to face her. Willow's small sobs turned to hiccups.

Rae-Lynn walked over to the hospital bed, glancing at the bouquet box. "So, did you see what it was? I'm sure you have some questions for me."

One question after another fired from a mental voice of irritation. Huh? What? Why does everything come back to this stupid gift? What the hell was it?

Blakely took this moment to answer for me. "We were about to open it. There is a card, but neither of us knew anybody by that name. Whoever it is left her an awesome poem too. I think they may have a crush on our little Alexcia here." She snickered at her jab at me. "I don't know much about rhyming, but I think it's beautiful."

Rae-Lynn looked puzzled. "So, you haven't looked at it? I thought for sure. You look so pale and your lips are blue like you're freezing..." Her words kind of trailed off into thought.

Yes. Finally someone gets it. I lifted the sheet and blanket up, "I would like to change out of this and maybe get something to eat. The package has waited this long, we can look at it after I'm clean and warm again."

Mom looked relieved as she walked over and picked up the box to set it on another table. Then she asked Blakely to pull the curtain all the way around for privacy. Rae-Lynn picked items up for my sponge bath.

Turning to Blake, I felt a little embarrassed. "Hey, Blakely if you don't mind stepping out for a bit?" I felt transparent for shooing her out, so I added, "Also, can you find a microwave in this place to heat up the coffee? I would do it, but I'm kinda stuck."

She replied with a nod, but I could tell she was waiting for a response to my earlier actions. I shrugged as an apology, and she picked up the coffees and sauntered out of the room and down the hallway. In muffled tones, I heard her speaking to someone from the nurse's station asking directions to the kitchen.

Mom brought me a bucket of hot, soapy water and a washcloth. She untied the gown, and I went to work. I used the wash rag to wipe everything and everyone out of my mind. Trying to erase the unwanted emotions from Michael and the frigid feelings from the mystery box, I scrubbed. I still wanted to peek inside the box to see whatever it was, but I wanted to face it with a warm body, inside and out before I lost feeling from holding it again.

While I worked on ridding myself of a few layers of hospital residue, Rae-Lynn did the same to the mattress. She changed the sheets by lifting each leg and at the same time telling me to not get water on the cast. Handing me a new hospital gown with little kitten faces on it, she smiled. I frowned. I wanted the old one back. Really, I wasn't ten anymore, so why did I have to get the kiddy one? Mom tied me into it, and I sat back while she took the mini bathtub away. She came back with a clean flat sheet and a blanket. Clean body, clean sheets, and a clear mind. I was feeling much better. All that was missing was my warm, toasty coffee and some food. Then, all would be right with the world.

After we were done, she walked around the edge of the bed and sank into the chair as best she could. Glancing at her watch, she craned her neck at the door and then back at me. She puffed, "Great, we're done in time."

"In time for what?" I arched an eyebrow.

"Your father should be here shortly."

"What, what are you saying? I thought he was still away on business? Unsticking his assets?" It sounded like whining. No, wait, it was, "Why is he coming if nothing is wrong with me?"

"Wrong? Who said anything was wrong?"

"Mom, be frank with me. Do I need a transplant? Does my arm have gangrene and needs to come off? Or worse, am I dying?" Apprehension widened my gaze, waiting for her to disclose my life-threatening diagnosis. I was answered by her laughter. I loved the sound of it when it wasn't directed *at* me.

"What an imagination you have. No wonder you always get A's in creative writing. Isn't it okay for your dad to come by to see his daughter when she's laid up in the hospital?" I must have struck her funny bone because she was tearing up again while she was laughing to herself. At least, the ones she was shedding now were the good kind.

When Blakely returned, she was wearing a broad grin as though she was pleased with herself. Holding two white blankets and the cardboard drink container carrying our coffees, she said, "Looky, what I got. You needed and I retrieved. I told one of the candy stripers you were on the *not so warm* side of things and she gave me two fresh blankets right out of their dryer. Quick, take them, I'm sweating to death." Mom got up to take them from her. When she opened them up, the dry heat hit me instantly and I felt elated. I was getting a tad emotional over Blakely going above and beyond her duties as a friend and motioned for her to come closer. I wrapped my good arm around her, squeezed and told her I was sorry. She smirked and shrugged one shoulder to indicate it was no biggie.

Well, no better time than the present to look at my gift. I was clean and warm again. The earlier thoughts about Michael and the box were just a dirty memory. I glanced from Rae-Lynn to Blakely. The action gave me an idea. One of them could hold the box while I opened it. I feared the chill no longer. I had it covered.

"Mom, can I look at the flowers now?" I held up both hands as if to say *please*.

She leaned toward me from her chair and played with a tie on the gown. Maybe hoping one of the cats from the fabric pattern would bat at it. "Why now, I thought you wanted to eat after cleaning up. And your father is on his way. He'll be here any minute."

Blakely jumped off the bed, briefly looking at her watch, "Oh wow. Look at the time. Well, I gotta jet for now. But I'll be back tomorrow to add to the picture on your arm." She grabbed her warmed up coffee off the table and reached for her car keys to the Lady, her salsa red, 2009 Volkswagen Beetle two point five convertible. Blakely has always had an obsession with Sharpies. *She decorates everything with them. She is a great artist. I've even had her draw on a few of my book covers.* Anyway, she used about five, thick black Sharpies to attack her car. It has big, huge, black spots, making it look like a real ladybug.

I was so envious that she could drive, but aside from that, she was leaving awfully fast. Max has always scared her to death. I knew the minute she heard he was on his way she would bolt.

"Mom was just going to let me open the present. Please stay, I promise he'll be on his best behavior." I was trying to give those big, wide Puss-in-Boots eyes. Batting my lashes, she giggled.

"I really should get going. I have a paper due and TV shows can't watch themselves, ya know."

Scooting closer, I whined. She caved. I clapped. "Yay."

"Okay, let's open the box. Then I gotta go." She sat on the edge of her chair. Mom hesitantly handed the box to us. I signaled for Blakely to take it from her. Then urged her to go ahead and remove the tissue paper from whatever was underneath.

I never saw a bouquet of flowers so beautiful. They rendered me speechless. Two conflicting impulses kept me still. Anxiousness and longing battled for the right to control me—touch or don't touch—left me from advancing further. The coolness was wrapping around the right hand, but I was holding my own at the moment.

The flowers were similar to a rose but with thinner petals.

I counted seven partially bloomed buds as they glistened and sparkled, resembling the sun hitting snow. Eureka. The flowers really did look like snow. Each one was sculpted out of a substance which looked like the winter white stuff but held their form like ice. It would explain why the box was so cold until Blakely commented on the bouquet.

"Oh, my gosh, Lex-Cee. They are gorgeous. I've never seen such a pretty color of yellow. How much would seven pale yellow long-stemmed roses cost with buds the size of your fist? These are amazing. I think the florist goofed though because there are seven instead of six. You still think they were delivered by mistake?"

I looked back into the box again. No, they were white. Their brightness made the dark hunter green stems appear almost black. Something surreal had happened as I watched the bottoms of the petals turn a light azure and got darker. The new color began to move up the petals, marbling in delicate swirls. *Someone swat the flies from my unhinged jaw. Hadn't anyone else seen this happening?*

Catching Rae-Lynn's hard gaze, she was clearly unhappy with the gift and had no problem showing it. Slipping a single finger up to her lips, she made a silent *Shhh as* I was thrown into a world called *not now*. I tried to lick my lips to keep from saying something I might regret.

A deep voice clipped from behind me, "So, I see you let her open them anyway? What were you thinking, Rae-Lynn?" Max loomed over my shoulder. *Can we say, I need a bath again?* And from the looks of it, Blakely needed to change her panties too. She sat still, ramrod straight. Her chance to scurry unnoticed was moot, but it didn't matter because she was too scared to leave anyway.

When we first became friends, Max had become terse with us over coloring on the walls in the playroom. His voice had a tendency to boom, and I guess it was too much for Blakely. She burst into tears and rocked while clutching the marker to her chest. Ever since then, she has been afraid of him. If I was in a confrontation with him while she was there, I was S.O.M.O, *so on my own* as far as she was concerned.

"I can't believe his audacity. He gave her Remembrance Roses? Are the two of you trying to speed up the upcoming events in her life?" He appeared confused, which was against his character. "How in flames creation did he manage to bring these to this side? You realize what will happen if she touches them?" Using two of his fingers he lifted my chin. "Where is her pendant?" His voice had almost hit the booming level. Why was he angry over my missing necklace?

Willow was crying again. Blake looked like she wanted too. Mom stood there with furious eyes. She was determined to not show him she had already been crying. I sat silent and in bewilderment.

Mom narrowed her eyes. "It is the least of our worries. And as you can see, she hasn't touched them yet. Max, can I talk to you over here… in my, ah, office?" She gestured over to the bathroom.

Max had a disconcerted look on his face. "Rae-Lynn, that's the bloody bathroom."

She stomped and pointed. He cleared his throat and obeyed. She then briskly walked over to the bed. "If you're wondering, these flowers are called the Rose of Remembrance. They are very special. I also read in an article, you should never touch them, especially the thorns because some people are highly allergic to them. Excuse me, girls, for a moment. Alexcia, I need these for a few minutes." She took the flowers, and my heart melted.

Why couldn't I touch them? They were only flowers. And I'd never had an allergic reaction to anything, not even pollen.

Those flowers changed in appearance… I know what I saw, even if Blakely hadn't seen it. I knew it was the reason Mom took them. But I wasn't going to tell Blake because she was freaked out enough already with Max there. The door made a hissing sound as she tried to slam it, but the pressurized hinge at the top was stopping her dramatic exit.

Willow was clearly upset by the outburst, and I felt it was my duty to calm her down before she called the nurses to complain. "I'm truly sorry for Max's behavior, Willow. He's really worried about his company and having me laid up adds to his frustration."

She sniffed and bit her lip, displaying the weight of whether she wanted to tell us what was really bothering her.

Blakely could clearly see Willow was as upset as her. Getting up and walking over to her bedside, she rested a hand on the elderly lady's shoulder. "It will be okay, Ms. Glasston. Honestly, her dad freaks the hell out of me too. I'm sure he won't be staying long."

"Mr. Stasis does make a tornado sound like a breeze, but he is not the reason I'm scared." Her lip trembled, "That boy, the one who delivered your package, he knew my name." She mumbled, "He knew my birth name… Willamina. No one has called me by my name for over fifty years, not even my husband, rest his soul. He wouldn't dare call me Willamina if he knew what was good for him. But, that boy, he knew it. And I didn't like how he looked at me… I didn't like it." She glanced back at the door. "When he spoke to me, I experienced piercing pain, and I thought I was going to have a heart attack right then and there. The pain was not gas. That's the excuse the doctors have been brushing me off with. He isn't really coming back to see me, is he?" Her last question held fear in it. I wasn't the only one having the creeps about Michael.

My parents' voices were rising in the small bathroom. I was

concerned the door was going to burst from the built up anger between them.

Then... *SLAP.*

Never heard that one before between the two of them, and it left me holding in a sob. Silence seeped from under the door and filled the room.

Blakely's eyes were bursting with horror, and I knew she didn't want to be around for the outcome. I signaled, with my good hand, for her to get the hell out of there. She patted Willow's shoulder, waved to me, then pointed at her watch, reminding me Jake and Dee were supposed to be there shortly. Great, they were going to walk into an ongoing war between the roses.

She was gone in a blink and the door to the bathroom opened slowly. The first to come out was Rae-Lynn, rubbing the inside of her right hand as her reddish blond hair veiled her face. Father sported a four-finger welt on his left check as he stepped from the doorway. He walked over to Mom's laptop case and pulled out her cell phone, then walked back into Rae-Lynn's temporary office and closed the door.

Max's voice was an octave above booming again, and I hoped whoever was on the other end didn't have the receiver up to their ear. I turned to Rae-Lynn, silently pleading for her to explain why they were so hostile to each other over a dumb cluster of frozen flowers. She was right, though. If I didn't have questions before, they were on my tongue now. Mom walked over to the window... refusing to look at me.

"Mom," my voice wavered.

She turned to face me, slowly pushing up a long, weak smile. "Things will get worse before they get better, baby. You'll have to trust me. Okay?"

Max opened the door while hanging up her cell phone. He briskly walked over to me without saying a word to Rae-Lynn. Placing the cell on the small table, he spoke under his breath. I couldn't quite make out the words, but their soft hush made me feel safe. He bent over and hugged me tight, so tight I wanted to cry because I thought it was his way of telling me goodbye. The coldness was back when he broke our embrace. Max stared in pause, then turned to leave the room. My heart filled with panic.

"Where are you going? You just got here."

Father's deadlock stare with Mom said it all. He was leaving because of her, or so I thought. Then his voice filled the room. "Don't worry, honey. I'll be back as soon as I can." He shifted his eyes to Rae-Lynn. "I just realized I almost missed my appointment with death." Max abruptly turned on his heel and stormed out.

Now, that was enigmatic.

11

TEVIN'S SIDE: THROUGH THE EYES OF A REAPER

*H*IS TONGUE WAS SHARP EVEN THROUGH THE CELL PHONE. MY EAR still burned from the onslaught of my name being used with a colorful adjective afterward. Alexcia's father was on his way to meet me. Uncorking a huge breath, I turned off the phone and shoved it into the back jean pocket. I raised both shoulders in a half shrug and spoke out into the wind around me. "Time to discuss a new Bond-Rite." It was a matter of time before they found out who sent the flowers.

Damn.

I told Michael to only give them to Alexcia, not Rae-Lynn, and definitely not leave them out in the open for her father to find. Why was he causing him so much trouble? First was the botched up job from the party, and now this. *Michael needs to get it through his thick, Ashen head that she is a part of our world whether he likes it or not. A Child-of-Balance is needed to maintain order to the Constants we govern and between the Houses of Light, Space, and Time.* The power must remain equal for creation to thrive. We agreed as a clan to make sure she remained safe in her world until she was of age. Why trip up now when her time to choose was near? He did not need to keep rubbing what I did in my face. We still had to work together for the same goal, to keep the waters of creation flowing.

The snow was piled high for this time of year with icicles hanging from the upper rim of our dwelling, reminding me of serrated teeth in the dual moonlight. I had a desire to run a finger down the length of one, and it drew me in. I've always been amazed at how something so delicate and fragile could otherwise have another side to it, strong and stubborn, determined to not let go or bend no matter how hard the winds tried to wear it down. I frowned, realizing they reminded me of her.

Alexcia needed direction. I presumed if she could remember the accident ten years ago, she might understand her importance to both of our worlds. I wear a cloak because it is part of what I am. All the while, she has been forced to wear hers over her eyes.

Time was ticking, not only her, but for all of us. So many lines had been drawn in the sand, and all the players seemed to be surrounded by them. As usual, Alexcia stood in the middle. Shrouded and completely clueless, she needed someone to cross first. I decided it was time for all of us to choose power or protect. In an attempt to be forthright, the clan was divided about the *protecting* part. In my opinion, they all needed to wake up and face our reality because eventually her eyes will unlock. I tried to help the process along. *May the House of Constants protect us when she does figure it out.* Maybe I could move us to work at one of the earth's poles by then? Colder was better instead of the possibly of our own reaping and recopying, I believed.

Speaking of frostier pastures, our domain was located on the side of a snow-capped mountain in the dimension of the Unseen. No one could tell from the outside, but our cave was gigantic. In the back, buried deep within the cavern, the Cauldron of Ending was located.

All Ashen clans have had one assigned to them and each one linked to the other. It was filled with the waters from our creator, the River Styx. When we ventured near the cauldron, the water would boil. That was how the River spoke to us, whispering the names of the damned through the steam, and it was how we obtained the time frame and learned where to retrieve them.

By definition, Ashens have always been bound to specific harvesting areas. Therefore, they stay close to it, by mirroring their same location with the earth's present state. That way, crossing between both plains was as simple as a thought. We were mirrored to a particular part of Sin City. It was a fitting nickname for a city full of tasty, tainted souls. Death was never without a job because the unique mixture of Vessels trying to co-exist together was delicious. One drawback, though, was during summer solstice because it was brutally hot. Winter was never cold enough for our kind, another reason we remained tethered to our own dimension.

In our world, we could summon our cloaks or stretch out our wings as Smolders and soar without being detected by the living. To an Ashen, it was the closest feeling to what the Vessels call being free, although we never were. Our bond to the River was the price for eternity.

Our existence is mostly mundane. We fill our time coexisting between both worlds and find ways to kill time between harvestings. One of our past times is sampling what the vessels call fast food. Ashens do not need to consume this food to exist but snacking on it gives us a quick fix between jobs. The Bond-Rite between the River Styx and all Ashens requires payment for performing the severing process. Our power is sustained by siphoning a portion of the Vessel's energy before their life force can be obtained. When we sever the spirit from the body, it is when we truly feed. A Vessel's last emotion is our sustenance.

The empty soul is then given to the Bridge Crosser. That particular daemon's job is designed to take the soul to the Ever After where the gondoliers ferry them back across the River Styx. In short, we recycle creation. It's not a glamorous occupation being a Grim Reaper. Our only purpose for existence can be summed up in one sentence; we kill so creation can continue.

I looked up at the sky and wished for the wind to carry me anywhere, as long as it was not here. Ashens were damned to remain between both plains for however long our eternity lasted. Death walked among Vessels for so long that some of us tried to find a way to take out our own being. *Even a daemon can lose its own way when facing the never ending unknown.*

Screeching from above alerted the Smolder within me. My attention fixed on the trees above the entrance, and I watched a Callcry take flight, its wing span becoming smaller until it was a speck on the horizon. The wind whipping through the canyon had not altered its flight path.

Like all daemonic creatures, Callcrys, or the River Styx's soul cages, were attracted to negative emotions and malicious dreams. These beasts were similar to a raven but larger, about the size of a three-year-old Vessel, with the same length of wing span. Their most impressive feature was to disappear from sight, blending into the cover of night. Feathers were painted a dull, abyss black accented by the two orbs of burning gold. In the presence of another daemon, their eyes would die out and fill with blood to shed tears for the damned. If a soul was beyond the evils of darkness, the River it would send the Callcrys to collect, contain, and destroy the container and what was left of its essence. I thought of them as the River's filtration system.

Michael had once told me that a small flock of Callcrys found refuge on our mountain. That was fine by me because they would take care of our Snip and Snap problem. Humans have always believed that they were mythical creatures called pixies or fairies. *It is laughable since they take on more daemonic nuance characteristics than anything else. Snaps, or fairies, create diseases and poisons. Snips, or pixies, breathe life into lies and steal emotions from nightmares. Six hundred years and I still cannot figure out their purpose.*

My chest was heavy with so many uncertainties. The biggest one was how I really did not want to deal with Max. He was an unreasonable daemon. No one could if you valued your existence. I had taken a gamble sending Alexcia those roses, and this rat was going to pay the piper. I chuckled at the thought. Oh well, it was worth the risk.

The elementals were getting bolder by trying to attack her with a chance of leaving witnesses behind. I was impressed by their tenacious manner, not much, but enough to make me have second thoughts about picturing her in a coffin. Plus, something had to change with our duties watching over her. Seven Ashens made up our clan, and it was our job to handle about one-fourth of the harvesting in this area. The River's demand for more souls was increasing. With Alexcia upping her chances to become one of them, we needed a new strategy.

Grudgingly, I had to admit that I might have misjudged the outcome of this last attack. Regardless, extreme measures were necessary. Alexcia's body was having a negative reaction, especially if we were working next to her. That sometimes affected our work with the dying. The risk was becoming a problem and a damaged soul could turn into a Caster, or what the Vessels call a Ghost. *In my opinion, we do not need any more ghosts.*

I looked up where the dual moons were rising. Max was running late, must have been gathering up more power to knock me into the next plain. I was getting anxious. If he really wanted to snuff me out, he could have ported himself from somewhere in the hospital. This was his way of playing the older daemon teaching the younger one a lesson by making me sweat it out in the deep freeze.

This mixture of sour emotions was pissing me off, as well. I knew he did not have to go along with Rae's Bond-Rite with me. Max could have made it nonexistent if he really wanted to. Our House's ruler, Lucifer, had given him so much power in his human state, it seeped from his pores when certain emotions heightened. In most cases, Max exited in haste because he did not want Alexcia to detect it, and it made me wonder how long he could perform the duties of Doom Guard and keep the charade going. When he transformed into that physical state, he would have scared her to death... literally. Inevitability had a way of eventually helping out those who were clueless. It was only a matter of time until she figured it out.

Uncontrollably, both feet began to pace from the current of thoughts. Still entertaining the idea... if we could jog her memory enough to crack the door, maybe she would allow us to teach her how to use such powers. Then the clan and I would get some confirmation that we were actually protecting the Chosen Child. I understood what Rae-Lynn wanted us to believe, but the clan was getting restless protecting a Vessel that may or may not be the River's chosen one. Another question borne from thought made its way out, "If there are special children born every three hundred and thirty-three years, what makes her so different from the others?"

"Good question, daemon snot. But what makes you think I would enlighten you after the stunt you pulled?" He had answered my thoughts with words, and his voice sounded like gravel sliding down the mountain, growing louder until it was directly above me.

Max landed on the cliff at the top of the entrance, causing the Callcrys to stain the sky in streaks of ink. In his present form as Doom Guard, the daemon straightened to his actual height of ten, maybe twelve, feet. He roared out of annoyance while swatting with open claws at the swirling mass of inky feathers. Swishing in erratic patterns, his black horns reflected small specks of the moon's glow off the snow. The forest was lit up, but we were missing the thumping music to go along with it. I felt something dark, yet humorous, as I watched the spectacle play out in front of me.

The Doom Guard opened and closed his massive wings to give himself space in the middle of the encircling birds. He must have been about fifty feet up. The whirlwind of Callcrys fluttered, and then became a frantic warning of dread. Max set his sights on me, both eyes expressing he wished I would spontaneously combust and disappear from his existence. I sighed. "Here we go."

The cloak's mist began to dissipate, leaving a feeling of apprehension and tension as a shield. My own minion was bailing on me, how in the *Hell of Creation's Tomb* did it come to this? I made myself more corporeal to ground both feet into the rocks below. Narrowing both eyes, I prepared for a verbal confrontation and decided to go first. "So, old daemon, care to give Death an answer? The clan and I have grown tired of Vessel sitting. Maybe it's high time she finds out what she really is?" Threatening me with his wingspan, he slowly opened both sides. Maybe it was his way of processing. His tongue danced across his teeth, indicating he anticipated me as his next meal.

I felt like a suicidal jumper, the ones who think halfway down that it might not be a good idea. Whenever I had the opportunity to show up next to them before they landed, I would answer their thought with an actual verbal question. "Really, that is going to be your last thought?" Unfortunately, I was never given an articulate reply. Screaming normally came last.

A blast, louder than standing on the edge of a cloud after it gives birth to a lightning strike, filled the canyon with its memory. The mountain shuddered from the shock wave of Max's presence. In his Doom Guard form, he became a force to be reckoned with. I did not even have a chance to snap for my cloak before he was on top of me. I tasted blood and knew the familiar slow moving tar was oozing from other areas.

The predicament I was in did not really matter. I was more astonished to find I had unsheathed my scythe. Before realizing what had happened, the blade was under his throat, curving through the chain, with the toe resting on his left horn. The only movement between us was our House symbol dangling in my face. I was in a permanent stalemate with the second-in-command of our house. It was difficult containing the shock, but I worked on it by locking the jaw muscles. I switched my focus to the blood trickling down the back of my throat. Swallowing forcefully, I used it as an offering to pacify my own daemonic, Smolder creature within.

Max was using one of his hooves to slice in between rib bone and sneering as he pushed his neck down the blade to fill the space before me. Raising his leather wings off the stones, his words scorched across skin. "Listen, you are not worthy of my time to explain myself. Nor are you one to ask anything of me. You are the lowest form of daemon. I would not even take the time to scrape you off my heels." Molten, orange blood began to pool on the beard of the blade and drip down the snath. It hissed and popped the same way lava flow meets the sea. Brimstone and sulfur filled the air with an angered stench.

Max had truly lost it. By design, an Ashen's tool was forged straight from the River Styx for the purpose of harvesting the living, and in a rare case, to use for defense. The irony of it was mind-bending. Only daemons approved to bestow death were allowed to use a weapon of pure creation in its rawest form. No creature, living or existing, could touch an Ashen's weapon, which pretty much covered everyone. Max, even in his Doom Guard state, was no exception.

Alexcia's father rocked the tip of his hoof to add injury to his insults, then bolted straight up, pushing away from me. His blood sprayed everywhere, leaving plumes of smoke with each drop. I lowered the scythe and called forth my minion. Its black mist covered me with the shroud of darkness and leaving only the thin edges of my minion's indigo outline darting around me displaying its anger. I was told when I was at my worst, the bright color in my eyes faded to points of endlessness. Beyond that was where I kept the daemonic Smolder caged.

I knew my minion was pissed at me for allowing myself to take on this kind of damage while it worked at healing the wounds. Testing each area with a harsh sting was its way of showing me disappointment. Before it moved to cauterize the open gash Max had made, it gave me another jab. *This unique pet of mine has an attitude problem. It amuses the other reapers to watch us interact. Imp likes to point out that we are perfectly matched. Both of us are stubborn and set in our ways. The symbiotic relationship I have with my cloak minion is exasperating.*

A low growl turned into a chuckle as I used the snath for support to help me stand. Something was biting my ass. I was struck with a quick memory recall while reaching into the back pocket. Great. I dug in and retrieved broken pieces of the phone. I have gone through so many of the damn things, I should have switched to Bluetooth earpieces. *It would at least cut back on the grief I get from Quint.* I dropped the broken phone, seething as I heard the plastic pieces hitting rock.

"I get it. So, you do not want me to work for your angel anymore? Hey, that's fine with me. Quite frankly, it's high time you and Rae acted more like humans caring for a young Vessel and not keepers of a recklessly wild, exotic, and potentially dangerous animal."

Max frowned but remained quiet, so I took the opportunity to justify my actions.

"You do realize all the dangers she puts herself in, right? You contracted me to protect her, but she is going to end up killing herself faster than any elemental could. Oh, and, by the way, you owe me a new cell. Something with Bluetooth capabilities would be nice."

His response was a ground trembling roar. I tightened my

eyes in reply and mentally said, "The truth hurts, eh Max?" Spinning the scythe over my head, he would have missed me swinging it if he had blinked.

The mighty daemon rolled his wings and shoulders forward in a hunch. How could he look menacing and worried at the same time? *Damn me and the cloak I cast.* I was what? Feeling sorry for Max?

Well, he looked like he wanted to talk now. Sheathing the weapon, I inwardly cursed, "Double damnation," Then I snapped at the cloak and commanded it to remain close so it would not abandon me again. I made a swipe through my hair. *Great, blood there too.* I gave an order to my minion, "Cloak and Hood." The death shroud formed, and I stood there, draped in its power. In my Grim Reaper stance, I was ready for Max, anger and all.

The sound through his clenched teeth made a low whistle escape from his nose. I came to the conclusion that it was not me who hit this daemon's core. It was either his daughter or his lover. I coughed, not really sure if I wanted his attention back on me, but he could not stay in that location much longer. The other reapers would be back soon. I did not want to lose any of them to his anger. *Some of them do not know how to hold their tongues.*

Max's neck wound began to mend, becoming a light tinge of red. He let his weight drop to the ground and leaned on his claws. "Be grateful you never mated. Sometimes I would beg for something or someone to smite me down so I would not have to go back. But I find it hard to stay away from both of them, and Lucifer delights in torment for entertainment." His dagger-like eyes lost their steel, and I was no longer in his crosshairs. He spoke again, "The Master anchored my growing interest and suspended curiosities to move me like a puppet. He encouraged it, urged me to make her mine. What I did not comprehend was the consequences for such a relationship to exist."

Alexcia's father, in his otherworldly appearance, looked down the canyon's ridge. An oversized grimace peeled back to display his pointed teeth. I did not understand most of what he was explaining to me, but I was not going to acknowledge our little communication problem. Instead, I nodded in agreement and approached with caution as his voice echoed from the past. "...Before Rae-Lynn was transformed into her human form, she created the closest feeling to purity I would ever dare touch. The emotion that danced in her eyes mesmerized me, and her caress was so gentle, I finally understood what tranquility meant. Her waters quenched certain cravings, and I was lost in her ability to calm the turmoil of always wanting more. To my misfortune, she enraged a new desire of want."

Max lowered his wings as they darkened while he continued to speak, "After this little stunt, I feel her own feelings have become clouded for our daughter's safety. She is now angered with me." He rubbed a spot under his eye with the back of his claw and stared at me. "I was told to fix this... this little mishap."

The Doom Guard's claw opened and motioned up and down in my direction. Wonderful, the focus of this conversation was back on me. I remained silent, but the Smolder beast I kept contained began to mentally pace.

"Can you explain to me why you gave our daughter the Roses of Remembrance? Think about it because if your answer is not about her safety, I will make your existence recycle until you have no power left, and the River will not accept your essence back into its currents." He took on a striking stance, and I heard his nails scratch against the rocks, creating sparks. "Choose your words with care, Daemon of Death."

With eyes closed, I cleared the air with a back throat cough to buy myself some time to contemplate his proposal before willingly placing my neck across this daemon's chopping block.

I presumed either explanation I disclosed concerning Alexcia would start the recycling process for me in the end. I had never been on the other side of death's coin. To face the possibilities of demise with its next flip was surreal, and the frown I wore felt heavy as the conclusion became clear. Being upfront with Max was the only option. At least I knew he would hold true to his threat if he didn't approve. This existence would not end swiftly.

"I grow tired of waiting, Tevin." He gnashed his teeth making me focus on his face.

With a weighted down sigh, I answered, "The clan and I are under duress. We reap, recycle, restore. That is it. Guarding a life who does not want to be protected makes our job beyond complicated. We are all frustrated." My boots made a crushing sound against the loosened debris from our tussle. Taking a seat on one of the jagged rocks we had managed to avoid, I figured it would come across less threatening if I were sitting. A few scythe handles away from him, I felt a searing heat rolling off his body, anger in its complete form. Positioning my right leg so I could lean on it, I assumed the *thinking reaper's* pose while taking a moment to pause. "I was rationalizing about the benefits for both parties. By breaking yours and Rae's curse, she would be free to remember what she is. Hell, she definitely takes after you. I don't know if you have noticed, but her abilities are beginning to leak out. Right now, it is a slow drip… but soon enough… Max, the walls you use to contain her will come crashing down and then what?" I picked at the heel of my boot, pulling bits of embedded stone from the grooves. "I know she has power, but what will she do with it with no one guiding her on how to use it?" That was when I took a chance to look at him.

His eyes were set on something behind me. Max was zoning out. I could not tell if he was taking into consideration the explanation of the *why*. I had been forthright with him. It was not a case of covering my own ass, but I had sent the tainted flowers. I meant for her to touch them, and was, in a way, looking out for her well-being. I scoffed at myself. The word irritated me and the creature within growled in agreement.

"And who gave you the right to tear the wool from the lamb's eyes? *We*, as her caregivers, have taken all events into consideration. Yes, her day of birth draws near but *we* also have discussed the consequences of revealing everything and *we* feel she is reckless and too immature to handle the responsibilities of her calling. You and your clan have acted upon your own assumptions. Your contract was laid out in the simplest form between you and my wife with her asking for your assistance to help protect our daughter from corruption or demise." The last part of his sentence held grit from animosity toward me.

"The dead are getting neglected, Max. Do not hold ill-will against us. I sent the roses to Alexcia to wake her mind up. She needs to be told who she is, the power she possesses, and her role in creation's cycle."

Max appeared to be listening, but I doubted he heard every word. Regardless, I continued, "Alexcia also needs to stop her destructive ways. She is becoming unstable in her Vessel form. Her erroneous behavior will be her undoing. Not me, not my clan, and not even the elementals can dream of harming her body or soul, thanks to us and your spells. I am not sure what has happened to change her way of reasoning, but these past few specks of time have been close to ending her life. She is mixed up in earthly potions. My powers, for the most part, are keeping her chained to her soul. Max, the Cauldron of Ending has given us her name on more than one occasion."

His dark lavender skin turned a deeper shade with his disdain. He took to the sky and disappeared just as fast. I had given him plenty to ponder, and he needed to know. Rae needed to know. Alexcia had been damaging her soul, with almost every form of abuse to her life force. If she extinguished her own life, the River would look upon it as suicide… a form of murder. Therefore, the soul would be seen as unholy and not worthy to be recycled back into creation. Alexcia was going to find out quickly if the Callcrys came for her before we could stop them. If it came to that, we would not be able to halt the chain of events. She would be missing too much of her soul by the time we kept the River's soul cages from feasting on her.

The Doom Guard manifested behind me. The deep purple mist consumed me and jerked me around to face him in an instant. His claws passed right through me. I reached for the only thing I could count on. Swiftly pulling at the snath of my scythe, the blade rang out, colliding with his left claw. Sparks flew everywhere as we growled and roared in frustration.

Max's wings swiped at the air in front of me, trying to knock me off balance and push me out of his space. A sound of amusement slipped out because, in reaper form, I was nothing but mist, a dark cloud to rain on your day. He could not touch me, but at the same time, I had the same disadvantage. Floating like a Caster, I was only able to strike out with my weapon and nothing more.

He swiped. I faded. I swiped. Both of us moved, swiped, faded, swiped, and moved again. I was unsure how long we danced to death's tune, but it seemed as if we were getting out close to a decade's aggravation. I made the mistake of getting caught up in the rhythm of swinging and blocking when he countered by spinning the opposite way. Max tried to grab the scythe's hilt, releasing all of his force in one final roar.

My mist form blew to the back of the cave where I had intended on staying when I heard Max speak to me from the entrance. "Tevin, I grow tired of your whining. My wife holds you and your clan in favor. Why, I am not sure, nor do I approve, but it is what she wants for Alexcia. I will speak to my daughter but will not unlock her mind to her powers." The expression on his face dared me to speak, but I chose to play it safe. "The Bond-Rite I agree to is this: You have from this time forth, until the thirty-first rising of the dual suns in the Unseen. On the thirtieth set of the earth's single moon, you will not let anything happen to Alexcia's soul. I don't care if you have to stir the waters to change the outcome. After your time is served, I will break Rae-Lynn's contract with you and the bond to our rite will be severed." Max leaned into the cave entrance, making sure I heard his sarcastic tone. "In short, you have one earth month, from this time forth, to kid-sit my daughter. Do you object to this, or do we have a bond?"

I secured the scythe just as swiftly as I mentally listed the pros and cons. The mist around me became stiff with uneasiness. The reasons I found, in a roundabout way, were for both of our worlds. I was expecting her to find out who she really was, possibly change her destructive behavior and test the level of her strength. Most of all, if we could get her to value her life force, it would solve both of our problems. She would be less of a temptation or target to other Unseen creatures and give the clan a break from saving her ass all the time.

For the past decade, I had been consumed with keeping her alive and focusing less on this existence as a death daemon. Occasionally, I could not help but question the intentions or real reasons I had agreed to the venture. Over the years, the *why* of it had been lost among so many other questions of *want to know* as opposed to the *need to know*. The Bond-Rite was nothing but an infested thorn. I wanted it removed. No matter how much I was intrigued with Alexcia's nature, the clan had not chosen this path. My duties were getting neglected by it. Not great qualities of a leader.

This new Bond-Rite, between me and Max, would give us the break my clan longed for. I would also have a chance to open her eyes and awaken her powers to see if she really was the River's chosen. The time frame was golden, giving me close to thirty days to help this creature from losing her way. It was doable.

"Agreed." I unsheathed the scythe and positioned my hands over the two silver roses and twisted. Amused at the discomfort it caused because the feeling was connected to so many issues, I glided toward Max and presented him with one dripping hand. With his teeth, he ripped open his palm and held out the wounded claw. We shook and sealed our Bond-Rite. Alexcia would only be a burden for one more lunar month.

Max peeled his teeth back to show me the full length of his canines, "And stop calling my wife, Rae. It's Mrs. Stasis to you. I will even tolerate Rae-Lynn if you have to speak to her in front of Alexcia. But, if you ever address her by your own pet nickname again, I will stick your scythe up your ass." With that... he was gone.

12

My Shattered Soul

Dreams are fairy tales
Opened by the heart's desires
Tasting the candy-coated lies
They place by your pillow
Nightmares are terror tales
Unlocked by an eclipsed heart
Broken from a shattered soul
Screaming truths into your pillow
~Alexcia

URING THE NIGHT, CHAOS CAME TO VISIT ME, JOLTING ME FROM slumber by using loud voices mixed with screaming machines. Instinctively, I used my good hand to wipe the sleep from both eyes as I forced them to focus on the scene playing out before me. A slew of medical personnel stood over and around Willow, fiercely working on her frail body.

When I sat up, one of the nurses noticed and came over to pull the curtain halfway on the track so I couldn't see what they were doing. Then it happened. It felt as though someone gave me a shot of adrenaline. A lightning burst of electricity hit me, igniting the back of my eye sockets. I couldn't stop the pain of the pressure. Physically, I wanted to scream in agony. Instead, a sense of reason took over. Release was the only option. When I permitted the sticky tears to flow...

My ears popped.

Everything stopped.

Silence filled the space. Slowly they gathered at the foot of her bed, all of them appeared drained and disheartened. I heard someone ask the time of death and a nurse behind the curtain replied, "Zero three thirty-three."

Willow was gone.

My right pinky finger was cramping. Halfheartedly, I cast a watery gaze down at the painful annoyance. Both hands had knotted my fingers around the sheets and blankets, causing the knuckles to turn white. The anger I felt made me realize how much I wanted to shriek at them... *see, she told you all something was wrong with her heart, but none of you listened.* And now Willow was dead... dead. The thought left me cold to the point of numbness. At that moment, I realized a familiar chill.

It was the same sensation I'd felt the night of the party, but only when I was around Michael. The feeling seemed to have taken on a life of its own as it slithered underneath the flat sheet, snuggling up to me. Locked down in horror, the icy breeze licked the bottom of my foot, softly lapping from heel to toe. Terror sparked a shout engulfing my lungs, as it burned up my throat to escape. I quelled it by zipping both lips. If I had reacted the way I wanted to, everyone would think I was freaking out over Willow's passing. The intense heat was burning. For extra measure, I clamped my fingers to stop any sounds that might escape and bit my tongue before they used a straightjacket on me.

A voice from within whispered fearfully, "Michael's here... It's Michael."

For some reason I knew he was there, somewhere in the room. The icy air settled next to me like an empty presence. Cautiously scanning from corner to corner, the desolation I felt turned to dread. Small droplets of dew fell from my eyes resembling snow. Deep down I knew he had come to visit her.

A SOUR TASTE FORMED FROM WILLOW'S PASSING. DEALING WITH DEATH AGAIN so soon hit too close to home for me. My life went from what I thought was a normal existence minus the nightly meltdowns... to a life turned inside out and upside backward. Did that make sense? Because if it didn't... good. *Why should anyone else understand my life better than I do?*

For the first time in two weeks, I felt the discomfort of negativity flee as my refuge came into view. I was almost home. Rae-Lynn straightened her turn, gliding her precious steed up the driveway. For a moment, I wished to be Sleeping Beauty, for evil to swoop in and lock me away in the castle and put me into a deep sleep. The last twenty-four hours had been nerve-wracking. Everything had stacked up against me—from lack of sleep mostly due to fear, thanks to an overactive imagination—to being deprived of food since last night. It all rounded out the conclusion that I was suffering from a severe case of homesickness. One of the side effects was my crappy mood. Forcing myself to snap out of it was making it worse.

Mom helped me out of the backseat of her midnight blue Lexus HR750. Both legs were sticking to the gray leather seats, leaving a burning sensation of peeled skin behind. Once I was in an upright position, she walked around the open door to the passenger's front door to pull out the crutches, my parting gift from the hospital. It was work to keep those damn things under my arms, especially while sporting the forearm cast. Irritation made me start to rub the sensitive skin, causing a frown to deepen as Rae-Lynn handed them to me.

"I don't see why you couldn't convince them a wheelchair would be more practical? And you didn't even press them for one. Geez, I can't feel my foot in this brace. I think you went past tighten, and straight to constrict on the straps. When we get inside, I'm taking it off, and then I want some food. My stomach is threatening to move to a different residence." I blew dirty bangs from my eyes.

Yes, I'll be the first to admit, my picture was right next to the word bitchy in the dictionary. I had eaten a breakfast consisting of half a can of warm soda and a leftover bag of lint-laced toffee peanuts because I was under the assumption I was going home by brunch. I had refrained from consuming the rubber open-faced turkey dinner last night. But thanks to an oversight, I didn't get one of those paper menus, so the cart passed by this morning for breakfast. The doctor was going to release me by seven o'clock. Yeah, right. He didn't wander in the room until ten this morning, and I saw him for a total of six minutes. The process to leave took forever, with the paperwork and getting the right prescriptions called in to our pharmacy. By then, lunch had come and gone. It was now 3:55 p.m., and I was running on fumes.

Through the opening between the trunk lid and the car, I saw Mom lift her head slowly and back away so she wouldn't hit the underside. She was gathering all my consolation prizes for not winning the *getting myself killed by a fuel truck* award, when she muttered, "Edgy much, daughter?"

Attempting to maneuver around the front of her car to get to the walkway, I made noises similar to a gasping sprinter. I bit the inside of my cheek to refrain the use of a colorful reply. Instead, the words deflated with a mumble as an alternative response. It was better than sparking a word war with her because, in the end, she would indubitably win by the rule of grounding. Max had already established my new stipulations in the hospital. If they added more rules to my grounded status, I would need a grave marker by my bedroom door.

The cobblestone path was going to make getting to the front door practically impossible. I readjusted myself on the crutches and continued toward my goal. The rubber feet on them only got caught once which gave me a ping of satisfaction. With perspiration dotting my forehead, the next challenge seemed to mock me. The stairs. I felt as if I were trying to win a race to the porch. After maybe moving a hundred feet or so, my left wrist began to throb.

I was rocking up the short steps to the door when I heard the backfire from Ghost's car. He must have turned down the street. The smell of smoke was already lingering in the air and it made me appreciate being out of the cell, even though it reeked of exhaust from his farting car. It wasn't cold, dry hospital air anymore. Trust me when I say, even smoke tainted air was better. For the past two weeks, I had wished for one smoke, and maybe a beer. I had to admit though, the cravings for the latter had curbed during my imprisonment, but I couldn't wait for Rae-Lynn to leave so I could light up.

Max wouldn't be home until after ten. So, Blake agreed to come over and hang out, unlike Jake, who was making an appearance before heading to his job. Maybe I could convince him to call in sick? I would have called Dee too, but she was working at the A & M: Accessories and More Jewelry, until eight. Since it was a school night, I knew she wouldn't be able to come over. Her mother was controlling like that.

Feeling a stab of jealousy from missing the Sip 'N Chug, I blew my bangs from my face again. I mean, who really likes working where people come in all uptight and bark out demands, instead of asking for what they want? Leaving my presence all relaxed and happy, I did like seeing them leave though. It was the best part.

My nose even missed going into work; I loved the smell of fresh ground coffee. I could even get away with being a little rude before seven thirty. Using some of the same excuses the customers did had granted me slip status. The best one was, *I hadn't had my morning fix yet.* Mr. Sipton, on certain days, would even let me get away with it until the mid-morning rush around eight. By then I'd normally had a few cups.

Reminiscing about the good old days, I sighed and made a quick mental note to call Mr. Sipton about putting me back on for a shift or two next week. Maybe there was some light duty work I could do with my cast? At least the leg brace comes on and off when I want.

Jake's car pulled up in front, and I heard his parking brake crunch. The Ghost had arrived. His dingy, yellow submarine, which was a Cadillac Eldorado 2000, made the top of the World's Ugliest Car list, but he called it a classic. What was it with guys and their vehicles naming them, washing them with shammies, and talking to them? It gave me the creeps when they spoke in goo-goo talk to the dashboard while patting it, like Tod… used to… do. Unexpected tears welled up in my lacrimal ducts. *I had paid attention in biology class.*

I tried to stand upright against the doorjamb to rid myself of the crutches. It was the only way I could stop the soon-to-be-falling drops from rolling down dry cheeks. Lightly pressing two fingers against the bridge of my nose, I forced myself to stop crying. This was retribution, and the guilt was leaving a huge emotional void. If I were lucky, the chest organ would soon implode under the pressure and turn me into a black hole. I had no right to live and face an unforeseeable future.

Ghost walked up the driveway next to Mom and helped carry some of the stuffed animals. "Don't worry, Mrs. S., I'll unload the rest so you can get Lex-Cee settled. Tell me where you want them, okay?" He always had a weird kind of smile when he was around Rae-Lynn. I think he had a small crush on her, but I wasn't going to say anything about it yet. If he ever started

talking to her chest or trying to sit by her when he'd been invited over to dinner, I'd have to inform Max.

I smirked thinking about how Max would handle that tidbit
of news. My father was very possessive where it concerned my
mom. As I watched Ghost follow her up the stairs like a well-
trained puppy, the grin he shot me was all it took. His smile per-
suaded against snitching because I didn't want him to become
an actual ghost. I liked him haunting among the living.

Rae-Lynn placed her keys and purse on the small table next
to the front door. "Jake, go ahead and take them up to her room."
She reached up and punched in the code to our locked key box.
It clicked, and she pulled open the small door. I watched her
hang up the ring of keys and silently wished that one day mine
would be hanging in there too just as she closed the box.

"Here, let me prop open the door, then I'll help you to the
couch." Mom held the door open with one leg and braced her
hand to keep me from falling forward. "I'm pretty tired too, Lex-
Cee. Is it okay if we order out for dinner?" Rae-Lynn turned to
face Ghost in the doorway. "Jake, would you like to stay for dinner?"

I saw the glint in Jake's eyes. "Only if it's dinner for two," I
said to myself using his voice mockingly in the back of my head.
Then I heard him right next to me. "No, thanks, I have to leave
in about forty minutes." He checked his watch to be sure.

After he had cashed his first paycheck, it had been the first
thing he purchased. The sharp looking wrist watch was a Fossil.
It was waterproof, and the numbers and hands lit up, complementing the metallic blue face and silver band. He loved it and
never took it off. I'm sure he would want to be buried with it,
and I laughed inwardly at the thought.

Ghost brushed past me, leaving a cool breeze in his wake,
taking the stairs two at a time as he whistled, carrying an arm full
of flowers to the bedroom. Rae-Lynn looped her arm around my

waist to help me across the mahogany floor to a large, navy blue couch. The crutches must have made a *come here* sound because I heard rapid clicking coming from down the hall.

"Oh geez, look out—" I braced myself against Mom. "Here comes Trigger," I yelled so Ghost could hear me from downstairs. This was his only free warning. My father's Rottweiler, Gigi, was making up for weeks of missed slobbery kisses. *Ugh*, her breath was so bad. It stunk as if she had been chewing on charcoal and burnt hair.

Mom issued a stern command for her to go lay on her bed by the door to Max's office. The dog may have her dumb moments, but it amazed me how much she understood, not just commands but full-on sentences. I could say, Gigi, go and get my slippers, the fuzzy green pair, and she would do it. They would be soaking wet, but she understood the request. Max claimed it was because the dog had been around for so long, she picked up on the language. I would give him a nonjudgmental wave and say, "Yeah, right." *I believe Gigi is about eleven or twelve. That is ancient in dog years.* I wasn't sure exactly when Max brought her home because I was really little then. And I think that memories locked away by time are funny creatures, misting over and becoming foggy. In short, you can't trust them.

When we finally made it to the couch, I plopped down onto the cushions as if someone had cut off my legs. Mom draped one of her favorite Afghans over them, handed me the TV remote, and picked up the house phone. She zipped through the stored numbers on speed dial, then stopped on each number to ask me if I felt like eating take-out from there. As Rae-Lynn recited a number and I repeated it with her, we knew we had a winner. She walked away already knowing what I wanted... the number six, Paper Wrapped Chicken and a Veggie Spring Roll. Reality weighed heavy as it pushed me back into the sofa. I was home. Mom was ordering Chinese food, and I was going to veg out in front of the television with Jake.

Catching Jake from the corner of my eye as he carried the last of my boxes, he seemed overly zealous performing the duties of a florist delivery guy. Blakely had helped me yesterday, picking up the cards and stuffed toys. At the time, she'd placed each of the vases into their own little coffin boxes so they wouldn't tip over during the car ride home. She really went above and beyond. I owed her big time.

Remembering Blakely, I tried to twist around to make sure Rae-Lynn heard me while she was on the phone. "Mom, don't hang up. Blake said she would stop by after we got home from the hospital. We should order her food too." Holding up four fingers and two thumbs, I mouthed the word six so she would order Blake the same entree as mine. Mom nodded, and I leaned back, probably thinking if Blakely couldn't make it, I would be set for tomorrow's lunch.

My pissy mood was fading fast with food on its way, TV Land playing an old episode of *Gillian's Island* and a haunting Ghost. I finished up the thought when Jake popped up next to me, sitting on the floor in front of the couch. Beholding his watch again and scratching the almost five o'clock stubble on his chin, he gazed back to me, smiled and leaned back.

"If I knew I had to work when I showed up today, I would have dropped by after work." His voice trailed off with a chuckle.

I punched his arm.

"Ouch. Hey, I should charge you for labor… but since you're a cripple, it's free this time." He rubbed the spot I'd tagged.

Rae-Lynn came into the family room carrying a bottle of water for Ghost and a Diet Coke for me. My lips curved as Ghost took the water from Rae-Lynn. I couldn't tell if he was blushing. The smirk graduated to a snicker when she handed me a soda.

Clearing her throat at my awkward reaction, she glanced

from side to side. "I'm going to pick up the food. Jake, can you stay for another ten or fifteen minutes? It's just up the street. I won't be long." He checked the time again. I rolled my eyes.

"Sure, I can stay for a bit longer, but I need to be on time this week. Management is writing up our reviews next week, and I don't want to give them any leverage for something negative to jot down. I think this one might be for a raise." The cracking sound of the water bottle lid indicated he was done explaining.

"Great, I will be back soon. If you want to grab a snack before you go, you're more than welcome to do so." Mom waved her hand toward the kitchen while walking over to the hallway entrance table. I heard the little beeps and the pop of the lockbox opening. With keys jingling, she called out one last time. "Okay, call my cell if there's an emergency." She used the shutting door to end her sentence.

I made a sound of exasperation. "You keep looking at your dumb watch. Do you really have to go so soon? I mean, we haven't had a lot of time to catch up on things. I've missed hanging out with you for the past two weeks. And you only came to visit me twice in the hospital." I proceeded to pout. My finger was making a ticking sound with the tab from the soda can. Pouting wasn't my forte, but I always tried. I could hold up on one hand the number of times it had succeeded, but, for the most part, I failed at it miserably.

Shocked, he looked at his wrist. "Dumb?" Jake's smile widened when I felt his hand drop on my head, tousling my hair. "Did little Lex-Cee miss me? I had to work. Plus, Mr. Grottal popped a grueling English exam on us in the middle of the week. You know I wanted to come by more often." He readjusted his long legs, Indian style so he could face me. "I promise to come by more often since you're laid up here. Besides, you'll be in school next week anyway, right? I'll pick you up for school on Monday, okay?" Wiggling his brows, I knew he was trying to lighten my sulking over the blow of his impending departure. "I'll get Dunkin'—"

Donuts were not going to cure how I was feeling. "Jake, I know you tried to come by, it's just that I was hoping we could catch up on things." I stopped *tinking* the Diet Coke tab and moved on to picking at one of the pulled strands in the lap throw. A slight prick of sadness tickled the back of my throat because I had missed being with him, sarcasm and all. Ghost had always been able to scare my problems away and I looked forward to his hauntings. I tossed the remote down in the middle of both knees. Feeling forlorn, I shrugged and pasted a plastic happy smile over the frown.

Jake appeared worried and bowed his head so I couldn't see his eyes anymore. "I do have some time, but I wanted to talk about something that I know you are not gonna want to talk about. To be honest, I don't know how to approach my concerns without you getting hostile." The way he was holding himself rigid made me uneasy. I couldn't stop staring at the top of his head. *It must really be bad if he wouldn't even look at me. Was I really that intimidating?*

"Alexcia, do you know how scared I was when I heard about what happened to you?" Jake's voice carried a small quiver as he continued, "For days, I felt as though the CMHS football team used me for a blocking shield..."

When he paused, I took the opportunity to interject, "Jake as you can see, I pulled out of it. I'm fine."

"No. You're not fine." Ghost scooted closer to me and immediately placed a hand softly on my arm. "Every time you would tell me you were going out or to one of your parties, I would brush the feelings of being an overprotective friend away. I would convince myself that you were pretty smart and knew when to stop. Back then, I thought you could take care of yourself. Alexcia, I was wrong. I was enabling you to become worse and not thinking of what you could end up doing to yourself. The smoking is one thing, there's time to deal with that. But the drinking. Your drinking. Needs to stop." His eyes glossed over, and I found his fingers intertwined with mine. Unmoving, I was dumbfounded and bewildered... unable to speak, breathe or even blink. He had turned up the fuel to my anger, feeling the intense heat rising to my eyes and I was about to boil over.

Everything became surreal, from Jake's condemning words to the fact he was holding back the shine in his gaze and the way my heart tripped over itself when he slipped his fingers away from mine. With an open mouth and flushed cheeks, I seized up.

While processing all of this, he whispered harshly, "I don't know what I would have done if you had died. You can't leave me too like *he* did. It took me years to get used to the hurt of his absence. Don't leave me, Lex-Cee, please stop being so reckless with your life. You don't have to be the life of the party to be someone. I'm... just... so..." Ghost couldn't hold it in. I watched a tear escape to commit suicide by slipping down the side of his cheek, falling to its death, landing on top of my hand. His eyes, normally a bright apple-green, were clouded over in a stormy emerald.

Caught off guard by the confession about his father, and his expressed feelings of losing me, had left me speechless. My tongue dried to the roof of my mouth, and I couldn't stop the pull his eyes had on me. The color of them was spell-binding, drawing me deeper into his emotional sea. I had never noticed how long his lashes were before, a light blond tint tipped each lash and then they faded to a deep brown. With heavy eyelids, I tried to refocus, finding Ghost hovering inches from me. He was so close, I could feel his breath caress lightly across my lips. What was going on? I wanted to be mad. I wanted to yell. I wanted to... I wanted...

WITHOUT REALIZING ANYTHING HAD CHANGED, I HEARD A MUFFLED JINGLING from far away as both eyes snapped open. Jake was gone. Sitting up as quickly as my broken body would allow, I scanned the room and heard the front door open. Unclear about what had transpired between us, I was left in a state of limbo. Was he leaving? Anger told me he couldn't finish what he had started and was now bailing.

"Hey, I'm back. Jake. Sorry if I made you late. There was a line." Through lashes, I saw Rae-Lynn use her foot to shut the door.

The sound of a rattle and clink of glass came from the direction of the kitchen. I brought a hand to my lips. What was I feeling? What had Jake been trying to say to me? I tried to swallow but found our discussion had made me parched. Frowning, I looked down at the can of diet soda. Surely, it was warm by now. I picked it up and reached over to set it on the end table behind me.

"Not a problem, Mrs. S. The patient is doing fine. She has been sleeping for the past ten minutes. I'll head out now before she wakes up." The refrigerator door shut. So, that was why I woke up alone, he was hiding out in the kitchen.

"Chicken," I whispered out loud. I leaned back and shut my eyes since I was supposed to be asleep. I scratched at my neck. That was the first sign I was starting to break out with red welts. Perfect.

"Tell Lex-Cee I will call her soon to find out what time she will be ready for school on Monday morning." His voice moved to the hallway.

"Oh, thanks, Jake. I will pass the message on to her. You're a great help. I have a morning meeting on Monday, so you're a lifesaver. Oh, and thanks for staying."

The front door quietly closed.

I found my friend, Mr. Anger, who introduced me to Mrs. Disheartened. Tears fell from closed eyes. Yes, I was alive, but Tod and the others were gone. It was my fault, and I would have to live with the pain every time I took a breath or felt the sunshine on my skin. I didn't need to be reminded, especially by Jake, of my irresponsible actions. Drinking had nothing to do with what had happened to the others. It was my unnecessary alarm that had distracted Tod, causing the deadly, delayed reaction. We would have been fine if I weren't so selfish.

By the time I listened to Rae-Lynn pulling out the plates and condiments, I wasn't very hungry anymore. The servings Jake had forced fed me, about my lack of self-preservation, was filling enough. I kept my eyes closed when I heard the house phone ring. After she had answered, I knew it was Blakely on the other end.

More tears worked their way through lashes as Mom wrapped up her conversation with Blakely. From Rae-Lynn's comments, it sounded as if she were on her way over. That gave me about twenty minutes to pretend I was still sleeping. We would have three hours to visit before Blake had to go home. Then my father would walk through the door a couple of hours later.

Ghost had left me holding my side of our conversation. I wanted to tell Blakely everything but didn't even know what really happened. Was Jake making the situation into more than what it really was? His explanations versus his actions didn't match, leaving me with a severe case of pitfall. I felt empty and alone.

Diverting my plan to tell Blakely and Dee, I decided that our future discussion would be just between him and me. He was going to get an earful come Monday morning. Leaving me seven more days to think about what I was going to say to him made me mad, and I spoke in a hiss as the lack of sleep finally caught up with me. "You wait, my Ghost, until I see you again, I'll be counting the minutes until then."

13

Showers wash all the unsightly dirt and grime away. The warm spray relaxes the nerves brought on by the stresses of the day. But no matter how hard I scrub, the darkness that clings to me will not go down the drain.
~Alexcia

IT WAS SATURDAY NIGHT AND JAKE STILL HADN'T CALLED. I had called him twice only to be instantly connected to his voicemail. This situation was so unfair. Why was I, the one feeling guilty about what had happened? I didn't even have a chance to explain, not that I really needed or wanted to. My reasons were valid, and they were buried deep in my closet, right next to all the skeletons. No one was going to label me crazy, insane or Looney Tunes, then sentence me to do couch time discussing the cloaked demons I see in the ink blots. I didn't want to think about any of this crap anymore.

Instead, I focused on the next problem... taking a nice, long shower. I was starting to offend myself every time I shifted position, plus I wanted to move back into my bedroom. The couch was killing my spine, and privacy was nonexistent in the middle of the room. Especially when I woke up crying and Mom assumed I was reliving the crash. *Not really looking forward to another discussion about how I was handling things.*

Mom helped me by getting everything ready for the shower. She was coming down the hall followed by her black shadow.

When Dad was gone, Gigi moved from the title of speed bump to the honored position of bodyguard. She fit the part too, all eighty-two pounds of her.

Rae-Lynn was lifting me off the couch to head for the stairs when Gigi started huffing with a quick growl. Mom nodded and Gigi took off down the hall. I had no clue about their silent communication and stared at Rae-Lynn for an explanation. She shrugged. "Gigi wanted to know if you were all right." I wanted to say *what*, but my mouth was stuck at the Wh... part. Exhaustion must be jamming my senses.

Together we headed for the stairs because I wanted to shower in my own bathroom. Since I was going to sleep in the bedroom tonight, we figured it was better than dragging everything downstairs. Halfway across the floor, my phone slipped causing me to step on Rae-Lynn's foot. She cursed under her breath, and I recovered the phone with a sigh. This was going to take a while. The climb made me feel like a mountain goat. When we made it to the top, the urge to yodel from our achievement was caught in my throat. *I knew I was delirious.*

Placing the crutches in the corner and setting the cell on the counter, Rae-Lynn helped me out of the leg brace. I worked at chiseling the nasty clothes from crusted skin. At first the right leg refused to bend, and I seemed to have left my oil can downstairs, so she helped me hobble into the shower.

At that moment, I loved hot water. Not so hot to scald your skin but hot enough to coat the bathroom mirrors with a thin layer of condensation. Never again would I ever take a shower for granted. Almost three weeks without hot water spraying on my skin was two and a half weeks too long. *If I ever use a sponge again, it will be too soon.* Whoever thought using a damp sponge could replace a hot, steamy shower was sadly mistaken. Feeling greedy, and looking at my plastic-wrapped wrist, I started counting down the weeks before I could take a delightful bath. The image of me soaking until I was waterlogged was inviting, but for now, I relished the simple spray of H2O.

Rae-Lynn stood close by as a shower spotter. My right knee tried to give out from time to time, but I was holding my own for the moment. She had decided to use a garbage bag to cover the cast. Who knew that some duct tape and a plastic bag could lead me to the path of cleanliness. Chalk one up for ingenuity.

Adding some shampoo, I heard Rae-Lynn trying to talk over the water, "Lex-Cee, I need to speak with you about a few things. Can you hear me?"

"Mmm hmm," I answered, focusing on the one-handed scalp massage.

"Alexcia, I need you to pay attention."

I blew the soapy foam from my good hand. "Yeah, I'm listening."

Mom kept talking as she opened and closed the cabinet doors looking for my after shower necessities. "You said Blakely is picking you up for work. Don't you think tomorrow's too soon?" She slammed a drawer, making me jump, and I grabbed the showerhead to brace myself from slipping.

"Mom, what are you trying to do, send me back to the hospital? Can't you see I'm going stir-crazy here? Mr. Sipton is going to put me on light duty. I'm restocking and cleaning the inter-chat room. It will be fine."

Using a loofah, I scrubbed two weeks of leftover grime off… amazed to find clean, pink skin. I considered how hairy both legs were but decided to dry shave later. My head was beginning to throb. This was the most physical activity I had done since I'd been released from the hospital.

After turning off the water, I held out a hand so Rae-Lynn could give me my robe and towel. When I was wrapped up to face the breeze of air coming in from under the door, I stepped out of the shower and fought the panic when my knee wanted to give out again.

Rae-Lynn helped me hobble to the toilet and closed the lid so I could sit. When Mom started to unwrap the plastic and duct tape, the damp air made me clammy. I stretched out each finger to allow airflow. That's when I noticed, she looked troubled. Not wanting to hear what she was mulling over, I concentrated on the throbbing arm. Rae-Lynn was examining each nail, but taking extra care with the broken pinky one. She let go of my hand and bent down to rest on her knees so we were eye to eye.

"I am sorry, Alexcia. I have been trying to do what's right for you for so many years. It's hard for me and your father to go back to the way things were before, especially after what has happened. It's a rude awakening for your father and me. We could have lost you. This world would be in chaos if something happened to you." She picked up both hands to caress them in hers. At that moment, what she was sharing with me made the back of my throat close.

I croaked, "But, as you can see, I'm fine. Why do I have to keep repeating myself? I'm here. I'm breathing. I'm living. Tod, Brad, and Melanie are the ones who are not here. I have to live with that every day and don't need everyone pointing out the obvious." I sniffed. "I know you and Dad care, but I also know you both are busy with your jobs. Nothing has to change. We will get through this. I will get through this."

The towel wrapped around my head was slipping off, and instead of fighting it, I pulled it over my eyes to wipe each one. *First, Ghost and then my mom… everyone must be taking a number to bash on me. What do they want me to say? I can't change anything.* Unlike Jake, at least my parents were not aware of my after-school pastimes, but I knew the direction her talk was heading. This was so unfair. I wasn't ready for any of it.

Her eyes filled with tears, triggering a tight sensation inside. My heart was trying to wring out what was left of the pent-up emotions. I knew it would take a while, but I needed to rebuild the wall, stronger than the one I'd left crumbled on the highway. It needed reinforcement, first by hardening the heart, followed by sealing off those weepy emotions because I longed for dry eyes.

"Alexcia, Mrs. Peston called two days ago. Tod's funeral has been scheduled for this Wednesday, at six in the evening. It's going to be open for the students too, since ... well... " Her voice trailed.

She didn't need to explain. I gathered there were going to be a lot of people in attendance... his family and the students from Cheyton Memorial. Tod had been very popular and the faculty bent over backward for him to play lacrosse for CMHS. Mom was worried I wouldn't be able to handle the funeral, let alone facing all those people with their silent accusations and insincere sympathies. Mocking voices stirred in thought. *Are you all right? How are you coping? Is there anything I can do for you?*

The warm shower had turned against me. All the exposed skin was raised with little bumps. I was so glad I hadn't shaved in the shower. Legs and underarms would have ended up with stubble from the chill. Inside this empty shell, the temperature was trying to readjust from the heat escaping my skin.

Teeth chattering, a sense of overwhelming tiredness rolled in like a fog. I felt dizzy from being both cold and sleepy, and a weak smile was all I could command. "Mom, can we talk later? Maybe tomorrow after work could be a good time. I need to get dressed and dry my hair. My brain has me frozen in first gear, and it's starting to grind. Blakely is also waiting to hear from me before I tumble into bed. I need to find out how early she's planning on showing up." I tried to use a reasoning voice with her. "We made plans to meet up with Dee for breakfast in the morning." Leaning over the sink to grab the cotton ball bag and bottle of astringent, I was even too tired to scrub those dirty pores. "Oh, and don't worry about helping me, Blakely is coming over early for that. She plans on dropping me off at the Sip 'N Chug before she heads to her job." Frustrated from rambling and the lame explanation, I pulled apart the little cotton puff. Then I used what was left to apply the stinging liquid.

Rae-Lynn walked over to the neatly stacked pile of night clothes and started unfolding in silence. Slipping my cell into the fluffy red robe pocket, she set it aside to hand me everything. Four dirty cotton balls went into the trash as Mom handed me the purple underwear with hot pink and light purple polka dots, a solid purple sleep tank top, and a pair of fuzzy white and hot pink striped socks. Evidently, I'd struck a nerve with her when I said I didn't want to talk about it. *I will face my demons when I have to, not when everyone thinks it's time.*

She helped me dress then reattached the leg brace. Turning to the corner of the room, Mom grabbed one of the crutches to hand me. For the past four or five days, I'd been getting around on one crutch. The fact I was getting better at it made me think I could handle a few shifts at the Chug. At the very least, it would give me something to do other than staring at the TV for hours. I was getting desperate trying to find ways to get out of the house. Even the thought of going back to prison, I mean school, was tempting. The thought of my butt getting flat from pressing into the couch, twenty-four seven was enough to spur me forward. I needed to move it and add to my stagnant back account. I couldn't save any money this way and the situation wasn't getting me any closer to attaining a Jeep. I had done the math... *job plus Jeep equals freedom.*

Starting the nightly rituals, I used the crutch to prop myself over the sink so I could brush my teeth. Mom stood guard while I did little circles over each tooth. I palmed water, to slurp it in, swished and spit. Glancing at the bathroom clock, I couldn't believe it had taken over two hours to take a stupid shower. I sighed but was finally done and ready to call Blake, take pain and sleeping pills and then slip into slumber.

Well, I hoped for sleep. I was back in my own room for the first time since I had been home. The couch had been a necessary first stop, and I'd stayed there out of convenience for Rae-Lynn. Her bedroom was on the first floor, so it was easier for her to get to me when I needed to go to the bathroom. But since I was getting better with the crutch, we figured I could move back upstairs. I was a tad bit nervous because I hadn't had one of my nightmares for almost three weeks and wanted this sleep streak to keep going. The plan was to take the pills and talk to Blakely until I couldn't move my mouth with a coherent sentence anymore.

Mom was still trailing behind in silence. She was as troubled over this as I was, although we were on the opposite side of the phrase *it could have been*. I was living with it, dealing with it and didn't want anyone handing me their two cents on how to manage it. The air between us was laced with unspoken words because I knew she had more to say about the funeral, but I was done processing for the night.

It was funny how things changed on a dime, or, in this case, a door. Jake had made a path with all the boxes, bags, and vases to my dresser and table. Piles of clothes were still scattered from that night by tornado Lex-Cee. A flood of feelings hit me, and I singled out the only one that mattered, making it to my bed.

"Alexcia, I've meant to ask you something. What the hell happened to your room?" Her tone had returned to the familiar, biting parental voice.

With a shrug, I answered, "Couldn't find a thing to wear. Anyway, my intention was to clean it the next day. I had no idea it was going to be three weeks later." I hobbled over a shirt and a clump of skirts to make it to the bed. "I will clean it after work tomorrow." Using the crutch as a broom, I swept the clothes pile onto the floor where they landed by the foot of the bed.

"Nice," Rae-Lynn's remark dripped with sarcasm.

"I don't wanna fight," I answered with a yawn while slowly scooting to the middle of my bed so we could work together swinging my legs up and under the covers.

"Okay," she said, blowing air out with her words in defeat. "But, ignoring what we were talking about in the bathroom will not make facing your feelings any easier." She pulled the comforter up and over the leg brace. Turning to pick up the glass of water and medication, she handed everything to me. I downed the pills and gulped the water. "Great, that was supposed to last you all night. I hope for your sake the bathroom doesn't call your name at two in the morning." She took the glass, kissed my forehead and with her eyes at half mast, said, "Clear your heart. Clear your mind. Clear a path that sleep will find." I smiled because the little girl in me had always loved Mom's bedtime quips. Then Rae-Lynn draped my robe at the foot of the bed and removed my cell phone from the robe pocket and handed it to me. "Don't be on it all night, okay?"

"No way, I'm ready for some *zzzs*. Just a quick call. Besides, I took a sleeping pill. How long do you think I will be able to stay awake?"

Her face had skepticism written all over it. "You have perfected the phrase *if there's a will, there is a way*, daughter."

"I wasn't aware that phrase ended with the word, daughter," I said, mimicking her facial expression.

We laughed and finished saying our good nights. As soon as she shut the door, I pressed the number three on the speed dial. It rang only twice when I heard a yawn come over the line. *Was it that late?* Through another yawn, she scolded me, "Do you know what time it is? I thought you were taking a shower not going to the spa." I heard her blankets and sheets crinkle and scrape across the receiver.

"Sorry, but I wasn't exactly having the time of my evening either."

"Isn't that, 'time of your life'?"

"I don't think that far in advance anymore, not that I ever did."

Mindless chitchat out of the way, she plunged into our plans for tomorrow. "So, we are meeting Dee around nine o'clock for breakfast. Is eight early enough to help you get ready? Her shift starts at eleven, but she wants to leave around ten thirty. What time do you have to be at work tomorrow? I forgot." Her voice caught when she tried to suck in air at the same time.

"Sure, eight o'clock is fine. I already have my work smock and a change of shoes by the bed. My shift doesn't start until three, but Mr. Sipton said I can hang out in the break room until then. Uh, Blake...?" I still didn't want to talk about this subject, but with the day looming, I needed a friend. "My mom told me about the funeral."

"I was wondering if you were going or not. You know me. I didn't want to press." I blew out the air I had held waiting for her answer. *She gets me.*

"Yeah, I need to go. There's something I have to do." I looked at my closet. In a hospital bag sitting on the floor were the clothes I was wearing that night. An item of Tod's needed to be returned to him. I didn't have the right to keep it after what I'd done to him.

"Well, what time is it? I need to make sure I'm free. Isn't your mom going with you anyway?"

"I don't know if she can come or not, and I really haven't given her the opportunity to talk about it." Several emotions from earlier that night seemed to make their way into our conversation as I explained how Rae-Lynn was treating me. I was fed up with the routine, and it was past time to reconstruct my emotional barrier. *Clunk.* First brick down.

"Blakely, if you can't make it, I understand. And don't try to shuffle your shift around. You have done so much for me. It's really wrong for me to ask more of you. Forget it, I'll be okay. Besides, I'm sure my mom is trying to clear her schedule for that day." A sigh turned into a yawn. The meds were kicking in. *Wooboo*. Sleep might find me soon. I sank into the pillows. "It's this Wednesday at six o'clock."

"I'll talk it over with Stanley and see if he can spare me. They are cutting back. Even though I need the money for gas, he'll probably agree to give me the night off. He's cool like that, you know." Her words drifted off in a yawn, adding to my own struggle to stay focused.

So, even though I wasn't talking backward yet, we needed to end our call or tomorrow she'll be a Gigi. I snickered at my own joke. "You need sleep, and your waves of slumber are pulling me under with you. So, I'll talk tomorrow with you, and night. Okay?" Too late, the tongue muscle was working in reverse, and I thought she might be snoring into the receiver.

I raised my voice. "Night, Blakely—"

Right after I said it, I thought a shadow zipped from one corner of the room through the open closet door. I blinked to refocus on it. I suddenly felt heavy, and every digit melted to the cell. No, I wasn't going to allow this crap to start up again. "Blakely, are you awake? Are you still there?" I made a small prayer of hope she was still on the other end.

A hard huff came through the phone. "Yeah, I'm still here. But, Lex-Cee, I really need to go. Oh, gross. The speaker and pillow are wet. What did I spill?"

I didn't have the heart right then to tell her the obvious. While I listened to her moving things around for the imaginary glass of liquid, I focused on the closest ceiling star and counted backward. A breeze skittered over my arm setting off the little alarm hairs. Something was different and I was aware of the change.

Scanning slowly around the room, I came to the conclusion it had to be the medicine. It made sense, the heaviness, seeing things that weren't there. After I had taken about a minute to convince myself it was nothing, I said goodbye again to Blakely. "I'll see you in the morning. Just use your key. Rae-Lynn will be gone by six, I think."

"Huh, oh, yeah, okays. See you."

My cell went silent.

I slid the cover over and placed it back on the nightstand. The plan was to count the glow-in-the-dark stars to fall asleep, but I needed to find a new method of relaxation. Maybe if I envisioned a fairy tale meadow, where I could lie down to count the sheep jumping over a wooden fence, and then watch them land in a mud puddle. The grin sliding in place was playfully evil as I pulled the sheet up to my chin, holding a breath and glancing around the room, carefully avoiding the open closet. The air around the bed felt colder than normal. Warm breath lightly feathered between my lips. Heart racing, my blood felt thick and heavy in my chest. Stealing myself, I stared into the black void and felt someone or something staring right back.

With a quivering breath, I spoke to the emptiness. "What do you want from me? What is our connection? Why are you here?" I narrowed my vision and in the darkness I saw two pinpoints of glowing indigo at the back of the closet. An inky mist slithered up the sides of the doorway and over the floor in front. A faint growl made me seize. I wasn't asleep, but logic was screaming nightmare. Within a few moments, I mustered enough courage to speak. That was when the shadow moved past the door and toward the window. Its movement was so fast, I didn't even get the chance to fully blink. Simply gone. The inward laugh resembled a movie trailer where the main character is headed for a crazy house.

The room became warmer and the heavy feeling lifted. A tiny sob slipped out while I pulled the covers tightly over my head. *Please. I chanted silently… do not dream… do not dream.* Willing myself to relax, I became the shepherd searching for sheep to count before the shadows came back to eat them.

14

Mr. Depression was no longer an acquaintance of mine. Positioning its presence on the edge of my bed, it filled my inner ear with emotional, crushing justification to support my grief-infested heart. Singing lullabies in the darkness, sobering hits titled: "You Shouldn't Be Here, It's Your Fault," and my favorite, "Death Should Have Taken You." When Mr. Depression was no longer able to console me, it would linger around the corners of my room, waiting for my sobs to cease. As my tears turned to ice, Miss. Numbness moved in and pushed my new friend away. I wanted our visit to last a little longer, but sadly it had business elsewhere.

~Alexcia

Sunday:

WORK WASN'T THE SWEET RETURN I HAD HOPED FOR. I WAS looking forward to getting out of the house, to see new and old faces in the café, but I wasn't thinking about how they would interact with me. Different voices penetrated through guarded thoughts during my entire shift, bombarded by so many variations of the same questions. The situation was driving me insane.

It started when some of the students from CMHS made

eye contact with me. The group came over and started pressing for more information. *What had I seen? What it was like? How I was dealing with it now?* Even the regulars cornered me while I picked up empty coffee cups and wiped down tables. The weight of my answers tired me out, so I asked Mr. Sipton if I could rest in the back room.

I carried my cup of Choca-Dunk to the back and realized there was no escape because my co-workers were also reciting from the same playbook, *Interrogations for Dummies*. And it didn't stop there; the questions followed me after I clocked out. As I stood outside, some of the late night bean fiends approached me while I waited for Blakely. One by one, they came over to give me a hug or express their fill-in-the-blank condolences, instead of goodbyes.

All the explaining wore me out, and I didn't say a word to Blakely after she helped me into the car. She seemed tired too and accompanied me on our road to solitude. After she had parked the Lady, Blake turned to me and muttered something about helping me to the front door before heading home.

Without a word, we both hobbled toward the brick steps as I attempted to multitask by digging out the front door key and trying not to trip over her plaid, Sanuk shoes. Blakely swung open the door and yelled, "Jello," instead of hello, declaring her chauffeuring shift was over.

She turned to leave and I mumbled, "Thanks for the help and the ride." After the hand-off, Rae-Lynn helped me up to my tomb.

Different stabs of pain hit me all at the same time. My right knee was burning… I assumed from being on it for too long. On the same side, my wrist throbbed from table duties and even my mouth had joined in the fun, giving me a headache. This was the one and only time I would admit I had used it too much.

Struggling up the stairs was exhausting even with Mom

handling most of our weight. She must have also felt my vibe because we moved together in an awkward step-clomp silence. At the top of the stairs, I carefully twisted away from her and hopped over the threshold. Using the doorknob to steady myself, I waved, in a nonchalant manner and mumbled, "Goodnight." Then I closed and locked the door. Not long after I settled into bed and relaxed, the nightmares welcomed me home with their choking embrace.

Monday:

GHOST WAS SUPPOSED TO PICK ME UP THIS MORNING, BUT HE WAS STILL MIA, which helped me make a very important decision. I was staying home. It was my only choice anyway because Mom had a morning meeting she couldn't rearrange or cancel. I really wasn't in the mood to be around the herds of sheep at school. All walks of life had tortured me enough for one day.

For the last few days he wouldn't return my calls to at least confirm, so I assumed he had dissed me. I had left about five messages yesterday, each one ending with a: (>.<), :P, :$, @,@, oh and lastly, (SCRW U). With no plans to beg for his attention, I knew he couldn't avoid me forever. The inevitable fight was coming soon. Thinking about it made me salivate for a taste of the first word I would use. Regrettably, my heart remained silent, causing me to reevaluate his peculiar actions from our last meeting. I couldn't get over how well he mixed his words of unsettling remorse with sprinkles of biting anger, although the emotional replay between us was a bit perplexing.

Every time I replayed the conversation, the more my mood slipped gears. First was my grinding anger. Second, would ease into blame. Third, was holding up confusion steadily. Fourth, found me cruising along with sadness. Fifth, would stick, and then I would find myself popped back into first gear again. Reverse was broken because I refused to be the one to apologize for who I was before the accident or for the person I had become. Besides being a little bruised and broken, I thought I was pretty much the same... sane by day... crazy by night.

Watching the thin sunlight stream in, inch by inch across the carpet, was the only highlight to most of the morning. And since I'd stayed in bed all day clinging to my cell phone, I didn't feel like doing much of anything else. Every now and then, I scribbled nonsense in one of my journals, texted Blakely or Dee to pass the time. They knew not to bring up any paranormal sightings with me.

Before I realized it, 11:57 p.m. glowed in purple next to me. A dark laughter bubbled up aimlessly as I remembered my last thoughts before we crashed. With a hefty exhale, I slipped the cell under the pillow while eyelids closed. Once I hit the wall of REM, I slipped into a pattern of, dream, scream, awake, rinse, repeat. *Lucky me.*

Tuesday:

EVER SINCE MY SHIFT AT THE SIP 'N CHUG, THE REALITY OF TOD'S FUNERAL loomed closer with every passing hour. I poured myself a cold cup of pessimism and topped it off with a layer of foamy penitence while spending most of my time practicing methodically what I would say to Tod's mother... if I built up enough nerve to approach her.

I dug out his letterman's jacket from the hospital bag and placed it on the back of my chair. It smelled burnt, but when I held it close, I could still detect the lingering scent of AXE. Occasionally, I would talk to it as if Tod were sitting there wearing it. Was it appropriate asking him which method of greeting was proper for his grieving parents?

Listening to my voice rehearse, it lacked the sorrow I was

trying to share with them. The distress in each word was mostly from guilt, considering I had a hand in his death. How could heartache compare? I had lost a fling, whereas they lost a son. I shuddered, wanting to cry, but reminded myself I was still undergoing emotional dam construction. Jake helped with rebuilding the wall by placing the first stone of silence down. It made the job easier so I could prevent those unwanted emotions from penetrating and containing the water where it belonged, inside.

Later in the day, Mom came in to check on me, making sure I had everything ready for tomorrow. She had given me a glass of water and some pills before she left.

Rae-Lynn helped me pick out an old dress from the back of her closet. It was clean cut, and definitely not for partying, instead, it whispered, *I'm a conservative church dress.* The scoop neckline was perfect for me to wear the choker I bought last month, but the memory of the purchase made me smirk, as I recalled window shopping at the Meadows Mall with Tod in tow. He didn't like shopping, yet he had more shoes than me and Rae-Lynn combined.

The polyester, rayon, and spandex blend filled all of my needs: warmth, look, and comfort. I wouldn't need a wrap because of the three-quarter length sleeves, and to provide even more coverage, the skirt hit above my knees. The slit in the back of the dress was high enough to make a quick escape. The flat black color would help me blend in with the background so I wouldn't have to talk to anyone unless I wanted to.

A trickle of water tickled down my nose, triggering a sniffle. The hiccup that followed made me grasp why I had picked it out to wear. Staring at the dress draped across the seat next to his jacket, the scene seemed ironic. The sleeves touched as if we were holding hands. Tod and I were going on our last date together, and I had decided at the end of it, I was going to break up by saying *goodbye.* I knew what I needed to do so we could both have a clean slate to move on with no strings attached from either side. I needed him to forgive me, no matter where he was.

I was being squeezed by an emotional boa constrictor, causing my breath to hitch and the trail of tears to become sticky and heavy. I didn't want to fall asleep because I knew what was awaiting me on the other side of those weighted down lids. However, this blanket of sadness I had wrapped myself up in was comfortable, and I was so exhausted. My body shut down against its own will.

Against the house, I heard soft moans singing in the breeze. It lulled me into a false sense of security. Just before my lashes locked together, I thought I felt a light trace of cold brush each cheek... wiping my tears. I sank suddenly into sleep.

The past few nights I had noticed the dreams becoming much worse. This one was by far the most obscure. Whatever had happened in my demented mind was now physically following me out, twisting reality.

I FELL INTO A DREAM, LANDING IN THE MIDDLE OF MY LAWN LIKE A CAT. FEAR grabbed my mind and panic slammed into my chest making it hard for me to breathe. From a crouch, I sprang toward the darkness encircling the house. The smoky mist felt threatening, and I was being drawn to someplace higher.

Rounding the left corner of the house, I was in a full sprint. The grass was slick from the mist causing me to lose traction. My inner brakes locked up. I fell forward, smacking into the base of a tree, my head tilted back at the welcoming refuge. The wind lightly swayed its leafy tentacles, urging me to get off the ground. Each branch seemed to be stretching down, extending to me a sense of trust. Arms and legs moved on their own pushing me up to the crown of the tree. I tried to suck in the moist air as I looked down. Recognition tapped into memory. I was climbing up the weeping willow at the side of our house.

Making it to one of the main branches, I wondered if the thickness could still hold me. I took a chance and kicked one leg over while silently cursing against time. Straddling it, I began to scoot across the branch. This one I knew all too well since I had used it as an alternative escape from my window several times before. The air sharing my space was spiked with a taste of chill. On this night, the dampness swept up the roots, covering the leaves with moist droplets. Rustling on the vined limbs gave me a sense of being unwanted, causing my heart to weep.

Something was about to strike. Realization hit me. I had nowhere to run. Trapped, I watched in horror as the frost began to form over the unearthed roots. Instantaneous cracking and popping, from the night's moisture, hardened, moving with increasing speed. I gazed through blurred eyes at the ice working its way up the bark of the tree. With doubt's shadow of damnation revealed, I knew it wanted to kill me.

The sound from the instant freeze seemed to blend in with someone who shared the same icy laughter. I craned my neck to locate the reverberations, and that's when I saw seven cloaked figures standing on my roof. I couldn't move. Each had different colored eyes, staring directly at me. One, in particular, caught my attention with dark, indigo eyes that seemed to covet me. A convulsion of quakes rocked from head to toe, but it wasn't from the instant drop in temperature. I dug my nails into the tree limb, fearing his unhinging stare might break my hold.

He separated from the cluster, floating down from the roof toward the branch with his hand held out. I had the urge to call him a friend but was too afraid to address the cloaked figure that way. The hood covering his head also concealed most of his face and the only features I could make out was from the moon's light whispering some of his secrets to me.

A mixture of light and shadow played across his face, revealing his skin color as a light gray, almost ashen in color. The smile that coiled up on the edges of his mouth displayed pure bright, white teeth. While I pondered his appearance, he cocked his head, enough for the moonlight to cast an ultraviolet black light glow on his face. I figured the discoloration was from the moon reflecting off his cloak. Shivers caused goosebumps over every inch of skin as I noticed the blackness wrapped around my house. It appeared as an extension of his cloak, approaching the tree. My sight swam in tears that would never be born because the crisp, night air dried them faster than I could shed. Even though he remained concealed under his cloak, I noticed he raised his head, maybe trying to understand why I wasn't accepting his help.

Maybe?

I had only two options because the tree was turning brittle from the ice, and would soon give way under the weight. If that happened, I would fall to my death or accept my fate into his unknown hands. I begged, with pleading eyes, for him to give me a small sign that I could trust him.

Even though we shared the same distance, his aura oozed of incontestable power. His cloak lost the indigo tints of mist, making his appearance seem more menacing. In direct conflict, the two orbs of the same color blazed with reassurance. His eyes said he was not a creature of myth or fairy tales, but of memory.

The branch beneath me made a sound of protest, which broke our spiritual connection. Coming up hard and fast, another wind gust tried to knock me off my perch. Long strands of hair blew around, whipping and stinging the sides of my face. The cracking and splitting sound echoed louder, and I glanced back at the cloaked creature.

A blanched hand remained extended. Deep down, I knew I should be afraid of him but had to make a choice. Should I grab onto the unknown or face demise? With my heart seemingly pushing out of its cage, confusion and anxiety made me start to cry again.

The soft voice didn't match his appearance. "I have given this much thought, watching you for the past three flips of the Nightglass, Child-of-Balance. Against my clan's wishes, I will grant you the answers you seek." His beautiful eyes narrowed.

I was drawn to them as he spoke, like a moth to the flame of death. *Why did it sound so comforting?* My subconscious socked me upside my cranium as I pondered his words. *Answers to what questions?* The main chest muscle momentarily stopped beating as bewilderment pulled back the shroud from my eyes.

"You once asked, 'What do you want from me? What is our connection? Why are you here'?" He shook his head in dismay, placing fingers from his free hand over the bridge of his nose, pinching. When he released it, his eyes seemed to fish around my soggy brain for one of my used memories. His frozen stare warmed my heart into beating again. Then...

Snap, crack.

The trance we shared broke a second time when the limb gave out from under me, and the sound of splintered wood echoed. I was hanging in midair, suspended on wires of apprehension, while he still held out his hand. Shock and trepidation overcame me. I hadn't fallen to the ground yet but panicked when I saw his fingers begin to curl into his palm. Eventually, he sighed and his patience embraced me as he spoke. "You need to choose, Vessel. But I warn you, either path you take will eventually end in death."

Fingers opening, he stretched out farther for my hand. In a nod of agreement, we clasped hands and with one swift motion, I was on the roof. A jolt of ice ran up that arm. My breath stopped. Wild-eyed, he embraced me and leaned his face close to my neck so I couldn't see his features. His breath sizzled and skipped over the hollow curve behind the right ear to my chin. Frozen, I could only watch as his cloak violently spun around us, weaving a foggy cocoon. Parts of it probed through locks of hair, around my stomach and traced swirls over exposed skin. Both eyes fluttered, trying to focus, as his presence settled in view. Then he fused his body to mine. Startled, I inhaled some of the cloak's mist which caused my temperature to plummet.

Floating beyond the realms of inner subconscious, my next thought was of a winter's wind, biting at bare skin. I pictured myself small, about five maybe six years old, skating on ice with someone very tall. We were bundled in winter attire all the way down to my light blue mittens and his hunter green gloves. This boy's smile made my heart skip in childlike excitement. When we were close, I didn't feel the cold surface beneath the skates. We held hands, moving in time as if this routine had been programmed into memory.

I was having a difficult time looking straight into his eyes. Once in a while, I would get a chance to steal a glance, but the dual suns in the afternoon sky blinded me. Sneezes gave away my intentions, causing him to laugh, knowing full well what I was trying to do.

We spun and glided, jumped and landed. My giddy laughter grew louder when he lifted me into the air. And then, he chuckled even harder when I clung to him, to keep from falling. His hair was thick and softly feathered in a messy wind-blown look. When he carried me, I would cling to his neck, and then playfully pat his short locks of silk.

Every time I got the chance to wrap my arms around him, I would breathe in a mixture of smells. The boy's raven black, rust-tipped hair was an intoxicating aroma of frost, kissed by the sun. Combined with his skin's rich, airy smell of rain before a storm, I'd never felt so connected to anyone like this before. Sheer joy filled me while fear controlled me. Something in the trees around us bobbed.

Time ceased.

I consciously forced my head to turn and take a good look around. Horror shook me as I came to the conclusion that I was very far away, somewhere with him in a world made solely from a nightmare. Trying to rip myself away, to get as much distance between us as possible, my small legs were no match for his. Sobs faded, and I found myself yelling at him about curses and magical powers I didn't understand. The tall boy turned into a dark, shadowy figure. He frowned. Skating away from the darkness, I stopped in the middle of the pond, eyes burning with red, thick tears. Protection from him was all I wanted now. Without thinking, I spun around and screamed at the sky, *"Eh-tu-nook, Callcrys."*

Gigantic blackbirds took to the sky, blocking both of the suns' bright light, casting everything in an eerie, red eclipse. The screaming I heard came from me more than the winged monsters from my teenage night terrors. I didn't want this. Really, I didn't. He reached out and grabbed me by both shoulders, but I tried to break free. I wanted to make a different choice. Although terrified beyond my own comprehension, the screams bounced along each rib unable to find their way out. My body collapsed in his arms.

The moisture in the air brought me back. We were so close his breath filled my mouth with hoarfrost.

Hard breathing was all I heard from either of us. Blinking at the stars, I was instantly back on my roof, still in his arms. He held me tight, in more of a protective way than a romantic intertwine. His slow laughter sent a rush of elation through me from the familiar tone. I dug my nails into his back, and he laughed harder from the pain. *If I was dreaming, why did he feel so real?* I wanted to speak, but my tongue burned from the taste of snow. It seeped into my parted lips, but soon my entire body went numb as we remained connected.

A chortle as quiet as a whisper escaped his lips, curving them slightly. "I forgot all about that day. Damn it, Alexcia. Ten years and you still amaze me. How did you manage to do that?" He'd taken on a unique demeanor when his eyes held a need of hunger, but I didn't know how I could fulfill his new yearning. Arms and legs began thawing, and I brought cold fingers to my lips. They were tingling from the rush of blood trying to warm them. We both shook with excitement and anticipation as we parted. He panted, trying to regain control over his normal composure while speaking to the other cloaked creatures encircling us. His eyes never lost focus on me.

"Ashens, we will accompany Miss Stasis tomorrow night from a safe distance. Quint, get in touch with one of the other clans to cover for us. K, Archer, and Imp, you will take scouting duties and report back every five shadows of the sundial. Michael and Raven, you need to join me to work flank guard." A few of them growled in disapproval. My head lowered, not wanting to see who had disagreed with his commands.

He continued speaking, apparently unaffected by his protesters, "Death is different for each Vessel, but in the end the outcome is the same. I wish to see more from the other side of death's hold." His hand grazed my cheek wiping away actual tears. "I do not understand why you cry for what cannot be changed." In the end, his tone sounded unfeeling.

I couldn't pry my eyes from his. The cloaked figure licked his lips when he was done speaking. Moisture mixed with the moonlight made them glisten. A feeling of possession overtook me. I was envious of the night's light, touching what I could not have. My eyes throbbed and stung with hardwired emotions, responding to inner thoughts. I longed to taste his emotions of fear, torment, power, and most of all, his new one… desire.

The pair of glowing eyes before me widened in complete

surprise as I advanced with slight trepidation. Raising my right hand cautiously to caress his face, I brushed my thumb across his lips. Molding his hand over mine, his voice became breathless and quivering as he tried to gain his composure.

Dropping his head until he was a whisper away from the cusp of my ear, he said, "The answers you seek from me are as follows: Balance, a Bond-Rite, and to protect you… especially from me." The other six creatures started to close in on us, and I barely heard his last words as I leaned forward, deeper into his embrace. The mist engulfed us, and I woke up whispering, "Balance."

LYING IN BED MOST OF THE NIGHT SHIVERING, I WATCHED THE MORNING'S light filtering in between the cracks of the black curtains. The day of Tod's funeral. Pulling the covers over my head, I wished Rae-Lynn would come tell me it was Thursday.

Thinking back to when I had woken up on Monday, I had told Mom I wasn't feeling well. Then I came clean and told her I needed more time to deal with everything. Going to school and having to discuss what happened to all of us that night certainly wouldn't be pleasing to relive.

She wasn't upset but approached me, concerned. I was acting out of character. Under normal circumstances, I would have become agitated from being so weak, hiding behind ire. Emotionally, I couldn't handle facing everyone on unrestful fumes of sleep. But, I also wasn't going to tell her about waking up with blood caked under my nails and the new shade of dried blood eyeliner.

Had all my sanity vanished with the dream?

The inner sound of a heartbeat brought me mentally back to my bed. I flipped the covers off and limped over to the full-length mirror. Squinting at my reflection, I made a disgusted back throat noise. I touched the puffy eyes, picking at the corners of dried blood. *What if I did try to scratch my own eyes out while I slept? You know what they say about crazy, you're not crazy if you say you are because crazy people never do. So, what does that make me?*

Raising both eyebrows in a show of skepticism, I answered myself, "Yeah, I thought so too." I blinked at the reflection staring back. It had lost the luster even makeup couldn't fix. The face in the mirror appeared thinner than I remembered. My hair was stringy and full of knots due to the climb through the trees branches while escaping the world in my head. Leaning closer to the glass, I noticed some missed blood crusties.

Wiping them away, I held back a yawn, settling for a muffled groan instead. Ever since I decided to move back upstairs to my room, four nights ago, I had survived on broken slumber and lots of instant coffee. The medication wasn't working anymore. Well, it did for the physical pain, but not with the nightmares. Regrettably, Mom kept the narcotics under lock and key. She was afraid I would overdose or become addicted. But, the way I felt right now, overdosing would at least grant me some rest in peace.

My life was full of torment. By day, I was reminded of death from the living. At night, I fought against it taking me. The nightmares were back with a relentless vengeance. Sadly, that part wasn't the only thing different about them. Each morning, fear stained the thoughts that controlled me from the repeated nightly onslaught. Dreading the morning outcome had become routine. Checking my face for the unexplainable or searching for new scratches down my neck, arms, and back. One morning, I found my hair soaked in sweat and blood. I must have attacked myself instead of fending off the misty shadow creatures. At this point and time, I doubted I would ever enjoy the peaceful slumber my body craved.

Looking back at the mirror and into my eyes, I noticed they had become a faded shade of green mixed with blue, a black ring circling each iris. I frowned at the stranger staring back at me. Growing up, I'd always been told my eyes altered color with mood change. What I saw now dried my tongue to the roof of my mouth.

Studying both irises, I actually witnessed how they changed in color. The black ring was growing thick, and I watched the blue become absorbed by it, leaving light green. My vision began to burn again, and out marbled the black filling where the blue had once been. The irises changed to a deep, dark green with thin black streaks. With lids closed tight, I pressed fingertips into them hard and crumpled to the floor—trembling from what I'd seen in the mirror. The overall effect appeared sinister.

What is going on with me? Not only am I insane, but I'm mutating too? The burning slowly subsided, and I released the pressure. The light in the room had faded, turning a darker shade that matched my detached mood. Unenthusiastically, I crawled over to the bed pulling myself up. Sitting on the messed up sheets, I grabbed my favorite zebra print pillow, placed it over my face and screamed.

I was tired of feeling like crap, of crying, hurting, not sleeping, scared, and most of all, of being unable to share any of it with anyone. Never so alone. *How did anyone deal with this pain?* Rolling over on my side, I cried and punched the bed over and over until I couldn't feel anymore. Why couldn't I have my old life back from before the accident? At least I could handle the bad dreams then. But now, I was living for the sheer purpose to survive them. Unsure if I wanted to endure it any more. This wasn't my idea of living.

Wednesday: afternoon

I HAD MANAGED TO CATNAP IN BETWEEN SNIVELS AND HICCUPS UNTIL I NOTICED the clock was telling me to get up. The display showed 4:05 p.m., and it took all my energy to rise up off the bed, lean over, and knock the clock onto the floor. Time no longer meant anything to me, unimportant at best.

Still unsteady and dizzy while I tried to get dressed, I secretly hoped I'd fall over and break the other leg so I wouldn't feel guilty for not going to say goodbye to my boyfriend. Yes, those thoughts about the situation were pretty ludicrous.

Rae-Lynn worked it out with my father to pick me up for the funeral and stay during the service, but I wasn't sure I wanted him to. Bad enough the entire ordeal would be unbearable. Why not make it awkward, as well? Plus, I didn't want him with me when I found Tod's parents.

Why was this dragging out for me? Tod had been gone for more than three weeks. I normally got over guys hours after a break up, not weeks. Then it dawned on me because I never did really break up with him. Fate had made the choice for me.

I was zoning out in thought when someone knocked on the door. Frowning down at my shoes, I already knew who was on the other side. *Was it time to go so soon?* I pulled down on the waistband of the dress to smooth it out. The knocking became louder, more serious, and I jumped slightly. A small quiver vibrated at the back of my throat.

If only Blakely could have gotten the night off to go with me. Her boss said they needed her for inventory. Also, two other employees had called in sick, so they were pretty busy.

Dee didn't drive yet and we bummed rides off Blake and Ghost frequently. Since it was a school night and Dee's mom was working, she had babysitting duties. The twins looked like her but in mini size. Calvin and Bailey were okay for kids. I'd even babysat them a couple of times when both Dee and her mom had to work. They were no trouble, but I was always worn out by the time I was released from guarding duties.

Ghost was still MIA. Then this morning, while Dee and I were talking on the phone, she slipped some information to me while brushing her teeth. Ghost wasn't only missing from my life but from life in general. He hadn't been at school for the past two days... three, if he didn't make an appearance in homeroom today.

A fist smacked against my door. "Alexcia, are you decent? I need to talk to you before we go."

Great. I wasn't really in the mood for a pep talk. *Let's rally for the dead. I don't think so.* I limped over to the door and cracked it open about two inches. "Sorry, was listening to music. What's up?" Max shifted his eyes to the top of my head and grumbled under his breath. Gigi sat at attention by his left side patiently panting, waiting for a command. She looked at me, grumbled low and bowed her head. *That was strange.*

I hadn't seen Max since he had stormed out of my hospital room the day I received those beautiful, creepy flowers. Come to think of it, I never got them back from Rae-Lynn. She had mentioned something about Max working on a project regarding some mismanaged funds in New York. Today, my father was dressed in one of his best black suits. He liked the dark-colored Italian suits the best. I always thought it was because they made him fiercer looking to his foes. Mom had once said she liked the dark suits because they accented the passion in his eyes. I studied my father while he stood in the hall. He was an enigma with a cloud of mystery masking his uncertainty. His blue eyes were close to black, and that worried me some. I did the math ... Max plus uncertainty equaled bad for me, maybe.

Backing up to let him in the room, I watched in anticipation as his massive frame squeezed through the door, and he glanced from corner to corner. "I see you have been spring cleaning." I grabbed a corner of my comforter and flicked it over a pile of laundry, then smoothed it out to make a place for him to sit. Max surveyed the room, his gaze remaining on the empty computer chair. I motioned for him to sit, regrettably he accepted the spot. Gigi chose to stay in the hallway by my door. Not following him into the room was abnormal behavior for her.

Dad tried to get comfortable as I rolled the computer chair around and sat across from him. "So, what's the occasion? You never come into my room. Gigi's in here normally drooling all over my clothes, but now she won't even cross the threshold. What's up with her?" I raised my eyebrows, whistled and patted my leg to indicate she was more than welcome to enter. She dropped flat to the floor and whimpered. *Okay, fine, stay there. I'm not begging for your attention either.*

Max cleared his throat. "I know we don't spend a lot of time together, but you do know I care for you, right?" He adjusted his tie. Clearly he was nervous about something.

"Yeah, I know." I pressed my lips together tight to lock my mouth.

"It seems your mom has expressed some issues about the way things have been between the three of us, and she wants us to spend more time together." *Ah, okay, then why was he looking everywhere but at me?* He was telling all of this to the dog with me as their mediator. The muscle across his jawline tightened as if he wanted to say more but was keeping it in like me. *Did we have to do this now?*

Without notice, everything gushed out of me. "Do we have to discuss this now, before... well? I don't think this is the right time to pretend to be dad and daughter. I need things to stay the way they were." I rolled my eyes. *Wonderful, here they come.* Small droplets slipped out. I didn't need this now. "My life has been turned upside down. I'm broken. I don't want to be around people when all they want from me is to relive what happened that night. I'm tired of being wet." I wiped angrily under each eye, glad I decided not to wear makeup. "I feel like everyone is attacking me for being me. That's who I am. I'm me." I used my hands in an all-over motion. "This way and I'm not changing. I'm not asking for you and Mom to change either. I understand you both are busy. So please, tell Mom we don't need to redo anything. Besides..." I sniffed. "I can tell it's hard for you to even be in here with me. I'm not going to force you to be around me." My voice was small, and I cupped my face to muffle the sobs. I had been shattered and couldn't even type into the search engine to purchase a repair manual from Amazon.

I was trying to replace some of the bricks on my wall. Slowly, I stopped crying and lowered my hands. Before I could look up, he had pulled me into a hug. A real, genuine hug. I was lost for words as he stroked my hair and sighed heavily.

"My daughter, I am sorry you are so lost. Unfortunately, I cannot give you any answers for what you are going through. Not yet, at least. I promise, though, when the time comes, all will make sense to your feelings of madness. It will only be a while longer." He scooted back to look at me. "But first, before we can decide if you are ready to know, I need some information from you. Like, what my daughter's been doing with all of her free time?"

We locked eyes, and I felt a quick jolt. Unlike static shock, the electric crack seared its way into the back of my skull. I couldn't shake the feeling of dread. *What had he said to me? Something about partial truth wrapped up in a riddle?* Damn, my teenage ears. I didn't get all of it but was afraid of ruining our moment if I asked. Everything became hazy.

He stood, I think—maybe it was me—but he seemed taller. Heat rolled off his deep caramel-colored hands when he let go of me. I thought he might be running a fever. My back and arms were covered in chicken bumps from the absence of his embrace. I sat, blinking up at him when something came over me. The figure in front of me seemed to morph and pace. Something growled, then my mouth opened, and I started ratting on myself.

"I was at a party the night of the accident. We had been drinking. A bunch of us decided to go to a gathering. The weather began to attack us. I wanted to go home. They wouldn't listen. I distracted Tod. He lost control of the truck. Another big vehicle was coming right for us. I knew we were going to die..." I believed Max waved his hand in front of me.

"How did you know you were going to die?"

I didn't want anyone to know about that night, especially what really had happened. *What the hell has come over me?* I tried to shake my head to make myself stop. *Who was I telling all this to anyway?* Short term memory failing, I heard my name, but in a rolling growl, I jumped. *Shit. What was that?*

"Stop fighting me, Alexcia Crystalline. How did you know you were going to die?" Another low snarl followed.

What was with my mouth? It seemed detached from my will, and I started in again. "My demon came to rescue us but only took me, leaving all my friends to die. It is my penance for killing them. For me to live and them to die. I should be dead too."

Stop, Alexcia. Stop talking. The voice inside kept screaming, but another growl echoed in the room, and I sat straight up waiting for another question. *What was wrong with me, and who was asking me to reveal all of my secrets?*

Terror overcame me. I didn't want anyone to know about the nightmares. No one was going to lock me away, no one. I dug fingernails into both palms and felt trickles of warmth flow down my fingers, sour words started forming on my tongue. I needed to spit them out.

"Cort-tak-meois-le-quic," my mouth hurt, and something

snarled close by. My ears popped, and I blinked. Confused, I found us still locked in our embrace as if he'd never gotten up. Max pulled back slightly from where he was kneeling. I looked him square in the eyes and asked, "Dad? What happened?" Then I thought, *wasn't he just in front of me?*

He turned to sit back on the bed but faced me and leaned over to grab the arms of the computer chair. Wheeling me closer, Max used a thumb and wiped some of the tears away while glancing around before using the one of the arms of the chair to rise into a standing position. Then he patted me on my head. *What just happened?* My mind swam in confusion. Walking to the door, he turned around slowly, holding the handle with one hand and placing another over his temple.

"I'm sorry, Alexcia, but I think your mom is right. We have failed you in so many ways, child. Things will get better in time. Finish getting ready. We will leave for the funeral in ten minutes." He turned to walk out, pulling the door with him, then suddenly stopped and spun around to face me. His expression froze my heart in mid-beat. "You must remind me to thank…" he ground his teeth as he said, "a friend of mine for his parenting advice."

His dark coal eyes ignited as if he were about to pass judgment on the damned. Straightening his body to fill the door frame, he inhaled sharply, then exhaling his words with force. "Alexcia Crystalline Stasis, you are grounded." He slammed the door.

What. The. Hell?

15

Seven ravens on my roof, not one of them were here to take my soul but to help me attend a funeral, not of my own.
~Alexcia

HE SPACE IN MAX'S METALLIC BLACK HUMMER WAS FILLED WITH outrage. Now, not only was I depressed but pissed off too. I kept pulling on the hem of Mom's dress to keep him from looking at me… anything to avoid making eye contact with my new prison warden. I could kick myself. Forget about the phrase *you're grounded for a week*, it was replaced with, *you're grounded for a year.* I went from no rules to a motherlode of them within the first five minutes of our drive. Some good came out of it—I stopped crying.

Anger burned up all of my tears because I was cured, for the moment.

The weather fit the venue too. It was cold and windy with a slight drizzle. I didn't need to shed any more tears; the clouds were doing the crying for me. While practicing wordlessly what I was going to say to Claire and Clarence Peston, I stared out the front passenger window. My father yanked on the steering wheel and the beast jumped as if we hit a speed bump going sixty, jolting me from sulking. I dug both hands into the folded jacket and quickly returned it to my face, taking in his smell. The

scent of his cologne was fading, and I couldn't detect the shampoo smell either. My heart tugged on the pull-string to the water
bucket attached, but the line had been cut, thanks to my father.

The funeral service was being held in the Peston's home,
followed by everyone driving out to the cemetery for the family
and friends' final goodbye. I wasn't sure if I wanted to go that far
yet. Maybe if I could unhinge my jaw long enough to say what I
came there to, it might be possible, someday.

Sighing at the thought, I stopped the pity party long enough
to notice the rain had increased as we pulled up to the gates of
the estate. Tod had been cocky and full of himself at times, but
he never made anyone feel cheap. He never spoke of his family's
wealth or what he was going to inherit when his parents died.
Once I had asked him, "What good is all that money if you can't
take it with you?" If only I could've seen his future, I wouldn't
have said it to him.

To refocus and keep the waterworks away, my hand instinctively punched my bad arm. I couldn't wait for the cast to come
off. I would miss Blakely's art work, but I wanted to feel whole
again. It was just another stupid reminder of the way I felt about
myself. And the brace on my right leg added to the weight of
emotions.

Max spoke to the front gate guard attendant, who checked
the list, expressed his condolences and opened the gates. I
couldn't wait for that to stop too. People were another reminder.

My father followed the driveway and parked where they directed him. He grabbed a black umbrella from the back seat and
slammed the driver's door to come around to the passenger's
side. While he opened the door, I glared at him, clutching Tod's
jacket to my chest to keep it from getting too wet.

"It's time. Let's do this. Give me your hand. I'll help you
out." He opened his free hand while holding the umbrella higher for both of us to walk under. Tentatively, I took his hand and

slipped in right next to him. He closed the door behind me, and we walked slowly in the cold, wet air.

My throat hurt from the new dam I had built on our way over. Right before we walked through the door, he closed the umbrella and gave it a quick shake. I watched the rain drops sprinkle to the ground and pretended they were mine.

We merged with the flow of people being herded into the main hall. Some of Tod's lacrosse teammates were handing out programs with spiritual passages and directions to the cemetery. The deeper I dug into the sleeves of his jacket, the whiter my knuckles became. I kept my head down low so no one would recognize me right away. Having avoided everyone for more than three weeks had been easy. I preferred the box of solitude and wanted to stay locked up awhile longer.

"Let me help you down the stairs." Max extended his arm for me to loop mine through. He took a program and immediately held it out for me. I declined to reach for it, so he folded it and tucked it into his breast pocket. If only things in life were that simple, if you didn't want to deal with it, you simply tucked it away. But then again, I would need several pockets for all of my issues. He held out his arm again, and we took it slow down the four steps onto the plush, white carpet.

We were met by one of the lacrosse players. Chase Masson held out his arm to steady me. His blond hair was cut military style, which I thought made him look much younger than eighteen, but it did pronounce his dimples more since there was nothing to distract you from noticing his face. His chocolate brown eyes looked at Max and the blood from his cheeks noticeably drained. *Yup, the menacing football player, in the black Emporio Armani suit, is my dad.* I glanced at Max to see if he was paying attention to the young man who was melted to his daughter's arm. I think I was holding my escort up now. A slight crack formed in my armor as the corners of my lips flicked Chase a reassuring smile.

Tod's teammate cleared his throat. "This way. The Peston's would like you and your guest to sit with the family."

I almost lost it right there. They wanted me to sit with them. That was like Leonardo Da Vinci asking Jesus if he was sure about adding Judas to The Last Supper painting. I tried to keep myself from shaking as I took Chase's arm. Taking the lead, I followed in silence.

While he escorted us to our seats, I focused on my feet. Clutching Tod's jacket close to me, I didn't notice the patent leather boot sticking out in the middle of the isle. Chase pulled me back and around the boot before I fell forward, but I caught some air and glanced to see whose foot I almost broke. *Oh, someone upstairs doesn't like me very much.*

Krista was turning like a snake, ready to strike as she faced me. While staring at the jacket under my arm, she inhaled between her teeth sounding like a backward hiss. Under her breath, she spat out, "Bitch. If it weren't for you, Tod would still be here." Two of her cheer-bots, sitting next to her, laughed. They must have had poor programming.

My voice was airy when I mumbled, "I'm sorry." As Chase and I sidestepped her barricade and proceeded to our destination, my ears picked up on a low hum. A guy had gotten up from his seat to speak to a man across the aisle. He glanced at me and then over my shoulder at Max. Nodding at Chase, he winked at me and stepped around us to walk toward the back of the room. I was taken aback by his eyes. They were a deep violet, almost black. The word *beautiful* was severely lacking in describing them. I was blinded by the thought when I heard Krista yelp.

"*Oww.* Hey, watch where you're stepping," Krista barked.

I clung to Chase while I turned to see who was next on Krista's list. The guy we had passed was formally bowing to her. "My apologies ma'am but where I'm from, a lady sits with her legs together." The young man chuckled and in a low whisper, spoke again. "So, as not to advertise her merchandise." He completed the gesture and left her wide-mouthed. People around her snickered. *Touché. I must look for him after the service and thank him for such a great quip.*

Chase led us around the front of the mournful gatherers. Stopping four rows from the podium, he deposited us at the end of the row. Well, one thing tonight had worked out in my favor. Dad and I were hidden in the front corner of the room which meant when it was time to leave we would be close to last.

Max held his cool demeanor while helping me shuffle to the seat next to him. Like a bodyguard, he took the outside seat next to me. I placed the jacket across my lap and stared straight ahead. Everything in the room was color-coordinated with our school's colors: red, black, and silver. I noticed Tod's favorite midnight blue was used as an accent shade in the flower arrangements. When I noticed the casket lying unopened in the front of the room, my eyes widened. I had been so overwhelmed with my own world, I hadn't even noticed it. A coffin, the primary symbol of death—for all to see—was displayed in front of us. To make matters worse was my knowledge that it was empty. I tried to conceal my facial expression, focusing on the floor so no one could see the signs of guilt and loss. I really didn't have the right to be there.

While I pulled his jacket to silence a sniffle, Max placed his arm around my shoulders. I was still mad but leaned into him, accepting his gesture of comfort. He whispered, "Sorry," in my ear, and I wiped the tears with the palm of my good hand. Then he handed me one of his silk handkerchiefs and told me to keep it. My neck itched under the skin. Wonderful, not only do my eyes give me away, but my skin does too. I should have asked Rae-Lynn for a wrap. For a quick second, my pride got the best of me when I thought about putting Tod's jacket on to cover up the welts. *But, I'm proud to say, I am not that conceited and squashed the idea.*

From the front of the room, two huge wooden doors opened and out walked an elderly, white-haired woman carrying a hymn book. She approached the piano and two other women followed in her path. One was carrying a flute and the other had a dark-stained violin. I recognized the flutist from some of the pictures in Tod's locker and the hanging family portraits up the staircase. She was Tod's older sister, Brittney, and probably had to rearrange her college schedule to fly here from England. On more than one occasion, Tod had mentioned how proud he was of her. She was studying to be a symphony flutist and was also composing a few pieces for her undergraduate work. I didn't know the young girl with the violin or the grandmotherly woman sitting at the piano but was sure they were family members expressing their feelings of loss through music.

When the door opened again, a priest entered with Tod's parents following behind. The crowd hushed, and all I could hear was the heavy patter of rain from above keeping rhythm with Claire's soft sobs. The musicians started playing a piece called "The Prayer." I remembered this song from a childhood movie. When I was little, I thought it was pretty and romantic. Now it meant letting go and saying farewell. The fragile tinkling I heard was every emotion I held for Tod.

When the service was over and everyone was heading out to meet up at the cemetery, each leg felt made of lead, and I was slow in getting up. Max pulled me forward and switched me on auto pilot. As I focused ahead, I saw Mr. and Mrs. Peston. Our gaze connected, and I found the strength to approach her. I had to do this, not only for Tod... but for me as well.

I asked my father to please wait for me at the back of the hall, telling him I'd catch up when I was done. He looked at me with a grave expression but gave me a pat and a quick head nod in understanding. I watched him walk away when I noticed three tall men in the back of the room staring at me. A sudden chill around my ankles made me scan the room before I found myself panning back to the three of them, drawn to the middle one in particular. The air was sucked right out of me as I looked him over. Each man had darkened features, but the one in the middle had violet eyes, raven hair, and ivory bone skin. The temperature in the room dropped noticeably. When I approached the Pestons', every nerve ending trembled, but not from the nip of the air conditioner. I couldn't believe myself. I was crushing on some stranger at my boyfriend's funeral. Appalled by my inappropriate behavior, I broke our stare and focused on the prearranged plan.

Turning on my heel, I limped away... head held low, his jacket in my hands. I tried to find my voice. "Hello." It was all I could muster.

"Alexcia, my dear, thank you for coming. We are so sorry we didn't come to see you in the hospital. It's been so hard..." Her voice cracked, and Clarence put a soft hand on her shoulder.

"I don't even know where to begin to say how sorry I am about all that has happened. I never meant to hurt anyone."

They both looked at me, flummoxed.

My heart had been severed by the sharp blade of guilt from thrusting us into this situation, and I was slowly dying. I was weary of being a sprinkler, watering emotions that would eventually wither. I deepened my grip on his jacket for strength. *Oh, goodness this is hard.*

"On the night of the accident, the weather was so bad, and I got scared sitting in the back of the truck." I sucked in a quick breath. "I caused the accident by distracting Tod, and he turned the wheel hard when he looked back at me." Eyes burning, I tried to let it all gush out. "I didn't know he would take his eyes off the road, but I guess he... he..." I sniffed. "I know that having me here is a reminder because I should have died with them too."

Then... *Slap.*

Mrs. Peston was holding the hand she hit me with, and my left cheek was on fire. A commotion in the back of the room caused everyone else's eyes to turn, but I didn't even glance in that direction to see what was going on. It wouldn't have mattered. I couldn't see. Instead, I pulled his jacket to my face for one last sensory memory of Tod.

I looked up, shaking, but held her gaze while holding up my arms. "I brought Tod with me. I thought it would be inappropriate for me to keep him when he belongs to both of you. He asked me to go steady the night of the accident and gave me his jacket to wear. It is all I have left of him and all I can give back to you." I felt light-headed as I whispered, "It's really all I have to give you. I'm so sorry."

The grieving mother draped herself around me and wailed. We let everything out right there, holding each other while the stragglers in the room watched. I didn't care. I came to do what I needed to do, and now Tod was home where he belonged. We broke our embrace and she took his jacket from me and smiled, drying her face with the tips of her fingers.

"Alexcia, don't ever say you should've met your fate with them. I have gone through all the negative emotions of wondering. Why all of them and not you? How come you were spared and the others were not? One morning, I woke up and realized I was asking the wrong questions because I was blinded by the loss of my son.

"You are special. I can feel it. My son thought so too. Therefore, you need to stop feeling guilty. It was a tragic accident, one that could've happened to anyone. Now you need to fight for your future. Your fate is in your own hands. Make something of yourself. Live for not only you but for the others too. Do not let sorrow guide your life because if you do, then I will never forgive you." Her eyes were so puffy and rimmed with the color of loss, I was sure we looked alike. She handed the jacket to her husband and reached out to take my hands in hers. Her thin fingers wrapped around mine and she squeezed.

Her husband smiled at me. I was looking at Tod's eyes through those of his dad. "Thank you for bringing our son home." They each hugged me again, then turned away and walked to the empty casket.

I couldn't believe what they did next. Mr. Peston opened the lid, and Mrs. Peston pressed Tod's jacket to her lips and placed it in the casket. When Tod's father closed the lid and locked it, Claire kissed the top and said, "Tod Regan Isaac Peston, my son, rest in peace." And with that, our sense of closure began. She turned to me, "Are you and your father coming to the cemetery?"

"Yes, we will be there."

"Be sure to tell him, it's the first left turn into the parking lot. Walk to the hill on the right and go thirty-three rows in. It's the eighth plot down. Thank you, Alexcia. I know what you did had to be difficult. I want you to know you will always be welcome here."

My father joined me, "Well, I think you've shown me something very important here." The glint in his eyes was special. He held out his arm, and I looped mine around it. "You ready to go?"

"Yes, I think that I'm finally ready to say goodbye." I had been very close to drowning in grief, but Mrs. Peston pulled the stopper out of my emotional bathtub. For too long, I had soaked in a toxic marinade of conflicting feelings. High time for me to get out.

The weather changed from dismal to nasty on the way to the cemetery. At one point, the Hummer hit a dip and hydroplaned. Max said the roads were slick and we lost traction more than once. I laughed and said it felt as if we had run over someone. Then he stared ahead grumbling about problems not taking care of themselves. It didn't make sense, but I wasn't going to press the issue. Since we left so late, we had to park at the farthest end of the parking lot.

When Max opened the door to help me out, I noticed the air smelled of tainted rain, not the usual freshly washed aroma. A musty mold smell crept out from under the Hummer. Scrunching my nose, I raised a hand to plug it.

"Don't you smell that? It's horrible. See, I told you that you hit something."

He held out his hand to steady me on my bad knee. "You can smell it?" He shook his head. "I mean, I don't smell anything but brake fluid. I'll take the vehicle in tomorrow to have the brakes checked." He leaned around me to pick up the umbrella. While opening it, he blocked my view and cleared his throat. "Alexcia, I'm proud of you and what you did for the Pestons."

Now, I knew why he had opened the umbrella that way. He didn't want me to see his face. A warm feeling from my past tried to surface. Max hadn't spoken to me like that in ages. I missed his voice when he used it with kindness. It reminded me of the narrator from the original movie of *Winnie-the-Pooh*.

He lifted the fully extended umbrella over our heads. We had just started heading toward Tod's grave when Max's cell vibrated. Pulling the silver phone out, he looked baffled and turned to me. "It's for you."

I slid the bar on his phone so I could read it.

Unknown #— LOOK UP

Hesitant to respond, I wasn't sure if I was ready to see who was waiting for my reaction. I knew Blakely was working. Dee would be with her brother and sister. So that left only one person who knew where I would be tonight. I looked up to see a Ghost staring at me.

I smiled through tears, *Jake.*

TEVIN'S SIDE: THROUGH THE EYES OF A REAPER

MY CLAN WAS SCOPING OUT THE CEMETERY AND ALL THE PEOPLE AROUND TOD'S grave site. Archer, K, and Imp were not only looking for anything threatening but listening to the human conversations about the young Vessel's passing. It was intriguing to some of us about how much death affected most of them. I still couldn't understand all the words Alexcia tried to express to the parents. When she was explaining how she felt, how she should have died too, it confused me. She had become more intriguing to me during the past few days. Her useless emotions ran deep, and it made a huge spark light my interest. Leaning against a tombstone, I scratched my head in thought.

"Fleas?" K asked.

I laughed. "I do not understand why we bother them so much?"

"We?" K looked confused.

"Yeah. They mourn the loss, but I do not comprehend the logic of getting so worked up over anyone's passing. It is the cycle. You live. You die. Do they not realize the River's code of creation cannot be broken? Why fight it?" I watched some of the humans start to leave the funeral party, scanning the crowd for my problem of interest.

"You know, Tevin, I think the female Vessel is looking pretty bad. Sickly almost. The child is very thin and her spirit is weak. That is not good. If she damages it any further, the River may not accept her power." K leaned against a tombstone and lit a cigarette… took a drag and continued, "Who is the tall Vessel with her? Is that something we should worry about?"

I watched Max, Alexcia, and the male walking away from us,

heading toward their vehicles. Max turned to make eye contact with me as the male put his left arm across Alexcia's shoulders, and then kissed the top of her head. For some reason, the outer corner of my right eye twitched. I tried to make the annoyance stop by nonchalantly scratching the area so K wouldn't notice. "The Vessel is a friend of hers. He is harmless, for the most part." The male walked slowly with Alexcia and dropped his arm to hold her hand. My brow creased, and that blasted twitch came back. I swatted the side of my head, and K backed up from me. Max glanced down at their hands, then back at me, making me wonder what he had noticed. At least he was the only one around who could see us.

Archer was doing a slow jog between the grave plots with Imp following him. They reminded me of the little Vessels playing that chasing game. When Archer ran and jumped into a puddle next to me, I punched him in the shoulder.

"Tag," I yelled.

"What the scythe was that for?" He rubbed the spot I had punched. I did not hurt him, but the follow-through was a knee-jerk reaction.

Imp was jumping up onto a stone statue of an angel. He kicked his legs over one of her marble, outstretched arms and hoisted himself up to interlock his hands around the statue's neck. "Okay, baby, your grave or mine?" He wiggled his eyebrows while his deep purple eyes glowed with an intense brightness. I thought he looked stupid with his long black jeans dangling over her arm.

Exasperated, I rolled my eyes. "Get the hell off that. I swear, I wish I had daemons in my clan instead of children Vessels." I reached for a cigarette and held a finger up to light it. Talking with it between my lips, I asked for everyone to report in. "Well, did any of you pick up on anything?"

They looked around at each other. Imp jumped down,

smoothed out his gray blazer and shrugged his shoulders. "I didn't even get a whiff. If a daemon, angel, or elemental are around, they have a damn good blending spell. But hey, it's not a total loss. Rain always brings some kind of elemental out. Maybe we'll get lucky and see some action before going to work."

Imp was not even done talking when Michael and Raven came running up. Both were equipped with their harvesting weapons, and Raven's left arm had a gash down the length of it. Blood the color and consistency of tar was soaking through his charcoal gray dress shirt. My face hardened from the iron mask of disappointment.

"Sorry, Tevin, they got away. Three water ones were tailing Max's Hummer. Raven wounded one, knocked it under Max's vehicle, but the other two pulled their powers together and blended before we could dispatch them. We lost them in the atmosphere." Michael put his double-bladed battle axe away. Raven threw both his kataras into the dirt, embedding both blades up to the hilts, clearly stating that he was pissed off.

Picking at his wound, Raven called forth his cloak. The red mist was so dark, it appeared like dying embers of burning charcoal as it draped over his form. A light sizzling came from inside his cloak. Laughing, he watched everyone through crimson eyes, glowing under his hood. "Good as new. Well, what now? I don't think they would be stupid enough to actually show up here. I think she's safe for now. Besides, Tevin, she is with Max. Who in the Unseen is going to mess with him?"

"Damn it." I wanted to kill something. "They're getting pretty desperate to keep trying attacks out in the open. Have all the entities of the Unseen gone mad? Why are they so desperate to see her dead? Who is going to try to kill her next time? Sure wish I knew when and where they planned the next strike." I rubbed my temples, filing away all of my questions because they were not going to be answered anyway. We needed to leave, and I required a recharge before another attempt was made on Alexcia.

The rain was pouring now, and we all walked in silence to the Vessel's grave. I bent down to read what was written on the plastic-covered piece of paper and spoke to the grave marker, but loud enough for all our group to hear.

"I promise your essence will always be Alexcia's strength. There was nothing I could do for you. The Cauldron gave us your name, and we must obey creation's call for death. But, so you know, Alexcia is not a mere human Vessel but a Child-of-Balance. I hope the words your human mother said to Alexcia will get through to her. She has mourned for you long enough.

"Your name is ironic, Tod. In German, it means death. So, in the spirit of the Unseen…" I looked up from my crouch as each one of them stood around me with their cloaks out, weapons drawn, waiting for my next command. I bowed my head. "Your job as a Vessel has been completed, and now I will take up where your life force ended. Alexcia will be taken care of, I promise, and your death will not be forgotten. So, Tod Regan Isaac Peston, in the spirit of my grim existence, I mean every word when I say, Vessel of Death, Rest in Peace."

I stood. Raven and K looked at each other. Michael rolled his blue eyes. Imp had grabbed one of Archer's arrows from out of his quiver and was picking his nails with it. Archer was talking on his iPhone X telling Quint we were done and on our way back. Michael was suddenly by my side, placing his hand on my shoulder, clearly looking confused.

"What were you doing?"

I shrugged. "Vessels talk to their dead all the time. I wanted to see what it felt like."

"Well?" He waited for my insight.

Sighing, "It felt like I was talking to myself." I straightened and faced him.

"You know, they can't hear them. Hello, they're dead. Now,

if you're done talking to the air, I'm hungry. Let's sever. We need to get to the Cauldron for the night's harvesting list."

We walked away from one form of death to go find another. I wanted to know more about the world Alexcia lived in. My plan was if I could understand her, I could protect her better. I only had twenty-three moon risings left, and then the contracts with both Max and Rae-Lynn would be undone. Just then, my cell rang, cutting through the silent cemetery. My mouth went dry. It was Max. I snapped the cell case shut, sending the call to voicemail. I needed to discuss some issues with him about our Bond-Rite, but not here.

Holding the phone acted as a reminder that Max was waiting for a reply. I needed to contain these contagious thoughts before they infected my emotions. The clan wanted this to end. I wanted this to end. At least, I thought I did. My pace slowed, adding distance between me and the clan so I could speak with the Doom Guard without their influence. They didn't need to know my plans, or my problems, yet. The River had acquired more of my power lately, leaving me drained, and I needed to recharge before I confronted Max about some real concerns. Reluctantly, I followed the others into the rainy night, not to harvest souls, but to clear my head of the unexplainable desires about Alexcia.

16

It's amazing what you can find out about yourself over one cup of coffee.
~Alexcia

UNDER THE CIRCUMSTANCES, MAX GAVE ME A TEMPORARY *GET OUT OF JAIL free* card. Mom must have filled him in on the quiet war I was having with Jake and suggested he let me clear the air with him before starting house arrest. He was grim about it but agreed to reduce my sentence for one night. I kissed his cheek, and he told me to be home before midnight. Since I hadn't been back to school yet, they were going to let me slide the rest of this week and start back the next Monday. Otherwise, he would never have agreed to let me stay out so late on a school night. *Oh, if they only had a clue.*

Jake and I decided to go somewhere that people didn't know us and we wouldn't be interrupted. I chose a small donut and coffee shop by my house. We ordered drinks and made our way to the back of the room. He pulled out a chair and helped me into it. Then he flipped his around to straddle and rested his arms on the back.

I watched quietly through the floor-to-ceiling windows as rain fell. As a time filler, I blew the steam away to cool my coffee. It gave me something to do. During the silence, my head filtered through the questions I wanted Jake to answer. Staring into the coffee, I waited for the little triangle to float up and give me an answer. *Not now,* came to mind several times, but I kept trying for a different outcome. The awkward quiet had followed us into the shop after our small talk on the way there. I frowned, not wanting to be the first to speak. I never knew how the absolute lack of sound could actually intensify ringing in your ears because I was about to explode and take all the bystanders with me.

Catching Jake from the corner of my eye as he took a finger to scoop up some whipped cream, I watched him wavering about putting it in his mouth. Then, he set the cup of hot chocolate down, reaching for a napkin. He clearly hadn't been eating either. Wiping his fingers, he cleared his throat.

"What?" I said, assuming he'd spoke.

"What? Did you ask me something?"

Yes, the voice spat out mentally. *I think we are on question thirty-three, but who's counting?* I narrowed my eyes, "No, I didn't. I thought you said something." Nervous energy forced me to turn away to watch the storm through the tinted windows. It looked like a scene from the Weather Channel. The silence was heavy, and I tried adjusting myself in the seat. Unfortunately, that made me even more uncomfortable. I squirmed, placing the warm cup on the table and using my good hand to scoot the chair closer to it.

"Do you want to sit somewhere else, a booth maybe?" His eyes held concern.

I wanted to snap back but clamped both lips together instead. I knew it had taken a lot for him to be here for me, even if it was out of guilt. We had been close friends for so long that I needed to give him the benefit of the doubt. Well, at least, until he gave me some answers, and then we would see if the rule still applied.

Steadying my voice wasn't easy, but I tried keeping to the

small talk. "No, the table is fine. How is your drink? I've never had the hot chocolate here. Any good?" What I really wanted to ask was, *Jake, where have you been for the last five days?* I raised the cup again, to see if the triangle made an appearance yet. No such luck. Damn.

"Oh, it's fine." He lowered his eyes to look at his shoes. I had never seen Jake wear a suit before. He must have borrowed it from his dad. It fit his length but hung loose across the shoulders. The dark navy suit made his eye color appear deeper, close to a sea-green, maybe? Looking even closer at his face, I noticed the dark rings under his eyes. His complexion was shadowed. *Jake, what is going on with you?* The questions kept coming, but they never passed my lips.

"That's good. Wow, some weather we're having, right?"

"Yeah, wet," he agreed in a low voice.

Okay, enough is enough I'm putting an end to this. "Well, you have my undivided attention, Jake. What's on your mind?"

He looked as if I'd slapped him. "Well, I umm, I..." The words trailed off.

I sat there wide-eyed while he stammered, waiting for him to get to the point. Then the inner voice texted me, *OMGoshness,* was I going to have to do everything? I cleared my throat. From somewhere inside, something was clawing at my ribs trying to get out. Then, I remembered its name... Mr. Anger. The raw emotion bared its teeth, and all the locks snapped into place before the beast broke out.

"Alexcia, I don't even know where to begin. I'm a crappy friend. You just came home, and I dumped all over you about things that well, well..." He was censoring himself, so I knew I was only getting bits and pieces. "I was mixing my past experiences with the present. All I can say is that I'm a jerk. I should have been thinking about you and not myself. You just went to your boyfriend's funeral and have been dealing with so much for the past few weeks. Here I was only focusing on how I almost lost one of my best friends."

I motioned to say something, but he held a hand up. "I know, the four of us said we wouldn't label each other, but it's how I feel about you, Alexcia. You are my best friend. I should have helped you work through your feelings, since… I've had to deal with shaking death's hand. I heard about what you did today for Tod's parents. I don't think I would have been strong enough for that." The last part was hard for him to say because of his past, I could tell. But his emotions had eroded our wall, and he was spilling, so I allowed his words to flow over me.

"On the day you came home, I was scared for you instead of being happy you were alive. I also know it was wrong of me to judge you when we had never spoken about the accident. I can't tell you how sorry I am." Jake's voice carried so much remorse, I was almost as choked up while he was trying to get it all out.

The anger inside me calmed down long enough to let a few tears escape. I knew he was laying out his feelings, but I had to guard my words with respect for his loss, and not hold the emotions he carried for his dad against him. Still, I couldn't disregard my instincts. There seemed to be more to his emotions concerning me than he was letting on. I picked up the coffee to help lubricate my jaw before I spoke. "Jake, I have been so worried about our friendship. I'm really sorry about your dad and for not respecting your past. I do miss him too. But mostly, I've been wondering what I'd done wrong? What had I said or done that would bring you crashing down on me? How did your faith in me falter?" I stared at him through wet lashes. "I never knew you saw me that way."

Jake sat up straight and almost spat his drink out. He started choking, and I tried to scoot close enough to pat him on the back. He waved his drink napkin, signaling me he was coming out of it. Sucking in a huge breath, he made little clearing noises trying to get more air into his lungs to speak. "Saw... you... what?" He was still struggling to breathe.

"I'm not trying to be the life of the party. Well, don't get me wrong, I like partying, sometimes, but that's not why I need to..." I didn't want to say it out loud and wasn't sure if I wanted Jake to know about the nightmares, yet. Now that I knew he thought of me as his best friend, I didn't want him to see me as an unstable loony with a drinking problem. I finished my sentence slowly, "...drink."

Watching him from under long bangs, I waited for the boom. His face said a lot, but I think he was trying to measure how he'd go about asking me the next question. I closed my eyes and waited. It wasn't the question that hit me but more like a confession of our problems.

"Not being with you that night, I was basing your accident on the past few save and rescues you had called us to. It seemed like you were getting out of control. I panicked and was afraid you would do something stupid if I didn't say something to stop you. But I would never let myself get close enough to say anything to you. I have been angry with myself for not trying to discuss this with you sooner."

I couldn't help how my face reacted. It went from half a smile to a flat out expression of disgust. He tried to recover, but irritation came through loud and clear. "You know I don't mind helping you out when you're in a jam. My hands are tied when I am at work, but you know you can always call Blake. Otherwise, you can count on me to bail you out."

A snide thought came close to slipping out. *Yes, please, let's reopen all of our wounds and use our words like salt.* Burning in shades of red, the telltale itching came out in patches between my collar bones. The sarcastic animal inside me roared, causing me to intensely clamp down once again on my tongue. The pain added the restraint I needed to hold back as the taste of blood pooled under my tongue. The level of vexation had blown my temperature to new heights. "I can count on you because you're my friend, or because you feel sorry for the poor, drunk, party girl who can't seem to get her life straight?"

Jake reached to place his hand on my shoulder, and I smacked it away. He was lucky my aim was too far away from his face. I sat there smoldering over the expression of judgment on his face about how I conducted my life. *Well, screw him. I can take care of myself.* I didn't want the coffee anymore. It was the wrong poison of choice for the situation at hand. I wanted a smoke and a beer. This made me even more upset because I knew I wasn't going to get the latter.

He had a lot of gall, sitting there, explaining that I was his best friend, then turning on me and saying I was a burden. So, which was I to him, a friend or some pain in the ass he needed to swoop in and save? I thought he liked me for the freedom-seeking spirit I was. *Turns out it was all a lie.*

"Alexcia, you took what I said the wrong way. Please, I don't want to fight anymore. You wanted to talk, so we are talking. Don't make me apologize for expressing my concerns. I felt you were going to end up in far more trouble than I could help you get out of. This accident proves that. I could have been there for you if you had been sober enough to call. I don't like speaking ill of the dead, but I bet Tod was drunk that night too, yet, you still got into his truck. You could have died while I was home sitting on my ass watching TV. I would have never forgiven myself if anything had happened to you. Alexcia, I do not like feeling helpless." The green in his eyes faded and took on a shine from past grief.

Even though I was still mad at him, the urge to hug him filled me at the same time. Since I couldn't bend my will to do either, I sat there, waiting for him to push me off the emotional cliff he'd helped me up from. I was so lost without him and now that I had found him again, it was my turn to go missing. In short, I got what he was saying. I was his best friend, but my actions were causing him grief and pain.

I needed air before we blew up the coffee shop, so I pushed away from the table to stand, but the bad knee protested against moving as fast as I wanted. When I twisted, the forward motion caused me to fall toward Jake. Kicking the chair out from under him, he moved with outstretched arms to grab me. The momentum knocked me into his arms, and we both went down. I fell on top of him and heard his head hit the floor. He blinked a couple of times and then closed his eyes. My good hand was holding me up while the bad one was resting on his chest, waiting to feel his heartbeat under my fingers.

I didn't even realize I forgot how to breathe until I leaned over his face and the words fell out of my mouth without air. "Jake? Jake, can you hear me? Are you okay? Jake?" I tapped his cheek with cold fingers. Anger took a leave of absence and was replaced with concern as some of the customers started coming over to check on us. "Ghost, people are watching. We need to get up." I started to shift away from him, but Jake's hand slipped under the curtain of hair separating us from the onlookers. He rested it on the back of my neck. Warmth blossomed in the pit of my stomach, and I followed the pull toward his face.

He whispered, "I'm sorry," directly in my ear.

I flushed with fever. Those two words meant so much to both of us. He wanted me to know he cared—to forgive him and accept him back. The heat between us was too much. We shared an awkward *friendly* moment, one not rated for viewing by coffee shop patrons. I was almost compelled to seal the deal in that way.

Instead, I nodded and the smile that eased into view across his face was unlike any I had seen before. It was brighter but with a hint of mischief. I found I liked this new grin but had a pang of regret for feeling that way.

As a lady was helping me up from the floor, Jake leaned forward and parted his lips. I kept chanting in my head, *we are just friends, we are just friends.* His breath smelled of chocolate with a hint of mint toothpaste, and my stomach growled looking at his lips with a sudden desire for dessert.

I shook my head to release me from the unwarrantable compulsion. He crawled out from under me and thanked the woman for helping me off him. We stood there, intensely staring into each other's eyes, trying to make sense of what had happened. He broke the silence. "Are you ready to go?"

Steadying myself using his arm while the chest muscle thumped like it wanted to beat again, I frowned. It was too soon for me to go down that road. I forbade my heart to respond to an unthinkable need. Anyway, Jake and I had a long road ahead if we wanted to regain the friendship we'd once had. This was going to take some time and I didn't need to add to our problems by falling for him.

The rain had stopped and I was taking in the crisp, cool air, to clear all thoughts. "I guess I should be getting home soon." We walked slowly, not because of my knee but because we always took our time saying goodbye. On previous occasions, it had taken twenty minutes or more to get to the door of his car. That pesky emotion of desire tried to get my attention, but I chose to ignore it.

"So, how did we end up here anyway?"

"You drove us here, remember." I laughed.

"Alexcia." He stopped walking, and I turned to face him.

My response was a smile, and then I added, "What?"

"So, are we good?" He gestured between us.

I figured I would make light of the situation, instead of downplaying our issues. "Yeah, but are you sure you don't mind me calling your ass for help, even if I can't walk a straight line?"

It was a test question I hoped he would answer truthfully.

His shoulders rolled back, but he kept his attitude in check. "I said I would be here for you. Look. Here I am, right? If anything, it gives me an important reason to stick around and hope for the impossible." Jake dropped his eyes and headed for his ugly, yellow car.

Between the wet pavement beneath his dress shoes and the glow from the overhead parking lot lights, he appeared ethereal, a dark guardian angel. The look was fitting since he said he wanted to be around to help and save me. He was only missing the wings… if guardian angels had wings.

Baffled, I recalled what he had said, "You know, hope is just a wish with added expectations, and last I checked, Aladdin was the only one with a magic lamp." I rounded the car limping toward him as he held open the passenger side door. "Hope? What could you be possibly hoping for?"

"When I find how to answer that, you'll be the second to know," he said while helping me into the car. I slid over the seat and he made sure my leg was in a safe place before closing the door. Looking up at him through the window, I watched his smile broaden, full of promise. That's when a distant voice from inside whispered, "Could his answer for hope be enough to rescue us both?"

17

TEVIN'S SIDE: THROUGH THE EYES OF A REAPER

THE TIME BEND DEPOSITED ME ON THE ROOF OF ALEXCIA'S HOUSE. My boots scraped across the shingles as I paced waiting for Max. Black, misty swirls fought to keep up with my stride allowing quick pockets of moist air through the cloak. I could picture the entrance to our cave with its mouth opened wide showing rows of icicle teeth. At the moment, I longed to be swallowed by it.

Nature needed to call a plumber or twist the faucet and let it pour. I was tired of the clouds teasing with a light drizzle. As I snapped at the minion, it obeyed by forming the hood to keep the rain out of my eyes. I preferred the snow-laced mountains, it quelled my alter personality. Unlike the snow, the rain only temporarily dampened the daemon's fight to break free from my will. The cooler temperatures kept it dormant and made it easier to control.

The feeling of restlessness was not helping the situation though, so I decided to lean against the chimney while I waited. Off in the distance, I heard a rolling rumble but knew it was not thunder. The Doom Guard's Hummer was approaching with a warning for me to beware. The growling grew louder, bouncing off the stationary objects around us. I quickly took surveillance to weigh out the best options, in case I needed assistance for an immediate escape.

The headlights lit up the surrounding area in sparkles, catching the rain before Max turned the black and chrome beast up his driveway. My throat muscles tightened as the engine revved, punctuating its presence, and I found it amazing that I had allowed this daemon to get under my cloak the way he did.

Cursing at the wind. *Why was I putting my existence through this?*

I thought I had buried the answer long ago, without so much as leaving an X to mark the spot. Even if I wanted to remember, I could not. But with my daemonic luck, subconsciously my inner daemon had dug up a few good reasons, leaving them exposed for me to find. The answers lied with Alexcia. I knew it. My clan knew it. Her parents knew it. I just stubbornly refused to accept it. Call me, Daemon.

I hated feeling controlled, even though I freely handed over my will to Rae-Lynn. Whenever I didn't jump when they told me to, I pictured them rolling up my Bond-Rites to swat me in the face like a misbehaved pet. Besides, I was not their Hellhound to control. They already had one of those.

Right on cue, I heard the plastic dog door flapping. *Good little minion, coming out to greet its master.* Then I toyed with the idea of owning one as my minion became agitated. Yeah, minions did not like sharing space, and I knew it was very territorial. When it stiffened, I waved my hand in the air to reassure it.

"Do not worry; I am not getting a dog." The air around the shroud completely stilled.

"Why not?" A voice from the shadows sounded indifferent. "Hellhounds don't eat much. They like their food well done and obey without hesitation. All-in-all, an excellent minion to have, I believe."

Max. I should have known. My minion had always been terrified of him. I did not even turn around to face him as he stepped from out of the darkness. The huge weeping willow, by the side of the house, had grown immensely over the past ten years. Examining its branches and massive girth, it covered a large portion of the roof. I added the tree to my list of plausible escapes.

"Max."

"Snot."

I did not move to face him. Most of the entities of the Unseen feared Ashens and I figured death deserved some respect, even if he was Lucifer's favorite. I especially was not going to respond to this new nickname for me. As he closed in his Italian shoes tapped against each shingle counting down to my impending doom. I slowly lifted my fingers to pull the hood lower, not wanting him to read my face. My eyes were my weakness. If you looked hard enough, they would show you everything and more.

His approach abruptly stopped. A shift in the air made the rain smell sweeter, and my stomach churned as the small hairs on the back of my neck rose. The roof felt crowded by another presence instantly appearing between us. Without even turning around, I knew the source of the aroma, Rae-Lynn. She had once roamed the heavens as one of the Angels of Water. I guess she had not lost that part of her powers.

She sighed. "No, but my ability to command is limited."

I froze. *Oh crap, she was in my head.* I forced my inner thought to go blank, but I had so many questions and couldn't delete them fast enough. My best option was to start talking, so she did not have reason to wander around where she should not be.

My minion started to turn in the opposite direction than I did, the back of it clinging to the brick and mortar column so I could not advance. I lowered my gaze because Rae-Lynn could read emotions faster than Max, another of her Angel-like powers. Fortunately, Alexcia did not know it yet, but her power had a stronger pull than her mother. She had the power to control an entity. *It would be great if Rae-Lynn lost that ability the next time she is recopied.* Pressed lips fashioned into a tight smile as the enticing thought tempted me.

"Tevin. That wasn't nice." Her lips coyly curved. "Would you like to take a chance to see if it's a possibility?" She tried to sound seductive, but it came out too playful. Max thought so, as well because his irises disappeared, and all I saw were two empty sockets staring back at me.

I decided to play back. Maybe not the wisest of moves… but it was entertaining, "Rae how are you doing? You are looking…" I bowed. "Exquisite." Her fire-blond hair was longer than I had remembered as I watched the wind lightly weave through it. The rain dissipated before it even could touch her skin or the light blue, silk robe that hugged tightly over her form, and from what I could tell, that was all.

Tugging on the string around her waist, she curved an eyebrow at me. I ordered the cloak to add more length to the hood. Max was standing behind her with streams of steam rising from the air around him. This occurrence was not from anger, although the reaction could have been from both. He was dry because the moisture could not exist in the heat of his presence. This created a misty sphere over his hair and matching black suit, thus adding to his menacing demeanor.

Alexcia's father aimed a finger at me. "Treading too close to your death, Ashen."

I could not help the resulting hiss. "You could try."

"If it weren't for my daughter's well-being, you would have met your maker ages ago."

"Well, if it were not for me, you would not have been able to use the words *daughter and well-being* in that unsubstantiated statement."

"Boys, enough of this." Alexcia's mother held up her hands

making the area drier by forming an umbrella out of the surrounding air. Water pelted above us like pebbles bouncing off hard plastic. The angel had our attention now, and the Doom Guard and I stood dumbfounded at the condescending way she addressed us. *Boys?* My scythe felt warm, and both hands were itching to hold it, but I refrained.

"Rae-Lynn, this is ludicrous. The Ashens are going to ruin everything we've done to protect our child. I believe it's time to terminate our rites with this creature and his minions. Their services have been fulfilled." Turning away from his love, his eyes narrowed when they met mine. "I see reprehensible actions that could end up harming instead of helping our situation."

"Last time I checked... she was still breathing."

"You are interfering, not protecting. There is a difference."

"Once again, you are blinded by your own convictions, and not looking at the whole picture. We would not have to bust our asses if the child knew what she was. If she does not start controlling her abilities, it is going to get unpleasant between the Houses." I faced Rae-Lynn with determination to get her to understand. "You are with her the most. I know you see it too." Her face fell, losing a few days of beauty.

"I don't know what you're talking about. Alexcia is a child trying to grow up between both worlds. I'm sure it's difficult for her."

Her mother was in denial. I could not believe it. "Your daughter is not just leaking power. She is also on the brink of self-combusting. I am not sure what internal battle she is fighting, but I sense her internal turmoil. Most of the time, we are saving her from herself, not from the creatures of the Unseen."

The Doom Guard lowered his finger to address his wife. "Rae, what is he talking about?"

She tried to appear ten years younger, using her power of innocence to influence him. Wide-eyed, she stammered. "It's...

it is nothing."

Mr. Stasis put both hands on his hips and hunched his shoulders, eyes bearing down on her. "Rae-Lynn, what is this daemon talking about?"

"It's nothing Tevin and I can't handle. You keep maintaining the barrier, and we'll take care of the rest," she said while batting her eyes in rhythm with the rain tapping on the air dome.

"What she is not telling you is that the binding spell you both placed on Alexcia is failing. I have not put my scythe on it yet, but I believe her emotions are what is breaking through and accessing her memories. If so, it will eventually unlock her powers. Max, the next time she is in your presence, take a whiff. The child reeks of raw magic."

A crease dipped between his eyes. "Are you sure?"

Memories of us crossing in the isle made me shudder, saliva pooling, "Intoxicating." I licked my lips.

Taking a few steps toward his angel, he said, "Why haven't you been forthright with me? She is my daughter too."

Mrs. Stasis huffed. "You're so wrapped up playing human. You would rather deal with your corporations than your home existence. Ever since the accident, you have walked away from what she is. I told you from the beginning she was different, beyond that. She isn't a normal Child-of-Balance. Her powers exceed our combined strengths. I believe if we keep her in the dark for a while longer, maybe we can figure out how to deal with her. Until then, we'll continue to keep her in a state of oppression." She glared at me. "It's worked for the past ten years. It will continue to work for another month. Just until her sixteenth birthday. Then she can choose a House and become an entity of the Unseen. Max, then we'll truly be a family." She beamed as tears welled up across her lower lids threatening to spill over.

It was sad. She believed keeping the blindfold on her daughter was going to solve the problem. My head slowly swayed from side to side. "Keeping her in the dark is going to kill her, if not by these hands..." I held up both grey hands as a visual and continued, "certainly by the Cauldron's. Or maybe another Ashen clan will try. I have kept my word. Whether or not you like our methods, is not the issue. Alexcia's power is growing, and I believe it will be her undoing if you do not disclose what she is and teach her how to control it. Max is right. I see a future of fighting, not against us, but your daughter."

I peered up at the night sky as they shared a look, holding a discussion in silence. The heavy moisture lifted, and I no longer heard the rain as Rae-Lynn lowered her hands. She anxiously rubbed her wrists while moving her bare feet toward her husband. Having the ability to control the water was one thing, but it seemed to take a lot out of her. Max smoothed her hair and kissed the top of her head.

He whispered, "We'll think of something." He sighed with the dead weight of guilt. "By the way, I grounded her right before the funeral." Glancing at me, he said, "That's what I was calling to inform you about. I figured it would be easier to control her actions if we knew exactly where she was."

"Oh, Max, you didn't? How did she take it?" She buried her head in his chest.

"As well as could be expected. We'll have to keep watch on her twenty-four seven. Even though I told her she could still work, she is only allowed to go from school, then to her job... or straight home, if she's isn't working. I allowed her friend to comfort her and take her somewhere to talk, but he is to bring her back shortly."

My ears burned. *He?* The itch was making its way into becoming that annoying twitch. I tried to play it off. "So, who is watching her?"

The couple looked at each other, and then stared blank-

ly back at me. I cursed under my breath. *May the River take me.*
"You're telling me she is alone, at night, in the rain, with any
number of the Unseen? Possibly even the same ones that tried
to attack her mere hours ago?" Still, they both stared. Frustrated,
I whipped out my cell, and madly started texting for someone in
the clan to comb the area for the Child.

"Max?" Rae-Lynn was not at the funeral so she had no idea
what I was talking about. I did not hold it against her, but Max
appeared hazy with his aura scattered all over the place. He
was pissed at himself, if not slightly more than I was. The area
around us went colorless as sick, gray smoke with a purple haze
plumed from under his suit.

Pulling his wife close, he kissed her hard and stepped away,
breathless. "I will find her." In his anger, he turned his back
to me and said, "By the way, Reaper, don't call my wife, *Rae.*"
Through the air, a dense vibration formed, creating a sinking
feeling of disorientation. His casting spell covered us in sulfuric
stench. When the smoke began to clear, I could make out his
wings—and then he was gone.

Ink-filled clouds encircled the house, adding to the dark
halo effect. The angel did not fight against the elements to keep
herself dry. When the water lightly drizzled overhead, slight
movement caused me to glance at Rae-Lynn's robe. The night
sky was so dark, I would not have been surprised if the drops
stained it the same color. She stared up at the heavens allowing
the water to drip over her face causing me to wonder how much
she missed it.

Her voice sounded sad and misplaced as she answered my
thoughts again, "Yes, I do."

My cell buzzed, and I glanced down to see Michael's reply.
He was out reaping and had finished with a jumper. He vol-
unteered his services and was heading in our direction. Next,
Archer's text stated he was going to meet up with Michael and

work the opposite direction. I relaxed for a moment before closing the phone with a click.

"I have to go. Two of my reapers are looking for her now. With Max searching and me joining the hunt, we'll find her soon enough."

She deliberately turned away, keeping her eyes from mine. "Tevin, what do you feel when you are near her?"

The question took me completely off guard. "Angel?"

"Any emotion you don't understand?"

I took this opportunity to lie since she was not facing me. "No."

The slyness of a smile started to form before she spoke. "You're still the lost daemon I met ten years ago, I see."

My cloak resisted when I pulled away from the chimney, getting closer to the half-breed in front of me. The minion was not afraid... it simply did not trust her. The response was *proceed with caution*, Tevin. I took her words as bait. She was trying to open old wounds. The smell of blood was the same between us, and I was not going to bite this time. With two contracts hanging over my head, I did not intend to make a third.

"What are you digging around for, Rae-Lynn? You know Ashens are not permitted to feel the positive side of things. Now is not the time to get into this with you. Do you want me to protect your daughter... or not?"

"How has the River been treating you?"

"I think you already know that answer."

"You helped me in so many ways, Reaper. By you agreeing to the Bond-Rite, I have been getting stronger since the River Styx hasn't been absorbing so much of my existence as punishment for saving her."

"Yeah, well, I would have appreciated it if you disclosed the repercussions of keeping her powers from the River."

"Power is given and taken in equal portions. You know that

Ashen? If you take from the River, it will take from you. Still, you chose to protect my child. Yet, the answer you've been searching for has eluded you."

The inevitable feeling of betrayal coiled around my chest. She was trying to provoke me into revealing what I assumed were feelings I could not comprehend. The twitch came back with a vengeance, adding to my already foul mood. To distract myself I began probing the inside of the minion for a cigarette, I needed something to keep me from grabbing my scythe instead. The weapon hummed, feeding on my disarray of negative emotions, speaking to me. *If you need me, I am right here.*

I lit the tip and pulled hard so the smoke filled my mouth instead of the useless words that would end up tying my tongue in knots. Standing, motionless, a scythe's swipe away from her, we silently gazed at the clouds. Soft, irregular breathing echoed in from the entity beside me, as awareness struck reason. Feeling the intensity of her intentions was as hot as the real thing. She did not want to be alone. The half-angel had picked a fight to save face but also to use it as an excuse to calm her husband's qualms about why I remained behind with her. A sick thought swept over me, and I made a quick plea to Lucifer to keep her from hugging me. I pulled my cloak tighter and took another drag.

"Tevin, I can't help but feel sorry for you."

I choked on the smoke. "Sorry, for me? You are crazy. You know that, right? I got it all. My existence was solid before I met you and your family, not to mention getting stiffed for my services. I should have read the fine print in the agreement before I looked into your daughter's eyes. That is what I feel sorry for... mostly." The last word drifted out as if more than two syllables and I did not know why.

Her sly smile was back. "I don't understand the reason, but I still have hope for you, daemon. The death of her boyfriend was tragic, but she didn't love him. I guess you both remain in the same boat in that aspect."

Ugh, see, she was using that L-word again, and I got the same sick feeling. *Please have mercy on me.* I pleaded for her to not make me say it. That sentiment is strictly for the Vessels to deal with, and it linked them to so many other emotions. It completely made me ill trying to sort them out. I took another, cleansing drag.

"I guess it is good she still has Jake to help her out during this time of need." She turned to me and sighed. "He'll be good for her until she can come to terms with what she has to do and what she is. Don't you think so?"

Why was she asking me? I had no idea what he would be good for, other than a door stop, maybe a hole in the wall designated for a window, or a coffin fill. Honestly... if a daemon could be completely honest... I had no real problem with the male Vessel. At least, I thought I did not until it dawned on me how I started seeing him spend more time around Alexcia. I was aware—as my facial features turned grim—they should. I was a Grim Reaper, after all.

I shrugged in response.

She laughed. The one I hated so much was loaded with unshared answers. The hairs on the back of my neck bristled with anger. She was toying with me. I tossed the cigarette butt on the shingle in front of me. It was time to find the child and move on from this useless, nowhere discussion.

"Before I go, Rae, what do you really want from me?"

The angel looked back up at the points of light trying to burn through the clouds. Whispering into the air, she said, "My dear Reaper of the Grim, I want what every mother wants for her daughter: Spindled Magic, in place of knocking on the door of want. Strength and Muscle, to willingly fight beside her and help bind Creation's future with her Balance. Love, although it may endure times of sorrow, only in its ultimate form is it the key to overthrowing even one of the Houses. I pray to the Light she finds all three."

Cryptic, more riddles and no straight answers. "Rae, what is my part in all this?"

"Well, it's really up to you."

"What?"

"Your role in Alexcia's life is up to you."

I pulled out my scythe to replicate my form of a Time Bend. Using the excuse of checking for messages, I turned to walk away from her. I stopped long enough to text Michael, informing him that I was headed to look for Alexcia by the school. Then I would head to the coffee shop where she worked. Slipping the phone back into my minion's tentacles, I held out the scythe to make the portal. As it started to hum, a hiss of air crept from me in a harsh whisper. "I think you are expecting more from me than I can give to your daughter, Rae-Lynn."

"It's simple, will you be the door, the ring or..." she paused in thought.

"...or what?" I inched forward sensing the need to find Alexcia.

Silence followed as I stepped into the Time Bend. The answers to Rae-Lynn's riddles would have to wait. Then as the portal began to close, I heard her voice echo through the churning darkness, "... the key."

Seriously? Was she trying to sever my last nerve? Here her daughter was out in the world, unattended, with only a mere Vessel as her shield from the creatures of the Unseen who hunted her. And Rae-Lynn wanted to play? Normally, daemons would jump at the challenge to show off their intellect, but I seemed to lack the desire. Or maybe I lacked the restraint to stop following what I desired. Then, a light feeling brought a memory into focus, and I saw her sea swept eyes and fire-blond hair.

Wait... what? *No.* What was I thinking?

I needed things to go back to the way they were before I met Alexcia and was suckered into making a contract with her Angel of a mother. Back to a time, when all I needed was nothing more than to harvest some souls for my grim existence. *I guess it is true what the humans say, "You reap what you sow."* I shifted my right arm slowly toward the left shoulder to touch the beard of the scythe for support. Time would continue forward to whatever end was waiting. With the inevitable looming, I thought, "You reap what you sow, right?"

Then, for Alexcia's sake, "*So shall I reap.*"

Scythes & Salutations

*A*LEXCIA AND I ARE OVERJOYED AND WOULD LIKE TO THANK YOU FOR joining us into the Unseen. I hope you have enjoyed following Alexcia's first steps into her future, Tevin's journey toward understanding humanity, and the places their separate paths will take them.

This story would have never seen the light of day if it weren't for the following people in my life. First and foremost, I wish to express my love and deepest gratitude to my hubby of twenty years. Thank you so much, Jeff, for giving me the strength and courage to press on, chase my dreams, and pursue my love for Storyweaving. To Josh and MK, for your smiles and encouragement, for staying up with me while I read my pages out loud for your input.

Special thanks to my second family at Clean Teen Publishing and to CTP's very own Graphic Arts Designer, Marya. I want to express my love for the cover and give a special shout-out for making Tevin look so good. Thank you Rebecca and Courtney, for understanding all of my midnight "sorrys" and detoured mishaps. My sincere gratitude to Melanie, for supporting Alexcia and Tevin by suggesting their story could be something special. Thanks to my editor, Kathy, I can't express how much your insight and expertise has opened my eyes. Amber, I appreciate you for listening to me ramble about my characters, staying up to rehash the same sentence over and over, and for trying to cure my affliction of useless words. My deepest thanks to Monique for accepting the task of Graphic Arts Designer, internet guru, niece, and friend. You've taught me that even when you trip, it is still your fate and your choice to pick yourself up and keep going.

To my dad and sister for their advice and harsh critiques that helped me open my inner ear and listen to reason. To Amy, Autumn, and Nathan for your love and support from afar. A special thanks to my adopted sis and her hubby, for allowing me to be me by crashing your parties with my laptop in tow and borrowing your beloved Gigi to be the next superstar Hellhound. I can't forget Hunter for inspiring me to never give up, being the crazy aunt, and learning not to worry about what I cannot control. To the rest of my friends and family who believed in my kind of crazy enough to not lock me up when I said I heard voices.

And last but not least, to all my readers, thank you for taking the chance on a new author, new characters, and the Unseen realm. If it weren't for your love of reading, my Storyweaving wouldn't have a purpose. The Reapers can't wait to meet up with you in the next installment.

Scythe ya later

About the Author

*B*ORN IN POMONA, CALIFORNIA, KATHY-LYNN CROSS LIVED THERE for twelve years until her family moved to Las Vegas, Nevada, where she resides today. Inspired by the backdrop of Sin City, Kathy-Lynn took her English professor's advice and wrote about the hometown she knew. Kathy-Lynn wasn't always a writer. In 2008, when her niece was hospitalized, Kathy-Lynn decided to do something special for her, so she wrote a short tale for her to read. After devouring it in a single day, her niece and the nurses in the pediatrics wing quickly asked her, "What's next?" That was when a new chapter in her life opened up, and Kathy-Lynn realized that she wanted to become a Storyweaver.

Kathy-Lynn loves the color red and uses it obsessively in everything, including her bottle-blonde hair accented with red highlights. She has a knack for baking and cake decorating—that is when her fingers are not busy writing mayhem. When recharging, she can be found curled up with a cup of coffee and a good book or spending time with her hubby of twenty years, two kids, three cats, and the family dog.

KathyLynnCross.com

You are

not alone.

I‍F YOU KNOW OF ANYONE WHO SUFFERS FROM ALCOHOL OR DRUG abuse or needs someone to talk to, here are some websites and hotlines to help.

Alcohol abuse hotlines and information
National 1-800 Crisis Hotline : 1-866-684-6303
http://www.allaboutcounseling.com/crisis_hotlines.htm
National Helpline | SAMHSA
www.samhsa.gov
877-SAMHSA-7 (877-726-4727)
800-487-4889 (TDD)

Phone Hotline for Teens | Help for Teens in Crisis
http:///www.pamf.org/teen/hotlines National Council on Alcoholism and Drug Dependence, Inc.
Helpline for finding treatment.
(800)-NCA-CALL or (800) 622-2255

The NIDA for Teens website helps educate adolescents ages 11 through 15 (as well as their parents and teachers) about the

science behind drug abuse.
National Drug Abuse Helpline
www.nationaldrugabusehelpline.com

Drug Abuse Hotlines: Find treatment options via ...
http://drugabuse.com/library/drug-abuse-hotlines/
Call 1-888-747-7155